THE
GHOST
CHRONICLES
Book Two

D1114004

MARLO BERLINER

THE GHOST CHRONICLES BOOK TWO
Copyright © 2017 by Marlo Berliner

Published by Teddy Blue Books

Print ISBN: 978-0-9969724-3-7

Cover Copyright © 2017 Marlo Berliner
Cover artist: S. P. McConnell
Interior formatting: Author E.M.S.

For my husband, Chris.

I love you.

For my parents, Maryann and Jerry.

I love you.

CONTENTS

THE
GHOST
CHRONICLES
Book Two

"Nothing in the entire universe ever perishes, believe me, but things vary, and adopt a new form. The phrase 'being born' is used for beginning to be something different from what one was before, while 'dying' means ceasing to be the same. Though this thing may pass into that, and that into this, yet the sums of things remain unchanged."

– Metamorphoses by the Roman poet Ovid

CHAPTER ONE

DISCUSSION

MICHAEL STOOD THERE, holding a phantom breath.

He'd waited so long for some kind of tangible answers, but he feared whatever his friend said next would only lead to more questions. *This had better be good,* he thought out loud, not caring if Tom overheard his thoughts or not.

His mentor gave him an indignant grimace. "You're right, I am a Protector," he said with a long, exhausted sigh. "What Vassago said is true. I protect souls both living and dead. Oh, and sometimes situations," he added at the last minute, "though I think Navigators have a great deal more to do with those."

Michael studied his face. "So that's why you always get that distracted expression and need to leave right away."

"Yes." Tom nodded, seeming almost relieved that he could finally reveal the truth.

"But who tells you?"

"Voices…indistinct. It's difficult to describe," his friend replied with a slight shrug of his shoulders.

He pondered this for a moment. "Then how do you know what to do?"

Tom paused to gaze at the ocean waves hitting the shore

before he answered. "They tell me what I need to do shortly before I need to do it."

This perplexed him more than anything else. "But how can that be?"

"I don't know exactly," Tom said with a smirk, as he peered down his nose at him. "I'm still learning, remember." Now, his wise mentor turned the conversation around to pose a question of his own. "Who told you about the five types of souls anyway?"

He knew Tom was eventually going to asking him that, so he couldn't help the cheeky grin that now slid across his face. "Abraham Lincoln."

Tom huffed. "Good old honest Abe...couldn't keep his mouth shut."

"And, I'm glad he didn't," he shot back. "At least now a few things are starting to make some sense." He chewed the side of his lip, as something else had just occurred to him. "Wait a minute, if you already know what kind of soul you are...then what are you still doing here?"

"Apparently, I'm still learning," Tom repeated, sounding a bit annoyed.

As the implications of that statement struck him, his mood crashed.

And he must've been wearing the disappointment on his face, for his friend now added, "Oh, oh...you thought that's all you needed to figure out was what kind of soul you are and then you'd move on. I'm sorry, Son," Tom said, patting him lightly on the shoulder, "but to tell you the truth that's only the beginning."

Michael's heart sank. *Only the beginning?*

Tom gave him a sympathetic look. "In order for you to understand," he said, "I think maybe it would be best if *I* start at the beginning."

As the two of them casually strolled along the sand, Tom began his story. "Just like you, I knew right away that I was dead. But here's the thing...*unlike* you, I had no reason to believe in anything otherworldly. I didn't believe in God. To tell you the truth, I can't even say I was an agnostic. I was, for all intent and purposes, an atheist," he explained. "So I wandered around lost and confused as to what I was going to do as a ghost the same way you did, except I felt even worse. Lucky for me, I only had less than an hour of suffering in that pathetic state before the first plane hit the towers. Then it started almost immediately—the music, the column of light...and of course, the ascension of the souls who perished."

He couldn't even imagine what witnessing all that tragedy must've been like. "What did you do then?"

"What anyone else would've done...I fell to my knees pinned to the spot," Tom said plainly. "And like I said before, I was filled with hope. But that hope quickly turned to frustration and confusion. So my time of turmoil came *after* I saw the light."

Michael gaped at him. "Why was that?"

"Because I thought I had it all figured out," Tom said. "I believed all I had to do was be closer to the light the next time. So I became an ambulance chaser. I stood by car accidents as people passed away. I waited in hospital emergency rooms and Intensive Care Units. And I saw the light come a number of times." The sadness in his eyes

3

spoke volumes. "If many died suddenly, like in a natural disaster such as a tornado, or in an attack like 9/11, then because of the sheer magnitude of the event, they would send a special congregation down to escort all the souls at once," he explained. "I would see the shining column, hear the music, and feel the presence of a whole entourage of angels, as we both just did. If not, sometimes a single soul merely passed quietly into the light."

Wow. The very thought of it made chills ripple through his soul. "But...chasing the light didn't work?"

"Of course, it didn't work," Tom replied, with a light-hearted chuckle. "And it didn't take long before I figured out I was being *prevented* from going. So I became increasingly frustrated and distraught, like you." He paused. "And then things got even worse. One day, I saw not just one soul, but also a demon emerge from the body of a dead man. He threatened me and scared me half to death before taking off. After that, I was terrified because well...that's when I realized there was something in the afterlife to be terrified *of.*"

He nodded in grave agreement. *I can certainly vouch for that.* "What did you do then?"

"Pretty much the same thing you have so far. I met other ghosts, asked questions, tried to learn whatever I could from them. One day when I was at my lowest, a spirit appeared who explained to me that there are five types of souls, Messengers, Navigators, Protectors, Seers, and Warriors, just as Lincoln told you. And he told me I was a Protector."

"And did he say what that meant?"

"No, he didn't," Tom responded flatly. "He took me to

the Elders to hear their cryptic covenant...and then he left me."

"So, you didn't get to ask any questions of them either?" Michael guessed.

"Nope, not a one," Tom replied with a shake of his head. "I tried to ask him who am I supposed to protect and how do I protect them...and all he said was 'you'll know'." He paused to roll his eyes. "After that, he abandoned me on the steps of Eastern State Penitentiary. Later, I had another encounter with a demon." He seemed to slightly shudder at the memory. "This time the demon was much closer and tried to grab me. I have no idea how, but the power to direct energy just came out of me. But it took time and patience to be able to control it."

He was beginning to wonder where Tom was going with this story. "Then what did you do?"

"Talked to more ghosts, observed all I could, and then wandered some more." Tom paused. "Until the night I met you. Don't ask me how, but I knew right away you were the one I was meant to protect."

"Protect me? Why?"

"I don't know yet," Tom replied, "but I'm guessing it has something to do with what kind of soul you are."

Again, a cloud of disappointment fell over him. "You mean you don't know? You're not the one who's going to tell me?"

Tom shook his head. "I'm afraid not. And it wouldn't do either of us any good to speculate."

He pursed his lips. *Great, just great.* "Well, is there anything else you can tell me about the five types of souls?"

"I can only tell you what I've seen and learned so far. The spirits I've met have been Navigators, Messengers and other Protectors," Tom said. "Obviously I'm still trying to figure out how to be a Protector. Navigators are a bit more complicated and I can't say I understand their role at all yet. Messengers are a bit more straightforward. They seem to do exactly that, deliver messages to both the living and the dead about what they should be doing or where they should go. Sometimes their messages are subtle, sometimes they're more direct."

Michael paused, trying to digest all his mentor was saying. Now, something Lincoln had said flitted through his mind. He decided to ask Tom about it while he had the chance. "I don't understand...if someone like Lincoln gives out warnings, then he must be a Messenger. But Lincoln said he was a Protector."

"I'm not positive," Tom replied, "but from what I can tell I think there's a fair bit of overlap in what the different types of spirits do, like shared duties and responsibilities for instance." He thought for a moment. "The other thing I can tell you is that the types of souls are closely related in life and in the afterlife."

Michael puckered up his face, bewildered. "What do you mean by that?"

"Simply this, if you were the type of soul in life that was a Protector, then perhaps you had a job as a banker, protecting people's investments and money. Police, first responders, security guards, insurance agents, all could be Protectors. Doctors tend to be Protectors too, because they protect people's health," Tom explained. "Messengers might be information processors like computer technicians, or mailmen, or delivery personnel. Navigators tend to guide people, so they might be involved in the travel industry, education, or have some kind of job as a director. Seers know what will happen, but I'm not sure what they do from there," he said, pondering. "In life, these might be the planners, maybe the entrepreneurs, things like that. Warriors...well, I'm guessing they're gifted with strength and they fight evil when necessary. So obviously, these are probably people in the military, or maybe activists who are fighting for causes, human rights, that sort of thing. Get the idea?"

He gave a small nod, but studied Tom's face. His friend was holding something back. Michael could tell. He'd seen it so many times before that he recognized it right away. That unmistakable down tick in his mentor's eyes. Not exactly looking away, but not exactly looking right at him either. Trying to read his mind only confirmed his suspicions, *he's still blocking me.*

For so many reasons, he couldn't help but feel hurt. "Why didn't you tell me any of this?"

"Because I'm not the one who was supposed to tell you," Tom said in a matter of fact way.

He still wasn't satisfied. "Then why didn't you at least tell me there was a heaven?"

Now, Tom turned to glare at him. "The answer is simple...I still don't know for sure if there is. I haven't been there yet either. I've seen no more or less than you have, so I have no idea what awaits us on the other side," he said testily. "All I'm following is my instinct here. I hear voices that tell me and take me where I'm needed, but only vaguely tell me what I'm supposed to do."

"But you still could've told me you had seen souls go *somewhere*," he said, sulking.

Tom gave an exasperated sigh. "Like I told you before, it's something you needed to see for yourself. Besides, how was I supposed to tell you that anyway? What was I supposed to say? Oh, by the way, yes, there is a place to go but they don't want you yet?" His words came out facetious and angry. "Given your fragile emotional state when I first met you, how well do you think *that* would've gone over? How do you think you would've felt then?" he said, almost barking the question at him. "All I knew was how discouraged I felt after realizing I was prevented from going to the light, so I had every reason to believe you'd feel the same."

Michael hung his head. "Okay, okay," he conceded. "I understand."

After getting that off his chest, Tom seemed to calm down a bit. "Believe me," he said. "I'm as relieved as you are that I can finally fill you in on some of the details."

"I appreciate that," he said, though he took special note of the fact that Tom said 'some', meaning he still might be withholding 'some'.

His friend fell silent, as if pondering something else important. Finally, Tom said, "One more thing I must tell you, Michael. Not only have I been protecting you from evil and falling into the hands of the demons...but to an even greater extent, I've been protecting you from yourself."

He swiveled around to give him an indignant glare. "What the hell do you mean by that?"

"I mean that you still have a lot to learn," Tom said.

Michael frowned. "Yeah, I think you've mentioned that once or twice before," he said with a pound of sarcasm.

Tom now gave him a hard look. "Have you ever heard a parent complain that they were having a difficult time teaching a child a lesson? That simply telling them something was not sinking in?"

He gave a slight shrug of his shoulders. "I suppose."

"Well, that's just the position I find myself in with you. I could tell you whatever lesson you need to learn, but it wouldn't be the same as if you learned it for yourself," Tom said with a long pause. "No one truly learns anything until they go through it themselves."

All of a sudden, his mentor got that familiar faraway look on his face. "I've got to go," he said quickly. With that, he gave a slight wave and faded away.

As usual, Michael still had so many unanswered questions. But at least now he knew the key to getting out of the afterlife might lie in figuring out what kind of soul he was.

Maybe then, he might finally be one step closer to heaven.

First things first, though. Now, he had to get back to the Angel of the Sea so he could tell Sarah the news...there really was some kind of destination after death.

CHAPTER TWO

HOLIDAY

SARAH JINGLED THE tiny silver bell ornament on the festively decorated tree in the parlor of the Angel of the Sea. "Tell me again about the light," she said, turning her hopeful eyes to him with all the innocence of a child asking to hear once more about Santa Claus.

Michael smiled and, for approximately the one-hundredth time, described the extraordinary experience he and Tom had witnessed in front of the White House Visitors Center. The spectacular column of light, the beautiful music, the overwhelming warmth and peace. He recalled for her every detail as best he could, searching for the perfect way to paint the scene for her, but failing miserably. "I think I finally understand why Tom didn't tell me earlier that he had seen the light. It's nearly impossible to put into words what we saw and heard, and do it any justice at all."

"Maybe, but I think it sounds wonderful all the same. I only wish I'd been there." She closed her eyes, and let out a contented sigh. When she opened them again, her expression had changed. "Except…," she hesitated, "I wouldn't have wanted to see what happened to all those poor people. It must've been so hard to watch them die."

He took her hand and gave it a gentle, yet reassuring squeeze to chase away the sorrowful thoughts taking root in her mind. Her sensitive soul was one of the many reasons he loved her, but he couldn't stand to watch her agonize over tragedy like this. "Come on you...it's Christmas Eve, let's go down to the Washington Street Mall and walk around the outdoor shops for a while."

Her eyes lit up. "It's cold, we're going to need something warm to wear," she said in jest. A split second later she had spun around and conjured the memory of her dressiest holiday coat.

He smiled, for he loved that about her too. How easily she could make him feel as if they were still alive. As if they were still two normal people. As if they could still enjoy 'life' together.

Hand in hand they glided down the side streets away from the Angel of the Sea and into the heart of the Victorian district. A light dusting of snow had fallen upon the parked cars, streets and houses, as if someone up above had sifted crystalline sugar over every inch of the historic seaside town. The entire length of the beach glistened with a fresh, pristine layer of white. Rolling waves revealed only the sand nearest to the water's edge.

With their pastel painted colors and scrolling filigree woodwork, it was as if the heavenly bakers above had sprinkled powdered sugar on a town of gingerbread houses. It was a rare, white Christmas in Cape May.

Michael decided there was something indescribably beautiful about a shore town in winter. Without all the crowds and the usual hustle and bustle, the beach had a peacefulness and stillness…and yet, the ocean complimented it perfectly with its gentle and steady rocking providing such serene comfort.

As they took a right onto Jackson Street, Sarah drew in a sudden breath beside him. He nearly did the same. Transported into an idyllic winter wonderland, each of the colorfully painted bed and breakfasts, inns and hotels they passed were decked out in holiday finery. Lights twinkled from every porch and softly shimmered through the fallen snow on every roof, wreaths hung from every door, evergreen boughs draped every staircase. If Thomas Kinkade could see this, he would've thought he had stepped right into one of his famous paintings.

That was one of the things he loved about the Jersey Shore. The coast was one giant Wonderland, but each of the shore towns had their own distinct history, personality and character. Cape May had a very singular feel, as if the place had been frozen in time, somewhere between the Victorian era of the late eighteen hundreds and the Golden Age of the Roaring Twenties. And in a way, it had been.

The hour was late, nearly eleven thirty according to the neon clock which glowed in the window of the Cabana bar on the corner. Only a few wisps of smoke drifted out of chimneys from lit fireplaces where tourists, friends and family still gathered around glowing hearths.

For a moment, his heart ached for his family, but Sarah's presence close by his side chased the feeling away as quickly as it came on.

When the two of them arrived at the Washington Street Mall promenade, Michael grinned. Since the shops had long since closed and the living had gone home for their Christmas Eve revelry, the dead had come out to enjoy the night's festivities.

And he'd been right all along. This old shore town had quite a few resident ghosts. Even though he hadn't seen any that first night he came to Cape May, a number of them had apparently decided to come out to celebrate the holidays.

Several drifted by in small groups talking, laughing, and caroling. Each of them appeared to be from different periods of time. By his estimation, at least the last three centuries were represented. And they were from all walks of life, too. Scanning the crowd he spied Navy officers and sailors, aristocrats, a policeman, a little Amish girl, and even the ghost of an old woman on a vintage phantom bicycle riding in figure eights around the square. The strange menagerie of spirits reminded him of the night he and Tom had gone to Salem on Halloween.

He stroked the back of Sarah's hand with his thumb to make sure she would be okay with so many unfamiliar ghosts around. "Looks like we're not the only ones out on the town tonight."

She chuckled, seeming completely at ease. "Apparently not."

He couldn't blame all the spirits for wanting to see this. Even though the shops were now closed, most of them had left their front windows illuminated. The promenade was magnificent with every shop, every tree, every lamppost, still aglow with brilliant white Christmas lights. The result— nothing short of magical. The twinkling lights sparkled and danced on every wet surface because of the freshly fallen snow, giving the length of the promenade an enchanted glow.

Passing the information booth in the middle of the Mall, he read the sign across the top out loud, "Welcome Friends Old and New, Linger Here A Day Or Two." He had to laugh. "I guess a lot of these spirits took that saying literally and have lingered here for much longer than a day or two."

"I guess so." She gave a warm chuckle. "I wonder what the townspeople would say if they knew so many of us were still lingering."

He tapped his finger on a poster advertising a ghost tour. "I think they do know," he replied, grinning.

As they strolled past each decorated shop window, Sarah pointed out pieces of fine art and handmade jewelry that caught her eye. All of a sudden, she stopped in front of a gift shop with a gold-etched sign that read, Whale's Tale. "Look at that gorgeous miniature carousel with the seahorses on the bottom and the glittering mermaids on top."

"It's certainly eye-catching with all that intricate detailing...I guess." The devilish glint in her eyes had him somewhat perplexed. "What about it?"

Before he could stop her, Sarah slid her hand through the front glass window of the shop without breaking it and set the carousel spinning. Drawing her hand back through the glass once more, she gave him a triumphant smile.

He stared at the rotating toy, wondering how she had managed to so expertly treat the glass as liquid and the carousel as solid. Going through the glass was easy, but having enough skill to then move the carousel with her hand at the same time was another matter entirely. All this time, he had been struggling with the flip-flop between things sometimes feeling solid and sometimes not. "When did you learn that little trick?"

"I've been practicing on the curio cabinets at the Angel when you're not around," she said with a satisfied grin. "I put my hand through the glass and knock over the little angel trinkets." She took him by the hand and drifted across to the Cape May Sweet Shop. A colorful replica of a red and white Ferris wheel sat on display in the front window amidst a rainbow of oversized gumballs on a bed of cotton made to look like snow. "Here, now you try it."

He arched an eyebrow at her. "Okay, how?"

"Let your arm slip through the glass and forget it's even there, then concentrate all your energy on the ends of your fingers," she instructed.

Cautiously, he allowed his hand to pass through the window until his fingers nearly touched the Ferris wheel. After a moment's hesitation, he tilted his head to the side in concentration, let his energy flow to his fingertips, and then pushed down on one of the red spokes towards the top. Much to his delight, the Ferris wheel spun clockwise.

"You did it!" Sarah squealed, clapping her hands like a schoolgirl. "I knew you would."

Michael turned to her to say something funny, but the antique pedestal clock on the sidewalk in front of the gift shop suddenly chimed midnight. As usual, time had once again moved forward at some wickedly irrational pace.

The wind had picked up and snow was lightly falling again, straight through both of them. He took Sarah's hand

and let the swirling wind direct him, spinning her around the tall wrought-iron clock as if they were ballroom dancing to music only he could hear in his mind.

Or so he thought.

Until Sarah started humming the same tune along with him.

He hadn't even realized it, but his mind must've been projecting the music, so he picked up the tempo now, humming louder. It took a moment before to recall the name of the tune, but then he recognized the song as "The Blue Danube", a famous waltz by Johann Strauss II. *At least I remembered something from middle school music classes*, he thought with amusement.

He twirled her around again with a big flourish then dipped her in his arms, before finally yanking her up into a tight embrace. A swirl of snowflakes danced softly around and through her wavy, red hair. Aroused by the warmth of her aura, he pulled her even closer to his chest, as spectral butterflies sprang to life in his stomach.

This was the kind of romantic moment any man, dead or alive, would remember forever. A thread of magic that would become stitched inside of a freeze frame of memory.

His fingers strayed across her cheek, relishing the softness of her skin. For a moment, her big, beautiful eyes held him spellbound. He could swear each time he looked into them they reflected an even deeper, more entrancing shade of green. "Merry Christmas, Sarah."

She leaned into him and whispered tenderly, "Merry Christmas, my love."

He let himself go, placing his mouth desperately over

hers, losing himself in the heat and passion of her kiss. As far as he was concerned there was nothing else on this earth, nothing else in this universe, except her lips and this moment in time.

Until a man behind them cleared his throat. Loudly.

With an audible grumble, Michael pulled away from Sarah and turned to find an older man with gray hair and a white beard glaring at him. The man was dressed in what appeared to be a World War II Navy uniform. Michael didn't know much about officer's insignia, but judging by all the stars and bars on the man's dress whites he must've been some type of Admiral. At least, he must have been when he was alive.

"What do you kids think you're doing?" the man bellowed, as if giving a command instead of asking a question.

Stiffening his body, he took a defensive stance in front of Sarah in case the ghost proved to be trouble. "What do you care?"

"I'll tell you why I care, you should be more considerate of the other spirits around," the man replied, waving his arm in a wide arc. "Some of us don't have sweethearts or wives to kiss tonight."

Of all the reprimands in the world, he hadn't expected *that* to come out of the officer's mouth. He thought for sure the man was going to yell about public displays of affection like the teachers used to at his high school.

Something about the heartfelt way the man said it though, made him relax his posture and begrudgingly mutter, "Sorry."

The bearded man shook his head, but his lips twisted into a quirky grin. "Don't be sorry. I'm just being a sour old curmudgeon."

Sarah chimed in to diffuse the tension. "I've noticed a lot of Navy personnel here tonight. Why is that?"

The officer awkwardly glanced down at his polished, black dress shoes. "Oh, that's because many of us were stationed here when we were alive, so we still come back to visit," he replied. "The US Navy had several bases here during World War II because Cape May's prime location at the southernmost tip of New Jersey was key to protecting ships along the Atlantic coastline."

The man now turned his kind, but weathered eyes to him. "Look, I really am sorry. I shouldn't have interrupted you like that," he said. "Let me make it up to the two of you. There's going to be a New Year's Eve Party in Congress Hall." He pointed up the street to the grand building whose North side could be seen from the Mall. "You both should come. Every spirit in town and many visitors from out of town will be there. You won't want to miss it. The festivities only happen once every thirty years."

Sarah got that cute, quizzical look on her face that he adored. "Why is that?"

"Because Thomas H. Hughes hosts the party and he only comes back to visit every thirty years." And with that, he tipped his white officer's cap to them and floated down the street.

Once the older man was out of earshot, Michael asked her, "Who do you think Thomas H. Hughes is?"

"He must mean the original founder of Congress Hall," she replied. "I think he was a Congressman at one time. I've seen his portrait hanging at different places around Cape May. Other than that, I can't say I know much about him."

He clasped her hand as they began meandering down the Mall again. "Interesting that he only comes back for a visit every thirty years," he mused. "I wonder why."

"Me too," she said thoughtfully. "And I'd be curious where he is when he's not here." She swung their entwined hands back and forth. "Maybe we should go to the party and find out. It'll be like a little adventure."

He smirked. "I don't know. I think we should check our schedules first and make sure we don't have any other plans. I mean...you know how it is, this can be such a busy time of year in the afterli–"

He didn't bother to finish because she had pinched him on the arm. Hard.

As they approached the northern corner of Washington Street, the melody of Sarah's soft laughter blended with the distant sound of people singing Christmas hymns. The music emanated from Our Lady Star of the Sea Church which sat facing the walking Mall. Made of large, gray granite bricks, the old building had a medieval presence about it and more closely resembled a gothic cathedral, with its high Romanesque round arches and tall, thick wooden doors. The light coming through the magnificent stained glass windows illuminated this end of the block, bathing the sidewalk and all its inhabitants in rich jewel-toned colors. The beautiful muted sound of people singing Christmas hymns floated through the air, so they stopped to listen. Obviously, inside the church midnight mass was still going on for the living. But outside, a crowd had gathered.

A crowd of ghosts. Dozens of them.

It didn't surprise him that so many spirits were here on the steps or on the sidewalks in front and on the side of the old church. What surprised him was that all of the ghosts were singing, right along with the people inside the church. Among the crowd, he noticed a Jewish man with a yarmulke on his head, a woman covered with a hijab, and a young girl wearing a cotton bonnet on her head and dressed in the simple frock of the Amish. No matter who they were—man, woman, child, young, old—every soul was arm in arm, or hand in hand, smiling, swaying to the music and singing. Every race, color and creed singing as one.

It was one of the most beautiful sights he had ever laid eyes on.

Still, a question formed in his mind. He leaned over to Sarah and whispered, "Don't you find this a bit strange? I mean, they're obviously not all Christian."

She stood thinking about this for a moment, before her mouth curved into a wondrous smile. "I guess they've just decided to respect each other's religion in the afterlife."

He nodded. Now that he was dead, this made perfect sense to him. What was the point in arguing about whose religion was the 'right' one anymore?

Sarah drifted through the church doors and he followed. He'd seen the Church on the Mall before when he had visited Cape May with his family years ago, but now he took a closer look at the stained glass windows and noticed that each one was etched with a name in the bottom corner. "I

THE GHOST CHRONICLES BOOK TWO

wonder what the names on the windows mean," he said to her.

Before she had a chance to hazard a guess, a woman next to them piped up. "Oh, those are the names of people who either donated the windows, or the name of someone in their family they wanted to memorialize." She pointed to one on the wall to the left of the main door. "See that one up there. My grandmother's family paid to donate that one in my uncle's memory."

As the song ended, he and Sarah drifted back outside. The joyous church bells rang out from the eighty foot high bell tower, echoing off the buildings and signaling the end of services.

The Jewish man he had seen earlier sat down to the side of the church steps and began to sing a Hanukkah song and spin a dreidel, along with the woman in the hijab, the little Amish girl and a young sailor. The three of them happily sang right along with the Jewish man as he spun the four-sided wooden toy.

This brought smiles to both he and Sarah's faces.

A moment later, the doors of the church opened and a slow stream of parishioners shuffled down the stone stairs. Bright smiles lit their faces and many exchanged Christmas greetings and well wishes with one another.

As Michael was about to ask Sarah where she wanted to go next, Tom suddenly materialized a few feet away, stalking toward them with an anxious expression etched across his face. "We only have a few moments," his friend said quickly.

He squeezed Sarah's hand protectively. "Before what?"

Tom had barely opened his mouth to reply when the ice-cold, sickening feeling crawled over Michael's flesh.

He already had his answer.

Demons.

CHAPTER THREE

BURN

MICHAEL GLANCED UPWARD and his knee started to quiver. He couldn't help it.

Above their heads, dozens of malevolent souls spilled out of a swirling, black vortex. It was as if the maw of hell had opened up. A dark, writhing horde of demons had descended upon the bell tower of Our Lady Star of the Sea and now enveloped the right side of the church. The inhuman figures didn't dare enter, but they were scaling the roof and walls, heading for the front entrance.

The rest of the dead must've finally caught sight of them too, for a few ghostly shrieks and screams now rang out across the Mall. Darting in several directions at once, every spirit in the crowd either dispersed or disappeared as fast as they could.

Unfortunately, the living continued to pour out of the church and onto the sidewalk, oblivious to the evil presence slithering closer and closer.

Michael tensed every limb, drawing energy from his surroundings. The lamppost to his left blew out, as he quickly sucked away all of its power.

Beside him, Sarah let out a frightened gasp. "Why are they here? Why now?"

"Because evil never takes a holiday," Tom declared, raising his arms to send a blast of pure radiant energy straight at the center of the circle of demons.

The blow struck, sending several shrinking away, but the flow of black shapes relentlessly kept on coming.

Michael harnessed the last bit of energy he could hold and sent a beam of his own radiating outward toward the approaching demons, as well.

His assault had virtually no effect. A few shrank back, but within seconds others crawled forward to take their place.

There were simply too many.

Ominously, the lights in the church began to brown out and flicker. He had no idea if the demons were responsible, but he wasn't going to wait around to find out.

"Sarah, come on!" he shouted. "We have to draw the demons away so they won't be a threat to all these people. You saw the destruction they caused at the school."

She nodded in agreement and thrust her hand in his. He would rather have sent her back to the Angel of the Sea, but with so many demons surrounding the square, he couldn't be sure she'd make it back unharmed. At least if she was by his side, he'd know she was safe.

They were just about to take flight when suddenly a commotion on the other side of the street caught their attention.

Sarah, Tom and Michael all turned to look simultaneously. But this time, the uproar had nothing to do with demons, or the dead.

Living men, women and children were screaming and running for their lives from an apartment complex across the street. Many stumbled out into the melting snow in their pajamas and bare feet.

It only took a second to realize why.

All manner of hell had broken out on the first floor. A fire raged on the right side of the apartment building. Whatever was going on had happened violently and without warning. Vicious flames leapt from the windows near the entrance, racing up the outside wall as if fueled by some unseen accelerant.

The blare of sirens already echoed faintly in the distance, but the fire was growing exponentially out of control.

As they all stood watching in horror, a window on the second floor suddenly exploded outward. A shower of fire and glass rained down on the crowd outside. More screams went up as the people tried to back away further and protect each other from the falling debris.

Chaos erupted in the square.

People who had been exiting the church now broke into a run.

Some charged across the street to help, while others, unsure of exactly what was going on, fled in terror.

A few priests and nuns from the church dashed into the rectory to fetch blankets and coats for the people who had evacuated the building and were standing outside in the frigid cold.

The demons swarming the church might not have caused the blast, but they now saw fit to join in the mayhem. Moving like a churning ball of hornets they took flight off the top of the church, thrashing and undulating their way across the street toward the roof of the burning building.

As the demon horde passed directly over their heads, all he could think was, *Oh, that can't be good.*

With lights flashing and sirens blaring, a police cruiser pulled up to the sidewalk.

Two officers jumped out and ran to give assistance. With outstretched arms, they began yelling instructions at the crowd of onlookers and evacuees. "Back! Get back! Clear the area here!"

Thick black smoke now poured from windows on both the first and second floors, as the flames advanced higher and higher up the side of the building.

A soul-shredding primal scream made all heads turn.

"Look there!" a young woman in the crowd shouted, frantically pointing to an upper window.

A small boy no more than four years old poked his round, cherubic head over the windowsill of an apartment on the third floor. Smoke billowed out around his tiny tear-streaked face as the child wailed in terror. He disappeared from the window only to reappear a moment later, apparently standing on something which had boosted him up. Wracked by coughing and clearly unable to take the heat and smoke, he placed one shaky leg over the windowsill and started to push himself over the edge.

Not wasting another second, Michael flew across the street with Sarah and Tom close at his heels.

The police officer didn't waste any time either. Grabbing the radio pinned to his chest, he relayed the dire situation to dispatch. "County 344, Officer 219. We have visible entrapment of a young subject on the *third* floor, need immediate assistance from fire and rescue with a ladder. Repeat, at least one entrapment, possibly more."

The response from dispatch was garbled, but immediate. "Officer 219, County 344 this is dispatch. Fire and rescue are en route to your location."

The officer now turned to the crowd. "Does anyone know whose child that is, or his name?"

A young teen stepped forward. "I live on the same floor," he said. "His mother works nights, so his grandfather looks after him. The kid's name is Emmitt, I think."

The officer spun around shouting up to the child, his voice calm, but full of authority. "Stay right there, Emmitt! It's gonna be okay. Help is on the way and we're gonna get you outta there. Just stay where you are!"

Overwhelmed with fear, Michael couldn't help but cry out to the child with his mind, *Listen to them, Emmitt! Stay right there! Don't move!*

The toddler paused for a second and momentarily slid his leg back down, but then, clearly confused and overwhelmed, he began to wail even louder.

Sirens ushering the arrival of the first Fire Department vehicle drowned out the boy's voice, as a red and white suburban skidded to a halt behind the police car. The Fire Chief emerged with a radio already in his hand, relaying information to dispatch, "Confirmed heavy fire, Engine 278 responding with a crew of six, ETA three minutes. We're gonna need two more alarms with ladders and rescue."

Sarah grabbed hold of his hand, her thoughts echoing his own. *My God. Hold on, Emmitt. Please hold on.*

Another garbled response came from the radio before the Chief looked up to see the child dangling from the window.

His eyes went wide. Switching gears, he quickly barked orders to his crew over the radio, "Upon arrival, first team take the thermo and a set of irons, begin primary search. We have a young victim visible on the A side of the building, third floor window, with heavy smoke. Second team, get our ladder in the air. Third team, drop supply lines on the A and B sides of the building..."

This time, Michael couldn't hear what else the Chief said. The sirens of the approaching fire engine blared as the ladder truck rounded the corner, roaring to a stop on Washington Street. In a flash, personnel hopped off the rig, darting about as fast as they could to grab gear, raise a rescue ladder to the window, and attach hoses to a nearby fire hydrant.

Help is here. His vice-grip on Sarah's hand eased, but it was short-lived.

Before the men could even get the ladder a few feet into the air the demons pounced, dropping from the sky like vultures descending upon prey.

Instantly, the ladder jammed. The confused firefighters had no idea demons had caused the sabotage, all they knew was the hydraulics had stopped working.

Seeing what the demons had done, he and Tom both shot bursts of energy straight at the black mass clustered around the base of the ladder.

As before, more demons simply took their place, as the frantic firefighters tried in vain to get the ladder mechanism operating.

Immediately, two brave firefighters laden with gear ran towards the entrance. Swinging an ax, they broke the glass of the front doors and took off into the burning building to rescue the toddler.

Despite the police officers urging them to get back, other desperate souls gathered beneath the window yelling at the child to hold on, arms outstretched in case they were going to have to try and catch him.

The rest of the bystanders, both living and dead, held their collective breath, all eyes riveted on the third floor.

The only ones who seemed to be enjoying the scene were the rest of the demons swirling above the roof. Whipped into some kind of frenzy, their nightmarish shrieking filled the night air. Tendrils of their dark evil energy stretched downward towards the window. Inching downward, downward, downward...towards Emmitt.

Enraged beyond rational thought, Michael shot a blast of energy directly above the roof to try and keep the demons away from the boy.

It didn't work for very long.

Again, Emmitt placed his leg on the windowsill in an attempt to climb out.

It was obvious what the demons wanted. For all he knew, they might even be urging the toddler to jump.

There was only a matter of minutes, maybe seconds, before the child would either burn to death or fall.

Sarah squeezed his hand once and yelled in her mind, *Go!*

He quickly glanced at Tom, who gave a solemn nod.

The two of them left her on the sidewalk, as they flew toward the burning building at top speed.

He had never flown directly through fire before. The

flames worried him a little, but the demons swirling over the rooftop worried him even more. Surprisingly though, they made no move to intercept them or attack.

Luckily, the flames had no effect on him either, other than to send a surge of energy coursing through him.

He reached the third floor first, with Tom close behind.

Fire and black choking smoke filled the hallway, as the two firefighters attempted to break down the heavy metal door. One inserted a pry bar iron into the door jam, while the other applied leverage pressure with the butt of an ax.

The door wouldn't budge.

Distant shouts and screams from the crowd telegraphed the worst—something awful was happening outside.

Oh my God, Emmitt must've crawled further onto the ledge.

A sickening panic swept through Michael like a tsunami. "They're not gonna be able to get to him in time!"

Tom hesitated for a moment, so that left him no choice. In a rush, Michael flew straight through the firemen and the door to reach the other side.

Spinning around, he discovered multiple dead bolt locks along the length of the door. *No wonder they can't get it open.* Gathering all his energy, one by one he unbolted each of the locks with lightning speed.

Once Tom heard the distinctive sound of the locks clicking open, he gently pushed on the door from the other side.

Michael stepped aside as the door swung inward a few inches.

The firefighters froze for a split second, staring in

disbelief at the open door before bursting into the room. One of them grabbed the crying child off the windowsill and threw him over his shoulder, while the other fireman swept the room with the thermal imaging camera. Picking up a human-shaped heat signature in the far corner, he found the grandfather lying incapacitated on the floor. Gingerly he scooped him up, and together the two firefighters followed each other through the smoke and flames to safety down the nearest stairwell.

Michael let out a heavy sigh, as a wave of relief reverberated through his soul. "You were told we could help protect him…weren't you?"

With a humble half-smile and a sheepish shrug, Tom waved him off. "They'll probably think the grandfather opened the door. Come on…let's make sure they get down the stairs with him."

In a blur Tom flew off to the right, through the now engulfed hallway, and disappeared around the corner.

Michael moved to follow, but stopped in mid-flight. Fingers of dread clawed their way up his spine.

Despite the tremendous heat of the fire surrounding him, what got his attention was the unmistakable surge of pure, ice-cold evil.

He spun around.

At the far end of the corridor he glimpsed three dark hooded figures.

Vampires.

With arms extended from their sides, a steady stream of white-hot fire shot from their hands as if they each carried a flame thrower—blasting the ceiling, hitting the walls, coating the floor. Behind them lay a river of flames and a path of destruction.

So, they had started the fire. *But why?*

The vampires must've now sensed his presence too. They whirled around at him, snarling and baring their pointed teeth.

Oh, crap.

Instinctively he tensed, preparing to draw in energy and do battle with the über-demons.

Much to his surprise, the three vampires did not engage him. Instead, they spun away from him into the flame-covered walls and disappeared.

Perplexed as he was by their mysterious departure, he wasn't going to waste any time looking that gift horse in the mouth.

Flying down the stairs, he caught up with Tom and Sarah outside.

He gave her a quick hug, relieved that she was alright. "What'd I miss?"

All she had to do was point at the sky and he had his answer.

High above the roof of the building, the inky, malevolent forms rotated clockwise, over and over again, agitating the air into a violent funnel. It only took a second to understand their devilish purpose.

Causing an updraft and directing the flames, they wanted the fire to intensify and spread to nearby buildings.

Tom's expression was grave. "Divide and conquer?"

Once more, he gathered his courage and nodded in agreement. "I don't have any better ideas."

"Okay, you try to draw them out of here," Tom said grimly. "And I'll stay and deal with those that don't follow you."

Again, he thought about sending Sarah back to the Angel of the Sea, but with so many demons around he couldn't be sure she wouldn't be followed. And with the fire about to jump buildings, there wasn't much time to consider other options. "Come on," he said to her, "we've got to lure the demons away from here. Now!"

Without a word and giving him all her trust, she obediently nodded, thrusting her hand in his.

Against his better judgment he took it and flew directly toward the mass of demons near the roof. He drew as close as he dared and then veered off to the right, taunting them so they would follow.

And they did.

Keeping Sarah within inches of him, Michael sped up Washington Street, banked hard left onto West Perry Street and then shot up Sunset Boulevard heading toward Cape May Point and Sunset Beach. Since it was so late on Christmas Eve, he prayed the restaurant and gift shop there would be deserted. He zig-zagged, he corkscrewed, all in an effort to lose the demons.

As they passed the old World War II Lookout Tower, he took a chance and glanced behind them.

He had no idea where they had come from, but the three vampires now joined the chase and were out in front leading the demon horde.

Sarah's face was horror-struck. "They're gaining on us!"

A few hundred feet more and they would run out of real

estate. The shoreline was closing in, but once they reached it they wouldn't be able to cross the water.

Now what do we do?

He hadn't had a specific plan, only a desire to draw the demons as far away from innocent people as possible and this was the most relatively uninhabited spot in Cape May he could think of.

But now that they had almost reached the beach, he had no idea what to do next. He could turn and fight, but they were sorely outnumbered. *And now I've put Sarah in terrible danger.*

When they ran out of sand, they were going to be over water.

Unless…

With the water's edge quickly approaching, he searched for something, anything that might provide some kind of sanctuary.

But he was coming up empty. There was simply nowhere to go.

Except for the dark silhouette sticking out of the water directly in front of them up ahead…

The shipwreck of the S.S. Atlantus, one of twelve concrete ships built during World War I. After several trans-Atlantic voyages, the ship was deemed impractical due to its enormous weight. The intention was to sink it to create a natural reef, so the Navy towed it to Cape May Point. But before they had a chance, the ship broke loose during a storm and ran aground in 1926.

He'd seen the remains of the Atlantus on a visit to Sunset Beach with his family years ago and heard about its strange history. Now, after all these years, the ship had sunk further and further below the surface of the water. Only a fraction of the skeletal remains of the ship's hull peeked out above the surf.

Seeing the wreck of the Atlantus, he suddenly remembered something his grandmother used to say, "Never question why God is taking you through troubled water. It's because he knows your enemy can't swim."

Oh, please let that be true.

It was their only chance, but it was a slim one. If they could make it across the water to what was left of the Atlantus, maybe the vampires and demons wouldn't be able to follow.

He only had seconds to decide. Whipping past Sunset Beach Gift Shop, he gathered speed and gripped Sarah's hand tighter.

She must've heard his thoughts. "Are we really going to try and *cross*?"

"Yes!" he shouted. "We have no other choice. It's only a few thousand feet out into the ocean. I'm hoping they won't be able to follow us over the water."

"But what if *we* can't cross it either?" she screamed in panic.

"It's our only hope!" he yelled back. "We've got to try!"

The demons were so close now, his legs had begun to sting with pain.

Whipping past the last streetlight, he tried to snatch one last bit of power to help them cross.

It wasn't enough.

For the second they reached the edge of the water and

flew out over the ocean, his energy deflated faster than a balloon with a hole in it. They continued to be propelled forward, but the air had become as viscous as mud, causing them to rapidly decelerate.

He couldn't risk using even an ounce of energy to look back and see if the demons had been able to follow. All he could do was pray they hadn't.

In his mind, he cried out to heaven, *we're taking a leap of faith here! Help us out!*

Their altitude dropped sharply and for a moment he was terror-stricken, sure they were going to plummet into the surf and dissipate, before ever reaching the Atlantus.

It took every last bit of his strength to propel them forward, but his feet gratefully touched down on the top of the shipwreck at the same time as Sarah's.

Landing on something solid restored a little of his energy. In one swift motion, he now whirled around to see if the demons had crossed.

Thankfully, they had stopped at the water's edge, but he was just in time to catch a sickening burst of green light as it surged from one of the vampires on the shoreline.

No!

He dove towards Sarah, but not before the blast hit her squarely in the chest.

Her face registered the pain and shock for only a second, before her legs buckled.

She pitched backward almost tumbling into the ocean.

He caught her limp body in his arms and went down on one knee to stop them both from falling. Hovering this close to the churning water below, and with barely any energy left, they couldn't control gravity's pull.

Gently, he laid her across one of the rusted beams of the ship's hull. The two of them now dangled precariously on the edge.

She slowly turned her face to look at him, but the pain behind her eyes was more than he could bear.

"Sarah! Sarah!" he screamed, willing her to stay with him, hoping her aura would remain whole, praying she would be okay.

But a breath later, her energy faltered and she vanished in his arms.

As his ghostly heart fractured into a million jagged pieces, he let out a scream so loud and so vicious, it practically shook the heavens.

He hoped it did.

CHAPTER FOUR

HOME

MICHAEL TRIED TO sit in one of the chairs in the parlor at the Angel of the Sea, but he only lasted five minutes before his leg bounced uncontrollably and he stood up again. It had only been a matter of hours and already he was losing his mind. He was grateful his plan to lure the demons away had worked and the evil beings eventually retreated, allowing him to escape, but he still blamed himself for Sarah getting hit.

All he could think about was waiting for her spirit to reconstitute and return so he could make it up to her.

The only problem was death still hadn't granted him even an ounce more patience than he had in life.

And so minute after minute, hour after hour, he paced.

And paced.

And paced.

Blissfully unaware of his presence, the guests had just sat down to afternoon Christmas tea in the festively decorated dining room. The staff had set the table with the finest holiday china and prepared a spread with all sorts of rich pudding, warm pies, and scrumptious pastries, each more delicious looking than the last.

For once, he couldn't even think about food.

Sensing an otherworldly disturbance, he glanced up to see a familiar face standing in the doorway.

Tom wore an expression of obvious and overwhelming concern. "Any sign of her?"

Michael paced back into the parlor. "No," he replied, giving it his best effort to fight off his annoyance. "I thought you said this was the most likely place her soul would return to?"

Tom placed his hand on the mantle, as if to steady himself. Clearly, even he was having a hard time with Sarah taking so long to reappear. "It should be," he said emphatically. "After all, she died here and she's been haunting this Victorian bed and breakfast for decades. Usually when a spirit's energy reconstitutes, it's in the place they frequented the most, or where they died because of all the emotions and energy they left behind from the event. Where their energy trail was freshest or strongest. I—"

Tom froze midsentence.

Out of the blue, Sarah's spirit had reappeared on the couch. Faint at first, and then becoming more distinct. She blinked for a moment or two, looking for all the world as if she had just woken up and didn't know where she was. Slowly, she put a hand to her head as if she was in pain.

Relief flooded through him, as he rushed to her side and knelt in front of her. He gently took her hand. "Sarah, Sarah," he pleaded. "Are you alright?"

She stared at him with a vacant expression.

No recognition at all.

This shook him to his very core, more than anything else that had happened so far. Even more than the terror of seeing her spirit dissipate before his very eyes on the wreck of the Atlantus.

He had no idea what to do. There was no playbook for this.

After a few minutes of awkward silence, his prayers were finally answered. Her eyes grew wider, as realization gradually dawned on her face.

She threw her arms around his neck, weeping into his shoulder.

He almost could've wept right along with her.

Once she cried it all out, he put a finger under her chin and raised her face upwards so he could look into her eyes. "Are you alright, Hon?"

She nodded, but winced at the effort. "I think so, but I've got the worst headache of all time. How's that even possible?"

He grinned. "I have no clue, but I had one too after this happened to me. One more cruel joke of the afterlife I guess." He eased her down onto the couch and laid her head on a pillow, before cautiously brushing a soft kiss upon her lips.

She threw her arms around his neck, kissing him back more fervently than he had expected. The warmth of her kiss filled him from the inside out. A tremendous feeling of love and gratitude washed over him. His universe was whole again, as if a wondrous planet had been thrown back into alignment.

"I'll leave you two alone," Tom said quietly, as he began to back out of the parlor.

Michael kissed her again, this time gently on the

forehead. "There. Let that soak in," he whispered in her ear. As much as he didn't want to let go of her, he stood up and called out to his friend, "Hold on a minute."

He drew Tom over by the dining room for privacy, hoping Sarah wouldn't be able to hear his troubled thoughts. "Why didn't she remember who I was right away?"

Tom's expression was grim. "I told you. That's what happens when you get hit by a demon. Your energy eventually reconstitutes, but not without some damage to your memories and your soul."

Michael scrunched up his face in confusion. "But it didn't affect me that badly when I got hit. I thought losing your memory only happened if you were hit multiple times, like three or more."

"Usually that's true, but it can vary," Tom replied. "It's different for everyone. For some spirits, one or two good hits is all it takes. Others might not feel much of an affect till after a half dozen. It depends on the strength of the hit, how direct it was, if it had to pass through anything…all these factors can affect how much permanent damage the hit inflicts upon a person's consciousness."

He shook his head and turned to walk back into the parlor, but Tom snatched him by the arm.

"Wait, there's one more important thing I need you to understand…"

The concern on Tom's face rattled him. He wasn't quite sure he wanted the answer, but he asked anyway. "What's that?"

Tom cast a sidelong glance in Sarah's direction. "No matter what…it *always* gets worse with each successive hit."

His mentor's warning sent a cold shiver through his soul. Something else still troubled him, too, though. "How did you know the demons were coming?"

That enigmatic expression he'd seen so many times before returned to Tom's face. "Let's just say I received a tip you might be in trouble," he replied vaguely.

Michael hated feeling like a child who was being babysat, so he changed tack. "I ran into three vampires on the third floor right after you left. I have no doubt they caused the fire, but what's really strange is when they first saw me they fled without a fight." He leveled his eyes on him, hoping to get a straight answer for once. "Why do you think they didn't come after me until I was away from the fire?"

"I'm not sure," Tom replied, pacing away from him. "I had the feeling from the beginning that this was all some kind of a distraction, some sort of a test to see what you and I would do…if we would fight the demons or save the boy."

He considered this for a moment. In a way it made some sense, but only led him to more questions. *Like…whose test was it? And had he passed or failed?*

He leveled his eyes on his friend. "You mean the demons could be testing us for weaknesses?"

"Exactly." Once again, that faraway look flickered on Tom's face.

"Let me guess," he said with a roll of his eyes, "you've got to go."

Tom nodded and slowly began to fade. "Oh, I almost forgot…Merry Christmas."

"Merry Christmas," he said, returning the sentiment, but

the moment his mentor was gone his intuition started niggling at him.

Clearly, Tom knew the demons would show up. But an uneasy question kept surfacing in his mind. Was Tom trying to protect him or lead him into trouble? He couldn't be sure. He'd had this same feeling on that Halloween night in Salem when they were attacked. This same uncanny sixth sense that Tom had led him to Vassago and his vampire minions, rather than leading him away.

He didn't want to mistrust Tom, but was he being a bit too naïve? Was Tom leading him astray from where he should go? He still had the sense Tom was keeping secrets. Could his friend be trusted? The bitter truth was…he wasn't sure anymore.

With a thousand questions still churning in his mind, he drifted back into the parlor to see how Sarah was feeling.

He crouched beside her once more, kissed her gently on the lips and wrapped his arms around her. Silently, he held her. There were no words for the emotions coursing through him.

She responded by nuzzling into his shoulder. "That was awful."

"I have to agree with you there," he admitted, holding her tightly to his chest. He let out a heavy sigh. "For oh so many reasons, we both better find our way out of the afterlife real freakin' quick."

Wrapping her arms around his neck, she whispered into his ear, "Don't worry. Even if we can't find heaven, we've found each other. And I'll walk through hell with you if I have to."

A tremor of anxiety rolled through him. Closing his eyes, he pressed her hand to his lips and kissed her fingers tenderly, as if he might never get the chance again.

With the utmost sincerity, he looked her deep in the eyes and said, "Let's hope it doesn't come to that."

. . .

They spent the remainder of Christmas day recovering from the madness of the night before, and watching the friends and guests at the Angel of the Sea enjoying themselves. Since the parlor was so crowded, he had to sit next to her atop the registration desk—it was the only spot in the room where they could be sure a living person wouldn't plop themselves right on top of them. And floating near the ceiling all the time got a bit too tedious.

By nightfall, he had grown restless again. As they listened to the living guests sing Christmas carols by the roaring fireplace, watched them pass around hors d'oeuvres and champagne, and felt the joyous emotions flowing out of them, his right knee jerked wildly and he couldn't keep his hands still no matter how hard he tried. Memories of holidays past assaulted him from every direction.

Naturally, his thoughts drifted to his family. This may have been his first Christmas with Sarah and his first being dead, but the fact that it was his family's first Christmas without him, hit him the hardest. He remembered those first few holidays without his dad and he could only imagine what his mother and brother must be going through. And ever since his last visit a couple weeks ago, he had more than enough reason to be terribly worried about them.

Sarah must've overheard his thoughts. "Michael, why don't you go visit your family?"

He hopped down from the registration desk and helped her down too. He was ninety-nine percent sure he knew what her answer would be, but he asked her anyway, "Do you want to come with me?"

She shook her head. "No, I think you should go alone. I'm not really sure I have all my energy back yet and you don't want to drag me along. I'll be fine here...really."

Touched by her understanding, he kissed her first on the forehead and then softly on the lips. To some small extent, he still grieved for his lost life and he was grateful she gave him what he needed most—the space to work it out on his own.

"I love you," he said with all his heart.

She squeezed his hand and let him go. "I love you too," she said. "Now hurry along. I want you back as soon as possible." A devilish smile played at the corners of her luscious mouth.

Taking her face in his hands, he couldn't resist kissing her one last time.

But if he didn't leave now, he never would.

Pulling away, he left her in the parlor and drifted out onto the porch.

After watching the ocean waves for a bit, he was ready. As he had so many times before, Michael closed his eyes and focused on the memory of his home. When he opened them again, he was standing on the sidewalk in front of his house on Fieldpoint Drive.

At his very first glance, his heart sank with disappointment. Since the two holidays came close to the same time this year, most of the houses on his block were lit up for either Christmas or Hanukkah.

Except for his.

Not only were there still no Christmas lights hung, but the normal porch lights which should be on at night didn't seem to be working either. Compared to his neighbor's, his house looked like a gaping black hole. And the window where the Christmas tree should be was still empty, too.

Michael steeled his resolve. He hoped there would be improvement, but deep down inside something told him the situation was probably going to be even worse than it was a couple weeks ago. But he ached to see his family. *How much worse could things have gotten?*

As his curiosity won out, he ghosted through the front door. Immediately he wished he hadn't asked such a stupid question. He now stood in the middle of the living room, *if you could even call it that*. The room was hardly in a condition anyone would consider livable.

When he had visited before, the house had been dirty.

Today, it was heart-breakingly filthy.

The little tree in the corner of the living room that had been dying last time he visited was now deader than he was. Not a needle left on the poor thing. Every branch lay bare and bending downward.

No sign of any Christmas decorations, or any Christmas presents, or any Christmas at all.

The pile of unopened mail had grown and toppled off the coffee table. The same newspapers still lay scattered all over the floor. The pile of shoes and dirty clothes had multiplied tenfold. Sticky red cups, used paper plates and take out containers lay everywhere. Anyone coming into this house would honestly wonder if it was occupied by hoarders. *Thank God, I don't have a decent sense of smell anymore.*

Turning the corner, he drifted into the hallway.

The grandfather clock was still stuck at eight fifteen. *Why am I not surprised?*

As he made his way into the kitchen, his heart nearly stopped for a second time. If he hadn't already been dead, he certainly would've gone into sudden cardiac arrest.

Must've been one hell of a rager. More liquor bottles, shot glasses, and beer cans than he could count littered the table and countertops. Some *one,* or some *thing,* had punched a basketball-size hole in the wall next to the refrigerator. Two broken cabinet doors hung pathetically from their hinges. Unwashed dishes and glasses lay stacked in the sink, half of them broken too.

He slowly walked back out into the living room, sat down in his father's favorite chair and put his head in his hands. How had things come to this? *This is the saddest and most depressing Christmas I've ever seen in this house.* Nothing like the holidays they used to celebrate as a family.

With no mercy, freeze-frames of Christmases past now flooded his mind. He tried as hard as he could to banish them, but the emotions ran too deep, too strong. These fond memories were part of the very fabric of his soul. Precious memories so vivid, so sharp, so sensory, they had been cut into his soul with the precision of a diamond.

Closing his eyes, he saw himself as a young boy,

chopping down his first Christmas tree at a local farm with his father and little brother. Running down the stairs Christmas morning to discover a shiny new bike beneath a brightly decorated tree bursting with color and sparkle. Tearing the glittering paper off boxes as fast as his fingers could fly. Helping his brother build the Connect-It roller coaster he'd wanted so badly, the one with forty-eight pages of instructions. Watching his mother hand his father a glass of eggnog, kiss him and wish him a Merry Christmas. So obviously happy, so obviously still in love.

The memory of an even earlier Christmas wiggled its way into his consciousness—the year he turned eight. That year was a turning point for him. The last year he truly believed in Santa Claus, the last year his brother was considered a toddler, and the last year he considered himself a 'little' boy.

For one of the briefest moments, he wished he was back there, wished he was that little boy who still believed in Santa, wished his father wasn't dead, wished he himself wasn't dead, but then…in his mind's eye he saw Sarah's smiling face. His love for her banished any regret or longing for the past. She was his steady satellite. If he hadn't died, he might never have met her. Now, he couldn't imagine being without her.

The sound of voices on the second floor shook him from his reverie and brought him painfully back to the present.

He followed the noises up the stairs and slipped through the door to his brother's bedroom. Right away he regretted it, pressing his lips together, as disgust washed through him. The sight before him made him want to wretch even more than anything he'd seen so far. He couldn't help but wonder, *can a ghost actually vomit?*

Nick Rossi lay across his brother's bed propped up on one arm. In front of him, lay rows and rows of flat white pills he was counting out into tiny envelopes. A few wisps of smoke rose from a nearby bowl brimming with pot.

Great, this idiot's gonna set the bed on fire.

Chris sat at his desk dividing a heaping mound of marijuana into plastic sandwich baggies.

So now he's selling this stuff, too.

Nick offered Chris the bowl.

Michael's heart broke in two as his brother paused what he was doing to take a big hit.

Chris passed the bowl back, snatching an open bag of Doritos from Nick's lap. The two of them started laughing and fighting like a pair of childish idiots. Half the chips spilled on the floor. As Nick got up from the bed he stepped on most of them, grinding the cheesy orange triangles into the carpet. "I've gotta piss," the dirt bag mumbled.

Classy. For a split-second, Michael considered following him, maybe even pushing him down the stairs on his way to the bathroom.

No, he hadn't really meant that, but the thought was tempting. Very tempting.

He left his brother's room before he got angry enough to really do it, and drifted further down the hall.

Peeking into her bedroom, he found his mother passed out and snoring on her bed, her clothes still on and her hand still wrapped around a fifth of whiskey. Tilting sideways, the bottle had partially spilled brown liquor onto the side of the bedspread and splattered on the carpet. On top of the nightstand, more empty bottles sat next to the alarm clock, which read only 9:15 pm.

Her mascara had run down her cheeks in black tear-stained streaks. She had been crying. Of course, she'd been crying. He could've guessed she would've been, but actually seeing her this way tore him apart like a grenade, the shrapnel of her pain tearing mercilessly through his own ghostly heart.

For a moment he stood frozen, his mind drifting back to his childhood. Another memory unwanted and unbidden slipped forward from the archives. He was six. Standing in the doorway of his parent's bedroom, much the same as he was now—frightened and needy, but for a very different reason.

He'd had a terrifying, vivid nightmare and awoken with the sweats. Now, he was too scared to go back to sleep or even be alone. Trouble was he was equally afraid of asking his parents if he could climb into bed with them, for fear his father would tell him to man up and go back to his own bedroom. His lower lip quivered, tears threatening to betray his cowardice. Luckily, in a moment of fatherly compassion his dad let him slide into bed between them. Enveloped in their safety and love, he had drifted off into a blissful sleep.

Now, he had once again had a nightmare. The only difference was this time the nightmare was real.

It took all his effort to choke back his emotions before the waterworks would come on full force and he would lose complete control. A phantom pain stabbed his gut, as he grappled with the overwhelming sadness for his family.

Without hesitating, he carefully slid on top of the covers next to his mother.

A small sob slipped out from her lips while she slept. He wanted so badly to comfort her, for her to know he was there, that he was okay. It was all going to be okay.

Wasn't it?

Tentatively, he reached out and touched her shoulder, pushing the comforter further over so it fell enough to cover her. She whimpered slightly in her sleep. Could she sense he was there? He tried projecting his thoughts into her mind, willing her to feel his presence.

"Mom? Mom, it's Michael. I love you, Mom. I'm right here," he whispered, as he stroked her bedraggled hair. "I'm okay. I'm alright. Please don't worry about me. You don't need to worry about me. I'm almost there. There really is a heaven...or somewhere to go anyway...and one way or another, I'm gonna get there. Please, take care of yourself and Chris." Tears welled up in his eyes and his jaw began to quiver uncontrollably. "Don't miss me. Don't cry for me. I'm alright. Really. I'm alright," he repeated. "Everything is going to be okay now."

For a moment, he thought to himself. *Who am I trying to convince, her or me?*

"I love you, Mom," he choked out. "I love you so much."

And for the first time in his afterlife, he cried as if he were six years old again.

• • •

His mother slept until noon the next day. All night long he lay next to her, wishing there was something he could do for her, wishing he could take away her pain, wishing he didn't feel so damned helpless.

When she finally got up, he floated behind her as she hobbled unsteadily down the stairs, all the while gripped by a terrible fear that she might fall. Luckily, she made it downstairs without incident.

He hovered off in the corner, keeping an eye on her.

She boiled water in one of the last clean pots, took out a chipped mug and made instant coffee. Her hands shook as she held the cup and sipped. She was gradually turning into skin and bones. How long had it been since she'd last eaten a good meal?

His brother came down a few minutes later, his eyes still bloodshot and glazed over. He didn't say a word to his mother, just moved around her as if she wasn't there.

Within minutes, the obvious truth smacked him painfully in the face.

They aren't even speaking a word to each other anymore.

It was all too heart-breaking to bear. There was no point in watching any of this another minute. Without a second glance, he slipped unseen through the back door.

Dark gray clouds hung heavy in the sky, blocking out the sun. They fit his mood perfectly.

Once outside, an odd thought struck his consciousness. Something he'd been too upset to notice before.

Where was his dog? Where was Samantha?

CHAPTER FIVE

FRIENDS

SAMANTHA'S CONSTANT HOWLING and snubs had been difficult to take in the days following his death, but he still longed to see his canine companion. Come to think of it, he hadn't seen her when he was here the last time either, but he'd been so distraught he never noticed.

Had they gotten rid of her? Was it too much for them to even take care of the family dog?

The thought had barely crossed his mind when a white mist moved into the corner of his peripheral vision. The movement caught him off guard and he whirled around as Samantha's familiar bark echoed across the yard. He fell to his knees as she bounded over to him, lapping his face with big, sloppy licks. He'd never been so happy to see her in all his life. Grinning from ear to ear, he grabbed her in a bear hug and clutched her to his chest. He stroked her fur and tried to calm her down. She seemed just as excited to see him.

But something was different. He knew it the instant he touched her, because she didn't flinch.

Samantha's dead, too.

As if she were reading his mind, the dog barked twice and shuffled toward the back of the yard. She kept turning around and giving a single bark, which clearly meant, *follow me you silly human.*

His eyes now fell upon a small plaque. Someone had placed it under one of the old oaks, not far from where his father had collapsed on that fateful summer day. With her tail wagging away, the German Shepherd barked at the wooden marker as if to say, *go ahead, read it.*

Samantha 'Sam' Andrews

Our Beloved Dog

"So they buried you here," Michael said solemnly, as he roughed up her fur around her neck and stroked his hand down her back to comfort her. *Was she even upset about being dead? About being stuck?* She didn't seem like it. This intrigued him though, because he thought animals didn't have souls. He made a mental note to ask Tom about this. Maybe Disney actually got it right? *Maybe all dogs really do go to heaven?*

He creased his brow, lost in thought as he pet the dog. His ghostly heart nearly melted as she nuzzled her head against his leg, even as his insides twisted with grief. "What happened, girl?"

Almost as if she could understand his question, she raised her nose up to touch his face. Instantly, a mental picture came into his head. Sam laying around lethargic, getting sick to her stomach multiple times, his mother driving her back and forth to the clinic. Mary receiving the grim diagnosis from the vet—it was probably Leukemia or some other type of canine cancer. And then finally, Mom and Chris saying their tearful goodbyes as the vet put the dog to sleep.

Michael bit down hard, as a fat tear slid down his own

cheek. He looked up to heaven and couldn't help the blistering anger that rolled through him. *Really, God? Really? You had to take the dog away from them too?*

He shook his head, trying not to be ungrateful. At least he got to see her again.

"But why haven't you moved on, Sam?"

This time in answer to his question the dog took off across the yard, up the back porch steps, pacing in half circles and barking at the back door.

Instinctively, he understood what his canine companion was trying to tell him. "You're staying here for a while because of them. To protect them."

His old friend barked at his words in confirmation. Even in death she was a faithful pet, man's best friend.

He smiled. "Wanna take a walk, girl?"

Sam barked again and promptly plopped down on the back porch. Her reaction surprised him. She would never have said no to a walk, but just like Sarah had been, the dog was obviously reluctant to leave the safety and security of home. He couldn't blame her. With demons after him at every turn, the afterlife could be one hell of a scary place at times.

He floated over to say goodbye to the dog, giving her another big squeeze and rub on the top of the head. "I'll be back again soon, Sam. I promise."

As he turned to leave he said to her, "But you're not gonna stay for too long now, girl, you hear? You're going over that rainbow bridge everyone's always talking about as soon as you can. Promise?"

In response, Samantha gave one short, crisp bark which made him smile.

Strolling through the fence, his mind wandered to the only other person from his hometown he cared enough about to visit.

Melissa.

Her house wasn't that far away. Only seven blocks or so. He could orb, or fly, or memory travel, but more than anything else he ached to feel normal for a little while, so he chose to walk.

As he passed his driveway and Mr. Jasinski's house, the front door opened and out spilled four children—Mr. J's youngest nieces and nephews, all of them younger than ten and wound up with sugar and holiday overload. The two oldest boys traded blows with glowing light-sabers, while the two younger girls took off down the sidewalk on Razor scooters.

He had to smile at how full of life and hyper the kids were behaving. *If only I could harness that kind of energy next time I have to battle the freaking demons.*

Next, a smiling Mr. J came out onto the porch. Obviously, he was there to make sure the children didn't kill each other with the weaponry.

Michael hadn't seen him since the funeral. A sickening hollowness hit his chest, as he realized how much he had missed his dear old neighbor, too.

Mr. J's laughter echoed down the street as the boys now took their battle to the lawn. The way they were playing reminded him of the many sword fights he and Chris used to have when they were that age.

He watched with interest, until all of a sudden a door slammed behind him.

Chris and Nick had just come out of his house, headed for the car in the driveway. A lit cigarette dangled obnoxiously from his brother's lips. To complete the dirt bag look, his filthy jeans sagged halfway off his ass too.

Nick passed within a few feet of him.

His jaw tensed, as his hands curled into tight fists. It was all he could do not to reach out and punch him in the face. Hard. Very hard. For that matter, the thought crossed his mind that he desperately wanted to deck his brother, too.

Mr. J glanced in Chris's direction as if he itched to say something, or throttle him also, but instead he simply shook his head. He didn't even bother calling out a friendly hello or Merry Christmas.

So Mr. J knows. The realization hit him like another sucker punch to the kidneys. His family was such an embarrassment. He couldn't watch anymore, so he slowly drifted down the street toward Melissa's house.

• • •

When he arrived, he found their driveway packed with cars. Of course, it's Christmastime. They've probably got company over.

He hated intruding, but he wanted so badly to see how Melissa was doing. After a few minutes wrestling with his emotions, he slipped through the front door and into their entrance hall.

Their house couldn't have been more opposite than his depressing home. Festive signs of the holidays were everywhere. As usual, Melissa's family had put up a real

Christmas tree, perfectly shaped and adorned with more ornaments than it could safely hold. Red fuzzy stockings hung from the mantle over the fireplace, evergreen boughs laced up the bannister, gold and silver decorations spread over nearly every inch of the living room. And since Melissa's mom, Karen, was half Jewish, a Menorah with three lit candles was also prominently displayed on a round table surrounded by presents.

A pall of sadness for his family moved through his spirit. *Now,* this *is the way a holiday should look.*

Happy voices and lively, pleasant chatter carried from the kitchen where the family was gathered.

He halted in his tracks, unsure if he wanted to go through with this. *How painful is this going to be?*

His curiosity won out over his fear though. He hadn't seen Melissa since that awful night in the hospital, so he wanted to be sure she had fully recovered from her fall.

The fall that was one hundred and ten percent his fault.

He glided over to the dining room just as everyone was coming out of the kitchen to sit down for dinner. Lit candles, bottles of wine, and white poinsettias graced each end of the elegantly set table.

Karen carried a platter of pot roast from the kitchen. Melissa came through the doorway next with a smile on her face and a glass of wine in her hand. Wearing a tight red dress that flattered her figure, she was as attractive as ever. Other than the soft cast on her arm, she looked perfectly healthy.

As the guilt on his conscience lightened up, he breathed a sigh of relief.

Next, Craig and his mother came out of the kitchen each carrying serving bowls of mashed potatoes and vegetables. Their presence at a holiday meal clinched it. *Melissa and Craig are still dating.*

While the rest of them took their seats, Michael stood at a distance in the corner, taking it all in. *This is the way a holiday should be*—hearty laughter, the warm company of close family and friends, a casual ease and a deep sense of belonging that comes from a lifetime of togetherness.

That should be me and my family sitting there. Any other Christmas it would have been. Yet, it didn't bother him as much as he had thought it would.

The conversation inevitably worked its way around to a discussion about college. Melissa's father turned to Craig. "So how did your first semester at Rutgers go?"

"It went really well," Craig responded confidently.

"That's good to hear. Melissa tells me you're considering a transfer to Pitt though," her father added, casting a not-so-subtle glance at his wife, Karen.

Michael had known Melissa's father long enough to know when he was fishing for information. Over the years, he'd been on the end of a hook a time or two, as well.

"Yeah, I am," Craig said, "I'm going to be changing my major to Neuroscience and I've heard good things about their program at Pitt. Staying at Rutgers is just too close to home for me." He shot Melissa a warm smile. "I've decided I want to go a bit further away for college." Meanwhile under the table, he nonchalantly grabbed Melissa's hand, giving it a squeeze.

All of a sudden, the obvious hit Michael like a sharp slap

upside the head. He could tell by how they were still holding hands. He could tell by the way they were looking at each other. *They're really in love. Maybe they'll even go the distance and get married.*

After dinner, they all gathered in the living room to exchange presents, drink more wine, and watch holiday movies.

He stood by, reading her emotions, and as far as he could tell, Melissa seemed one hundred percent happy.

And he couldn't have been happier for her.

As the evening drew to a close, he followed her upstairs to the guestroom, watching Craig kiss her goodnight. Her mother stood outside at the end of the hall, making sure they parted and slept in separate bedrooms.

He chuckled, thinking about how Karen would probably never change. *If you only knew the things Melissa and I had done in your basement.*

Craig gently brushed a hair from Melissa's face. "What's wrong, sweetheart?"

"I was thinking a lot about…about Michael today," she confessed.

He held his breath expectantly, but much to his surprise, instead of being jealous or angry, Craig pulled her into a great big bear hug. "I figured you were," he said with a heavy sigh.

She titled her head and looked into his eyes. "Are you mad?"

"Of course not," Craig replied, as he wiped a tear from her cheek. "He was my best friend. I miss him, too."

A phantom lump formed in Michael's throat, as he fought back more tears.

God knows he should be jealous. He has every right to be mad.

"You know," Craig continued, "I always thought he was the luckiest guy in the world because he had you. Who would've ever thought he'd be the most unlucky of us all."

Michael was both impressed and humbled by his friend's words. All that time, Craig had obviously been admiring Melissa from afar. Probably crushing on her big time. And yet, he was a true friend and never put so much as a toe out of line. Never made a play for her. Never acted jealous. Not even for a moment.

They both hugged each other hard before Melissa said, "Look, I'm sorry for being so bummed out. I don't wanna ruin our weekend. I'm really looking forward to this ski trip. And I'm so glad my mother let you stay here tonight so we could leave early in the morning."

Craig smiled and kissed her on the lips. "Yeah, me too. But you better get outta here before she knocks on the door. I'm sure your mother's counting the minutes you've been in here," he said with a chuckle.

Melissa grinned. "She'll never change."

Michael turned away and slipped out through the door.

A moment later, Melissa emerged from the guestroom. She went into the bathroom for a few minutes while Michael waited in the hall. He sat on the floor with his head resting against the wall. He thought about leaving, but there was still one more thing he desperately wanted to do.

As Melissa entered her bedroom, he slipped in right behind her.

She changed into her pajamas, crawled into bed, and as

usual, curled up with the latest best-seller. Finally, her head lolled to the side and her eyelids drooped shut.

Rhythmically her chest rose and fell, rose and fell. When he was sure she was sound asleep, he sat down on the bed beside her and gently stroked her hair. He couldn't feel it, of course, but he was hoping she might be able to sense his presence on some level. "Melissa," he whispered, "it's me. It's Michael. Don't be frightened or anything. It's all good."

He paused to chew on the side of his lip before continuing. "I want you to know I'm happy for you. I really am," he said, completely sincere. "Craig's a great guy and I'm sure he'll be good to you." Still, he couldn't help mumbling under his breath, "He better be."

Reaching out, he lightly touched her cheek. "What we had...it was super special and I'll always remember it." A pleasant sigh slipped from his lips. "But what Sarah and I have is...something more. Much more. Something like what you and Craig have, I think. I wish you both all the happiness in the world."

He bent down, closed his eyes, kissed her gently on the forehead, and left her to her dreams. Deep down inside he knew it would be the last time he ever kissed her. She wasn't his anymore.

But for once, he was okay with that.

He crossed the hall and drifted back into the guest bedroom where Craig was already snoring. A smile crossed his face, as he sat down on the chair beside the bed. To say he was proud of his loyal friend would've been the understatement of the century.

Leaning forward, he carefully projected his thoughts into Craig's mind. "Hey man, it's Michael. I'm hoping you can hear me, bro. I don't really know if this whole talking-to-living-people-while-they-sleep thing works, but in case it does, I just wanted to say…I'm really glad she landed on her feet with you and not some schmuck," he said in all honesty. "I wish you both all the luck in the world. Take good care of her, man. Be good to her."

He rose to leave, but at the last second swiveled back around. "Oh, and one more thing, don't you dare ever do anything to hurt her. If you're always good to her, then you have nothing to worry about. If you're *not*…better sleep with one eye open cause I'll haunt the living shit out of you."

Satisfied he had made his point, he glided out into the hallway and back down the stairs.

Suddenly an emotional vibration rattled through him the likes of which he'd never felt before. His thoughts abruptly shifted to Matt. In his mind, his friend's panicked voice echoed, calling his name.

He didn't know what was happening so he tried to shake it off, but a sharp pull and tug at the very center of his soul gave him the undeniable answer, *I'm being summoned.*

Obediently, he closed his eyes and allowed his consciousness to take him where he needed to go.

He had finished all he had come to do here anyway.

CHAPTER SIX

PAWN

A MOMENT LATER, Michael materialized on a tree-lined street in a cozy neighborhood on the other side of Branchburg. Matt stood on the sidewalk directly across from what must've been his house, a center hall colonial with a three car garage.

It took only a second to realize what the trouble was.

The entire house was surrounded by a tangle of demons. Dozens of them slithered from the rooftop to the ground floor. So many black figures covered the house it was nearly impossible to see inside.

"Thank God," Matt exclaimed when he saw him. "I'm sorry I had to summon you like that, but I didn't know what else to do. My sister's trapped inside!"

Michael looked up at the house which was nearly eclipsed by the undulating mass of demons. "Where the hell is she?"

"On the second floor, I think," Matt said. His voice trembled as he gestured toward the house. "If I look hard enough and the demons move at just the right moment, I can see her every once in a while in the front bedroom window."

Michael trained his eyes on the house, straining to see.

"There!" Matt exclaimed, pointing frantically.

Sure enough, he caught a glimpse of Emily's terrified face pressed up against the window.

As the demons closed around the gap once more, Matt's eyes went wild, his voice desperate and full of hysteria. "I don't understand what they want! It's like they've barricaded her in. They're not entering the house to hurt her, but they won't leave either. And every time I try to get close they start reaching out to come after me."

Just as he finished, the demons seemed to increase their frenzy.

"It's weird. But they seem extra agitated now that you've arrived," Matt said in a worrisome tone. "Maybe they know we're going to try and bust her out?"

We are? Michael thought in alarm. Mustering his courage and his wits, he replied, "Ummm, okay. But I think we're going to need a bit more help."

"Whatever it takes," Matt said. "We've got to get her out of there before they do anything to her."

Michael closed his eyes, concentrated, and in his mind as loud as he could, he called out one name, *Tom Wright*.

Instantly, his mentor materialized beside them.

"That was quick," Michael said.

"I was finishing up with something and started to get this niggling sense you needed me," Tom replied matter-of-factly.

Matt pointed to his house across the street. "You've got that right."

The frenzy of the demons seemed to further increase, their wild shrieks and screams growing louder.

"Let me see what happens if I try to approach the house," Michael declared. As he began to draw energy from the streetlights surrounding them, he turned to Tom. "Got my back?"

"Of course."

In one swift movement, Michael flew across the street and delivered a stream of energy directly at the demons congested on the porch.

Instead of shrinking back like they usually did, they ignored the blast and came straight for him.

Tendrils of evil energy whipped and grabbed at him, close enough that they burned his limbs with an ice-fire pain that threatened to bring him to his knees.

From behind him, a white flash zinged right past his head. So close, the heat of it nearly burned his ear.

Another shot of energy. This one from Tom.

Michael managed to make it back to their side of the street without the demons capturing him, but he was drained. Still shaking, he turned to Matt. "Is that what happened when you tried to get near the house before?"

"Sort of, but they didn't come after me as viciously as they came after you," he replied, his voice unsteady. "And look at them now."

Clearly, he'd poked the hornet's nest. The demons had gone wild. Spinning round and round in an unholy dance.

"They seem even more interested in capturing you than they were in me," Matt said.

Tom's expression was grave. "I'm afraid he's right," he agreed. "There's something about your presence that's making them extra crazy."

Matt addressed Tom, pleading for answers. "But I don't understand. Why don't they just grab her?"

"Yeah," Michael added, "they're not even touching her. Why hold her hostage, but not go near her?"

"Because they'd hurt her if they touched her and I get the feeling she's not the one they're after," Tom said. "They're sending Matt a very clear message that they won't hurt her as long as he surrenders himself. They're basically only using her as a pawn."

Michael narrowed his eyes on Tom. "Why can't she just orb or memory travel out of there? I never did get to ask you that."

Tom met his gaze with concern behind his eyes. "Because the demons are too close. It would be too easy for them to capture her energy while she's in that form, easier than capturing a fire fly in a bottle," he explained. "And she can't pass her energy through theirs in any way or they would only absorb her. She needs some kind of an opening in order to escape."

A hole in their defense. His father's advice echoed in his head, *play to your strengths.* As he would've on the basketball court in the heat of battle, Michael steadied his nerves. "I think I know how to get her out," he said excitedly. "Maybe we can use their interest in me to our advantage. Since I seem to agitate them the most, I'll go around to the back of the house and pretend as if I'm trying to punch a hole through their barrier, while the two of you use the distraction to drill a hole in through the front and get her out."

"We'll give it a try," Tom replied. He glanced at Matt. "Are you ready?"

"I'll try anything if it'll get Emily out of there," Matt replied with determination.

"Okay," Michael said, "give me an extra few minutes once I get around back, then start your assault on the front. Matt, try to get through to Emily's mind and let her know what we're doing so she knows to head for the gap in the front."

He placed his hands on a nearby lamppost. As he drew in energy, another thought hit him. "One last thing. Even once we get her out, we may still not be safe." He turned to Matt. "Is there a church or any type of religious building around here?"

Matt gestured up the street. "There's a synagogue about two blocks in that direction. It's next to the park. You can't miss it."

"Perfect, that'll do," he said. "Once we get her out, everyone head for that synagogue."

Matt clenched his fists, drawing in energy. "Let's do this."

Let's roll, Michael thought, as he zoomed across the street, making a wide arc around to the back of the house.

Getting as close as he dared, he let loose with all he had.

It was working. The demons began massing at the back of the house.

But now he had another problem. His clever ploy had worked too well.

The demons now had a new target.

And he was it.

He poured every bit of energy he had gathered into a continuous stream at the back of the house.

But he couldn't fend off all of them. There was no way he was going to be able to keep this up forever, so he prayed his friends were successful at the front side of the house.

Not a moment too soon, someone up above answered his prayers. In his peripheral vision, three white streaks zoomed past—Tom, Matt and Emily—fleeing in the direction of the synagogue.

Thank God, they got her out.

He spun around to take flight and follow the others, but pulled up short. He had to blink twice to believe his own eyes.

His father now stood in the middle of the backyard, directly in his path.

Overcome with emotion, Michael rushed towards him with open arms, but Eric was already fading out. "Dad! Dad!" he yelled.

His father's lips didn't move, but his thoughts came through loud and clear. *I love you, Son. I'm sorry but I can't stay. I not supposed to be here. I'm putting you in more danger.*

Desperately, he reached out for his father's hand. "Dad, wait! Don't go! Please, don't go!"

Again, Eric's voice faintly echoed in his head. *Don't trust.*

Michael took a half-step towards him. "Don't trust what? Don't trust who?" he mouthed in frustration.

All that remained now was Eric's faint outline, but the last thing his father managed to do was cast a quick sidelong glance in the direction Tom and the others had taken.

A milli-second later Eric was gone.

Michael's ghostly heart spasmed in agony. He wanted to

scream at the top of his lungs. His father had been so close, so damn close…again.

But he couldn't dwell on it now.

The feeling of cold prickles stabbed his back. He didn't even need to look. The demons were right behind him ready to pounce at any moment.

If he wanted to save his soul, he didn't have a second to spare.

Leaping into the air, he took off in the direction of the synagogue, flying as fast as he could.

Immediately, the demons gave chase, raking at his heels.

As he swerved and zig-zagged through the streets, a million questions whirled around his head. *Was Dad warning me about Tom, Matt or Emily? Can I even trust my father's warning, or was it a trick of the demons? Maybe it wasn't really my father at all. Are the demons capable of planting false visions and thoughts in my head?*

It took every ounce of his effort to focus on losing the demons and not get caught up in the tangle of thoughts unraveling in his mind.

He barely made it into the synagogue, darting straight through the side entrance.

Luckily, the demons stopped on the doorstep. Their angry, nightmarish shrieks and screams echoed into the foyer.

He caught up with Tom and the others in an office on the first floor.

Matt had his arm around Emily, who still seemed disconcerted by her ordeal.

As Michael approached them, she turned her tear-streaked face to him. In a shaky, but sincere voice she said, "Thank you. My brother told me what you did."

At a loss for words, he gave a humble nod and mumbled, "You're welcome."

"What kept you, though?" Matt asked. "I thought you'd be right behind us."

Tom now turned to him without a word, but his eyes bore a questioning hole straight into his soul.

He couldn't take a chance on tipping his hand. Instantly, he blocked all three of them from his thoughts, putting on his most convincing poker face. He didn't want any of them to find out about his father's warning until he had some idea of exactly what it meant.

"I took the scenic route," he replied nonchalantly, "had to fly around a bit to try and see if I could ditch them first."

It could've been his paranoid imagination, but Tom looked unconvinced. Especially, when all his mentor said was, "Glad you made it back."

After what seemed like a few hours, the demons finally gave up and dispersed.

Once they were sure the demons had retreated, the four of them cautiously left the synagogue.

"Thanks...again," Matt said sheepishly. "I thought for sure it would be you who needed my help first, so I'd at least have a chance to pay you back for what you did for me and Emily the last time at the school."

"Don't worry about it," he said. "I know you'll be there for me when I have to call on you."

Matt dropped him some daps. "You can count on it."

It had been a long day, even by ghostly standards, and all

he wanted to do was get home to Sarah. He'd been gone so long, she must be worried sick.

Matt shook his head. "I never expected them to use someone I love as a pawn to capture me."

All of a sudden the two thoughts collided, detonating in his mind.

Using someone I love as a pawn.

Sarah's alone.

Oh my God.

CHAPTER SEVEN

DANGER

BY THE TIME he reached the Angel of the Sea, panic overwhelmed all rational thought as he flew wildly from room to room, floor to floor, screaming her name.

Unexpectedly, Sarah poked her head out of Room 26 and peered into the hall. "I'm right here," she said, startled. "You were taking so long I was beginning to get anxious, so I decided to pass the time playing tricks to keep my mind off of my silly worries." She floated towards him with an impish grin. "I was just sliding a vase of fresh flowers to the other side of the dresser to see if anyone would notice."

Her happy demeanor dissolved the minute she saw the way he was visibly shaking. "What's wrong?" she asked with concern.

Rushing forward, he wrapped his arms around her in a bone-crushing embrace. He kissed her lips, her cheeks, her eyes. "Are you alright?" he choked out.

"Of course, I am." She pushed away from his chest far enough so she could see his face. "I'm fine. What's the matter?"

For one brief moment, he contemplated blocking his thoughts and not telling her the truth. She might be frightened if she knew the demons could target her to get to him, the way they had just tried to do with Emily.

Sarah being drawn into danger with the demons because of him was something he'd been terrified of all along. He couldn't stand that she'd already been caught in the crossfire and hit once. And now that he'd witnessed how the demons had used Emily as a pawn, he was out of his mind with worry that they might try to do the same with her.

But he also couldn't lie to her.

"I think you'd better sit down," he said with a heavy sigh, as he floated with her downstairs to the parlor. "I have a *lot* to tell you."

So, he spent the next hour or so catching her up on all that had happened on his visit home and also, with their rescue of Emily from the demons. Last but not least, he told her about this latest mysterious visit from his father, along with his cryptic message.

When she heard about his father's warning and sudden departure, she jumped up from the couch and threw her arms around him. "Oh my goodness, Michael. I'm so sorry," she said in a heartfelt way. "I know how painful this must be for you."

He closed his eyes, losing himself in the warmth and strength of her hug. *How does she always know exactly what I need?*

It took every ounce of energy he had left to let go of her, but they still had so much to talk about. "I'm not gonna lie, it did upset me that he was so close again, but the weird thing is...this time I got the distinct feeling...not that he was leaving, so much as he was somehow being pulled away. It seemed as if he wanted to give me that warning, but something or someone wasn't giving him the chance."

He paced back and forth between the fireplace and the couch, deep in thought. "And I'll tell you something else," he said finally, "I'm not surprised by my father's warning."

Sarah perched herself on top of the registration desk. "How come?"

He rested his hands on her knees, looking her deep in the eyes. "Because I've felt from the very beginning that something was off about Tom."

Apparently unconvinced, she frowned at him. "But you don't know for sure who your father is warning you about. It could just as easily be Matt," she pointed out. "I mean, look what he almost did to you before."

That very fact had been the marble rolling around the mousetrap of his mind all the way home. "I know…and I hear what you're saying…," he said, slowly shaking his head left and right, "but for some reason my gut tells me the one I need to worry about is Tom." If he was honest with himself, for quite some time he'd had this niggling fear he might find out at any moment that the great and powerful Oz was simply a fraud lurking behind a fancy curtain. Or worse yet, that Tom wasn't only a fraud, but perhaps a free agent of evil.

She wrinkled her eyebrows in obvious concern. "So what are you going to do?"

He carefully weighed his options. Was Tom the enemy? Vassago had said as much, but then again, demons couldn't be trusted. There were no easy answers here. Then he remembered a line he'd heard before, *keep your friends close and your enemies closer.*

Sarah must've read his thoughts because she now asked, "Where did you hear that bit of advice?"

"From Michael Corleone in The Godfather Part II," he replied matter-of-factly.

"Who?"

He stared at her, suddenly worried again about her memory. "Michael Corleone...The Godfather Part II? A bunch of classic movies about the Italian mafia?"

When she still looked puzzled, he smacked his forehead as the realization hit him. "Oh, I forgot...the Godfather movies came out after you died. Sorry about that." He snorted. "Sometimes I forget we have a generation gap."

"Hush your tongue," she reprimanded, jumping off the registration desk and stalking towards him.

Uh oh, looks like I've riled up that Irish temper of hers.

And it's adorable as hell.

"Just because we died decades apart, does not mean we suffer from any *generational* gap. Never. Say. That. Again." She poked him in the chest and gave a little pout. "It makes me sound older."

He laughed at her, but planted a tender kiss on her cheek to show he was sorry for the vicious insinuation.

She smiled back, letting him know all was forgiven.

"Anyway," he continued, "it's an old saying about keeping an eye on your enemies by making sure they stay as close to you as possible." He paused for a moment, lost in thought. "Which brings me to my next point. Now that I think about it, we're going to have to teach you and Emily how to fight by yourselves."

"But we already know how to fight," she said with a

touch of renewed indignation. "Or have you already forgotten what happened at the high school?"

"Of course, I haven't forgotten. I already know Matt can fight. But you had my help, and Emily had Tom's help," he pointed out. "I want to make sure the two of you are able to fight on your *own* if you have to. Or at least defend yourself if you're alone and come under attack."

Picking up on the heat of her aura, he slowly wrapped his arms around her. "Not that I'm ever leaving you again if I can help it. From now on, I want you to stay right by my side at all times."

She leaned up against him until he could feel her firm breasts against his chest. "I have no problem with that," she whispered, "since that's exactly where I want to be."

Slipping his hands down low on her waist, he suddenly pulled her up so he could reach her mouth. Pressing his lips to hers, he kissed her fiercely. His hands tangled in her hair and roamed over her back, while his mouth devoured her luscious lips.

Everywhere their bodies touched flared with heat.

Too much heat.

As the boundary between their auras began to weaken, he forced himself to pull away.

They both sighed, as he set her down on the floor once more.

Doing the right thing and following the damn rules required a tremendous amount of restraint.

I sure as hell better *to go to heaven for this.*

• • •

A few days later, right after sunset, he summoned Matt and Emily to the Angel of the Sea. Once Matt heard his idea about teaching the girls how to defend themselves, he was all for it.

At first, Emily was a bit skittish about learning to fight, but after they reminded her of her harrowing ordeal, she quickly relented.

Of course, the girls spent the first hour together chatting up a storm. Sarah gave Emily a full tour of every single suite in the two buildings of the Victorian bed and breakfast. Many ooohs and aaahs could be heard as Emily followed her from room to room, taking in the beauty and romantic ambience of the place.

While the girls were busy doing that, he used the time to talk to Matt and see if he could read his thoughts. All the while, he got no impression whatsoever that Matt was blocking anything from him. As far as he could tell, Matt's mind was an open book. His friend wasn't hiding a thing.

Finally, Michael had to remind the girls that this wasn't a social call. Actually, more like defensive boot camp. He yelled up the stairs to the second floor to get their attention. "Hey, I think it's time we summon Tom. He taught me how to fight, and I think he'd be the best person to help teach the two of you."

As the girls drifted back down the long staircase, he concentrated on willing his Protector's presence.

It only took a minute for him to appear and once Tom heard his plan he readily agree to help. "But I think it would be safest if we conduct the training on the beach," his mentor suggested. "That way we won't hurt anyone. And this place

is way too nice. I'd hate to see any harm come to it either."
He arched his eyebrow. "I still remember how you set that
bush on fire outside the hospital the night I first taught you
how to direct your energy."

He snickered at the memory. "Yeah, you may have a
point."

Together, the five of them half-floated, half-walked
across the street to the sidewalk adjacent to the beach.
Before they made their way down the ramp leading onto the
sand, Tom said, "There won't be any sources of energy once
we're on the beach, so everyone grab onto the lamppost and
absorb as much as you can hold. If you're not used to doing
this, it may feel uncomfortable at first, but eventually you'll
get used to it."

One by one they each took turns holding the metal pole
of the street light. Michael did too, just in case he would
need to help with the lessons. When they were ready, they
proceeded onto the beach.

Tom stood in the center of their little circle. "Okay, now
most likely each one of you has been able to at least turn on
electronic devices, correct?"

They all nodded in unison.

"Good," he said. "That's easy enough to do because it
takes very little energy and it doesn't have to be terribly
precise. Sending a surge of energy is much the same, except
it's more focused and therefore, it can carry more power."

Tom paused for a moment to look around. "We still need
a target of some sort...I hate to vandalize, but that will have
to do." He pointed to a lifeguard stand a few paces away and
they all glided over to it. "Now, Michael and Matt I know

you two know how to do this, and every one of you has seen this in action, but it bears repeating," he instructed. "Use your hands to help guide the direction of the surge. Otherwise the discharge will be haphazard and ineffective."

"Stand back and pay attention, as I demonstrate." He raised his hands, talking them through the process step by step. "I concentrate, harness the energy inside of me, and send it outward, converging on a single point." As he finished saying the last word, a bolt of white energy shot from his fingertips.

Michael hadn't really been paying attention, until the flash rocketed straight towards him.

He ducked just in the nick of time, as the light skimmed past one of the front legs of the lifeguard stand leaving a blackened scorch mark on the wood.

What the hell? That was a little close.

Tom now turned to Sarah as if nothing odd had occurred. "Would you care to go first?"

As she nodded in agreement, Michael held a phantom breath. He had all the faith in the world that she'd be great at this.

Raising her delicate hands, she confidently thrust forward, directing all her stored up energy at the lifeguard stand.

And nothing happened.

Barely a ripple of energy moved through the air.

So she tried again. And again. And again. And again.

He could sense the frustration rolling off of his beloved in waves, but also her patience and savage determination. On the tenth try, a weak squiggle of red light sprang from her fingertips but quickly fizzled out.

Deeply troubled, he turned to his mentor. "What's wrong? Why isn't it working for her?"

"I'm not sure," Tom replied, equally perplexed. "What she's throwing off are called sprites. Taken from the lightning of the same name," he explained. "Short, quick, bursts of energy that hold no real power."

Michael threw his arm around Sarah and pulled her into a hug. He could tell she was disappointed and on some level he was too. Perhaps it would just take time.

"Emily, why don't you give it a try next?" Tom suggested.

Matt glanced at her and nodded encouragingly.

But after a few minutes and several attempts, it became obvious Emily was having exactly the same results.

She turned to Tom with a look of consternation. "I just don't understand," she complained. "Why did it work for us at the school?"

"It didn't," Tom declared matter-of-factly. "You and Matt only helped me draw in energy. I was the one delivering it. And the same is true for Sarah. But now that I've seen Matt fight, I can tell it works for him. For some reason though, you two girls simply can't do this on your own. At least, not now."

Michael racked his brain for some rational explanation. "Could the proximity of the water be affecting them?"

"Perhaps," Tom replied. "In order to rule that out, why don't we move off the beach, away from the ocean?"

"Okay, we can have them try it in the center of the street over there," Michael said, pointing. "The town is pretty quiet in the middle of winter, so there hasn't been much traffic on the roads lately anyway."

Each of the girls now took turns standing in the street and trying to hit the square, green garbage can near the entrance ramp to the beach.

Both failed miserably, same as before.

Emily turned her hopeful eyes to Tom. "Maybe if we work at it?"

Tom shook his head. "I hate to say this...but even with practice...that may be all you're capable of. I've seen this kind of thing before. Some spirits have the ability to harness and channel energy, others don't. I don't truly understand why."

Matt didn't look too pleased. "So where does that leave us? Is there no way for them to protect themselves?"

Tom was quiet for a moment. Finally, he said, "Things like evasive flight and defensive movement can be as important as offensive strikes." He cast a sidelong glance over at Michael, his thoughts unreadable. "Why don't we show them?"

"You mean fight each other?" The suggestion caught him a bit off guard, but he found himself saying, "Sure. Anything if it'll help the girls protect themselves better."

He and Tom now moved to the middle of the street, while the others stood around them in a circle at a safe distance. As Tom turned to face him, Michael couldn't help but feel as if they were two cowboys about to square off in a gunfight. Tom's enigmatic expression and serious gunslinger posture did nothing to settle his unease.

"Ready?" Tom asked.

No sooner had he nodded, than Tom fired off an expert shot that zinged right past his head.

So close, the heat stung his ear.

What the hell?

There was no time to think. Raising his hands, he sent a bolt of energy straight at Tom's arm.

In a whirl, the older ghost spun to his left. The blow missed him by mere inches, colliding with the door of a nearby parked car and sending a shower of sparks into the air. As Tom glanced over at the singed vehicle, an unusually chilly smile crept across his face.

Before Michael even had time to react, a flash of energy came rocketing towards him again. He narrowly dodged it, but not before it ricocheted off the black top within inches of him.

So, the gloves are off.

Michael tensed, drawing in more energy from his surroundings. In rapid-fire succession he sent three blasts directly at his mentor's chest, head and legs.

In answer to the threat, Tom moved so fast he appeared as nothing more than a blur. For a moment he seemed to almost disappear and reappear ten feet to the left of where he'd been standing.

His eyes were murderous.

They were no longer just sparring.

This was a battle.

Everything became fair game. As they darted back and forth trading blows across the thoroughfare, they drew in energy from anywhere and everywhere—street lamps, porch lights, living room televisions. Before the night was over, the people living on the block were going to think their neighborhood had been hit by some freak electrical storm.

They were firing off so many shots at one another the air crackled with electricity.

One of the bolts of energy grazed his leg. For a few brief seconds he couldn't move his limbs, but then he rallied, firing off three shots in rapid succession while flying left and right to avoid being hit.

Each time, Tom managed to dodge the incoming fire and answer with a quick volley of his own.

As Michael struggled to keep up and return fire, he couldn't help but wonder, *is he really out to hurt me?*

Almost in answer to his question, another bolt of light charged towards his lower torso. He barely managed to duck and roll under this last blow.

Taking a risk, Michael paused. *Let's see what he'll do if I don't fire back.*

At this point, he was quite literally a sitting duck.

Tom cast off one last bolt of energy, which missed him completely and fizzled out into the night air.

As quickly as it began, their friendly little training abruptly ended.

"And that kids, is how you use evasive flight and defensive movement," Tom declared, sounding oddly triumphant and full of himself.

Slowly, Michael rose to his feet. *What the hell just happened?*

Eyes wide, mouths agape, every one of them looked stunned.

In awkward silence, they meandered back to the Angel of the Sea.

The minute they stepped foot on the wraparound front

porch, Tom got that familiar faraway look on his face again. "I have to go," he said in a flat tone, as he quickly faded out.

The rest of them exchanged uncomfortable glances, but no one said a word about the so-called 'training'.

After a few brief goodbyes, Matt and Emily departed, as well.

Once everyone was gone, Sarah grew unusually quiet.

"What's wrong?" he asked, full of concern. "Are you upset about what happened with the training?"

"A little, but it's more than that," she said with a troubled look on her face. "I can't quite explain it, but I got a really uneasy feeling when you and Tom were fighting each other."

Drained of energy, he leaned up against the wall. "Yeah, I kinda thought his behavior was a bit bizarre myself. Like he was enjoying battling with me *way* too much."

She nodded in agreement. "You better not turn your back on him," she said significantly. It was the first time she had ever advocated not trusting Tom, and this fact was not lost on him.

"What makes you say that?"

"I don't know…," she murmured, "but I'm beginning to think you might be right…Tom may be the one you have to worry about after all."

• • •

It had been Sarah's idea to get dressed in Room 27, her old bedroom. For all intent and purposes, the spacious corner room on the second floor had now become their own master bedroom. Even if guests were staying in that room, it worked out perfectly for everyone.

By day, while the guests were busy doing the touristy things like enjoying the beach, fine dining, and shopping that Cape May had to offer, Michael and Sarah lay in each other's arms for hours. Resting together on the bed during the sunny summer afternoons was the closest they came to sleep. Many times as they lay cuddling side by side, fond memories of their past lives would flow between them, which was the closest thing they had to dreaming. He now knew the truth—memories are reflections of reality forever etched into the heart and soul. And he loved sharing them with her.

By night, when the guests needed their bed back, the two of them were out and about –walking hand in hand along the beach, strolling through the shops of the Washington Mall, or hanging out in the parlor or the attic of the Angel.

Now, Sarah kept floating back and forth through the bathroom door, showing him the different hairstyles she was conjuring up until he picked one he liked best. After that, they spent the better part of the afternoon deciding what dress she would wear.

He couldn't believe that even a dead girl could take this long to get ready. She must've shown him fifty dresses on hangers she conjured from memory, all of which looked virtually the same to him. All he could say over and over again was, "That one's pretty. That one looks nice. That one too." Finally, almost in subconscious self-defense, he must've somehow said the magic words, "That one. Definitely that one."

"Oooh, I agree," she squealed in delight before darting back through the bathroom door.

He flopped on the bed with a heavy sigh of relief, proud of himself that he must've gotten something right, even if he didn't know quite what it was. Dead or alive, there were still some things about women that would remain an eternal mystery.

Finally, with her hair properly coifed and off her shoulders in a sweeping updo, Sarah sashayed out of the bathroom in her dress. She gazed at herself in the tall mirror, twirling around in the flowing, green velvet ball gown with the low-scooped neckline and plunging back. "What do you think?"

His eyes roamed over every inch of her as he sucked in a phantom breath. *Yes, I definitely did something right.* His eyes strayed to her gold locket perched just above her uplifted cleavage. He swallowed hard, as his knee began to quiver. "You look absolutely breath-taking..." he said, his voice trailing off.

"And?" she said, questioningly.

"And I think there's one helluva good chance I'm gonna get in a fight at this party."

Sarah smiled a wicked little smile.

Now it was his turn to get ready.

In less than sixty seconds, he conjured up the memory of the formal, black tuxedo he had worn once for his older cousin's wedding.

The only thing that gave him fits was the damn, choking bow tie. Turning to the mirror, he grimaced as he adjusted it for the one-millionth time and pulled at the sleeves of his tux. "Are you sure we're not going to be overdressed?"

She laughed and took his arm. "Of course not. You look dashing, now let's go."

He glanced at the clock on the nightstand, *9:30 pm*. It felt odd to be worried about the hour. After all, it had been a while since he needed to be anywhere at a certain time.

But there was simply no point in arriving after midnight, to a New Year's Eve party.

CHAPTER EIGHT

CONGRESS HALL

SINCE IT WAS so late, he and Sarah could walk to the party without getting drained by the light. They could've flown, but they both agreed, *when you have all the time in the world...you take your time.*

So, they strolled down Beach Avenue past the Hotel Macomber, the Marquis de Lafayette Hotel, and all the other stately old Victorian mansions which sit facing the beach and the Atlantic Ocean. Finally, they reached Uncle Bill's Pancake House and made a right onto Perry Street.

Immediately, the enormous oceanfront hotel known as Congress Hall came into view, impossible to miss with its bright, sunshine yellow façade and towering white colonnades. The sheer size and grand architecture of the L-shaped structure gave it the air and sophistication of a Southern-style plantation.

A huge Christmas tree with multi-colored lights had been erected in the corner of the grassy, open-air courtyard. The evergreen's sparkling branches danced with the winter wind coming off the ocean.

"That tree must be at least twenty feet tall," Sarah commented.

"Not quite as big as the one in Rockefeller Center, but this one still looks amazing," he agreed.

As he looked around taking it all in, he noticed several other ghosts relaxing in the wooden rocking chairs which faced the courtyard. Others milled about the promenade in front of the high sweeping windows of the first floor. Most were dressed in early twentieth century garb—the women in ornate ball gowns and white gloves up to their elbows, the men in black tux and tails complete with shiny, black top hats. A few of them, since they must have been military men, wore their Class A dress coats and uniforms. Many of them looked like they could have walked right off the deck of the R.M.S. *Titanic*.

Michael nudged Sarah's arm. "I guess you were right. We're not overdressed at all."

She grinned, triumphant.

Just then, he heard someone speaking Spanish behind him. A group of four men had crossed over from the beach side of the street to enter the courtyard. They were dressed in some type of formal, military uniforms, but not like anything he had ever seen before—black leather boots, white-plumed caps, and bright burgundy coats with shiny buckles. They went directly over to the right side of the lawn, each one taking off their feathered hats and bending down to reverently touch something that seemed to be partially sticking out of the ground.

Once the men had drifted some distance away, his curiosity got the better of him and he pulled Sarah over to see what it was the group had been looking at. As the two of them reached the spot, they realized it was a rusty old ship's anchor. Next to the huge scrap of metal, a white plaque was painted with big black letters—'JUNO'S ANCHOR'. Michael was about to read the rest of the inscription when an older woman with a round face approached them.

"Welcome," the woman said with a stately, yet friendly presence. She extended a white gloved hand first to Sarah and then to him. "My name is Annie. Annie Knight. I owned Congress Hall from 1904 to 1931, during the Roaring Twenties, as they've now come to be called."

"It's nice to meet you," he said. "I'm Michael and this is my wife, Sarah." As he shook the gray-haired woman's hand, he pointed to the four men who had just walked away from the anchor. "Who are those men?"

Annie smiled in a kindly way. She seemed to be enjoying their curiosity. "The two of you are new here, aren't you?"

Sarah nodded.

"I thought so," the woman said. She now turned to him to answer his question. "Those men are the last remaining spirits from the wreck of the Juno, a Spanish man o' war which sunk in a storm off the coast of Cape May in 1802 with four hundred and twenty-five souls on board. The Juno was a treasure ship, carrying four hundred thousand dollars in silver, along with other jewels, on her way from Mexico to Spain," she explained. "It's been said that the loss of the great ship and its priceless cargo may have affected decisions in Europe on behalf of the New World." She gestured toward the men who had walked away. "The ship's captain, his first mate and two highest ranking officers still feel responsible. They believe the Juno should be raised and the treasure found, so their crew at least did not die in vain.

Every so often, they toss some of the Spanish coins into the surf so they wash up on the beach to serve as a reminder."

Sarah looked disturbed by the tale. "How sad," she whispered.

"Not really," Annie replied simply. "Their day will come."

Something about the story now troubled him too. "Wait a minute," he said. "If they drowned in the sea, how is it that their souls are able to separate from the water? Didn't the water disrupt their energy?"

"Oh, it's a complicated affair I'll grant you," Annie replied with a nod. "I've asked them that very question myself. All I know is that somehow they've become a part of the water and it's become a part of them."

As he watched the men tread across the sidewalk of the promenade, a trail of wet footprints appeared on the cement behind them.

Huh, how weird.

"Come, let me show you around," Annie said, ushering them toward a set of double doors. "This is the back of Congress Hall. Most of the spirits are coming in this way tonight, because the living folks are entering through the main entrance on the other side of the building." She clapped her gloved hands and rubbed them together. "Oh, I do get so *excited* when company's coming," she said with a childlike enthusiasm. "It's our motto, you know. Our staff has been instructed to treat each day as if this place is their own house and company's coming."

This made some sense to him. His mother used to make the house perfect and clean like a fiend whenever company was coming.

Annie led them into the building, then to the right and into a great-room with tall windows, white pillars, marble floors and a small marble fireplace. In one corner, stood a colorful flocked Christmas tree. "This used to be the front desk area, but now it's a lounge," she said. Along the walls hung various framed maps of New Jersey from several different time periods. In the opposite corner, stood a pair of old-fashioned elevators marked Cab 1 and Cab 2. Two antique mirrors, at least twelve feet high with attached resting benches, sat along adjacent walls.

"Such a welcoming room," Sarah remarked appreciatively. "Love the bright Kelly green."

Annie smiled. "I do too," she agreed, as she walked over to another doorway. "And over here we have what we call The Brown Room, another one of our cozy places for guests to gather."

He and Sarah both peeked inside. With its rich chocolate brown walls, dark wood floor-to-ceiling fireplace, comfy leather chairs, and an ornate wraparound bar in the far corner, the lounge had a very distinct Gatsby-esque feel to it.

Suddenly, Sarah rushed forward into the room. "Is that the pianoforte from the Christian Admiral Hotel?" She reached out and ran her hands lovingly along the top of what looked like a square piano set inside of a wooden case. "It has to be," she said, answering her own question. "I know every inch of this wood, every nick and every scratch." She turned to Annie. "I should…I had to dust it every day."

Annie gave her a graceful smile. "Yes, it was saved and brought here when the Christian Admiral Hotel was demolished in 1996."

"What's a pianoforte?" he asked, befuddled.

"It's Italian and it means soft-loud," Sarah explained. "Because that's how this piano can be played, soft or loud depending upon how hard you strike the keys."

This set his phantom heart aglow. He was always impressed by how much she loved music as much as he did.

She caught his smile and returned it with one of her own.

He pointed to another doorway off of the Brown Room that led to what looked like a dining room with bright pink and white striped walls. "What's in there?"

"Oh, that's our Blue Pig Tavern," Annie said with a chuckle. "It's a restaurant named for the gamblers who used to frequent the casino here at Congress Hall. Back in the day, they used a pink and white tent on the lawn, and the gamblers in the club called themselves the Blue Pigs."

He laughed at the funny name. "I never made it to twenty-one, so I never got to gamble or even step foot inside a casino," he said, leaning over to Sarah. "One of these days we should go up to Atlantic City and see some of the casinos there."

She nodded. "Sounds like a wonderful idea."

Once more, Annie led them back through the green lounge and out into the main hallway, which was decorated with four foot wide red and white floor-to-ceiling candy canes along with lit up evergreen boughs. A table off to the side of the foyer even held a large replica of Congress Hall made out of gingerbread, detailed with tiny people, realistic scenery, and white frosted pillars.

He stopped for a moment in front of the display. "Man, I loved gingerbread."

"Is there any food you didn't love?" she said with a cheeky grin.

"No, not really." He shook his head. "I'm hoping heaven is like a cruise ship with a twenty-four hour buffet that never runs out of all my favorite foods, and I can eat and eat all I want and never gain a pound."

Sarah laughed so hard that for a moment, he feared the living might be able to hear her.

Annie grinned. "This is Founders' Hall," she said with a wide swish of her arm. "The walls are covered in historical photos from every owner and time period of Congress Hall's illustrious history. Over the years, Congress Hall hosted many opera singers, band leaders and famous heads of state. Normally, the various American flags line the hallway, but during the holidays the flags get taken down in favor of something festive."

As they walked along admiring all the photos and historical items on the walls, Sarah asked, "Why is this place called Congress Hall?"

"Oh, it wasn't always named that," Annie said. "When Thomas H. Hughes first constructed the hotel as a wooden boarding house for guests to the new seaside resort of Cape May in 1816, he called it The Big House. With 108 guestrooms, local residents thought the hotel was much too big to be successful, so they dubbed it Tommy's Folly. And the name stuck for a long time. In 1828 when Hughes was elected to the House of Representatives, he officially changed the name of the hotel to Congress Hall." Annie laughed. "Now, we simply call her our little survivor because no matter what happens, she always manages to survive. There have been times the hotel has fallen into such disrepair it was almost a ghost town, but she always comes back. For instance, the place burned to the ground in Cape May's Great Fire of 1878, but within a year its owners had rebuilt the hotel in brick, making it the first brick building in all of Cape May."

As they continued down the hallway, he couldn't help but appreciate all the history and memories. The tremendous spirit and dignity of the place seemed trapped within its very walls.

To their left, a group of living guests were making their way up the grand circular staircase. Its steps had been painted a gleaming white and carpeted in royal blue with the signature Congress Hall crest in white and gold—the letter C overtop a diagonal key with a letter H below.

In fact, as he looked around he noticed the symbol for Congress Hall was emblazoned on nearly everything—the carpeting, the doorknobs, even on the doorman's podium near the front entrance.

Clearly, the C and the H stood for Congress Hall. The only thing he couldn't figure out was what the key stood for, so he asked Annie.

"Oh, my master key," she said wistfully, as if referring to a long-time friend. "It came back to me, you see. My key was always very important to me." She manifested a thin chain from around her neck which had been hidden by the high collar of her blouse. On it, dangled a tarnished old-fashioned key marked with her initials, A and K. "I always had this skeleton key with me, because it was the only one that opened every single door in Congress Hall. One day I lost the key, but several years later it was miraculously found during a renovation of the building. Now, I never part with it. And that's how the story of my master key made its way into Congress Hall history and onto its crest."

Up ahead, a few spirits, young and old seemed to be dancing, twirling straight through the walls on either side of the hallway.

"Why are they passing back and forth through those walls as if they aren't there?" Sarah asked, inquisitively.

"Because at one time, they weren't. This entire floor was one giant room, called the social arcade of Congress Hall. In fact, if you look here on the floor...do you see that line where the marble stops and the wood begins?"

Sarah nodded. "Yes."

"This was the beginning of our wooden dance floor. Every weekend I would teach the children how to dance. The foxtrot, the waltz, all the popular dances of the day. They had to be dressed in their Sunday best, though," she said, raising an authoritative finger. "I never married and didn't have any children of my own, so teaching my young guests how to dance brought me great joy."

Leading them back the way they had come she said, "You're welcome to visit another day if you'd like to see more of the hotel, but for now I'd say it's time for us to get to the Glitter Ball. My guests will be wondering where I've gotten to."

Annie turned down another corridor and opened the ballroom doors revealing hundreds of living guests packed onto a dance floor.

"So sorry, my mistake. Force of habit," she said, closing the doors once more. "Let's try that again, shall we?"

Once the ballroom door closed again Annie said, "This way please, follow me." With that, she walked straight through the doors this time.

As they ghosted through the double doors behind her, Michael's jaw dropped. Sarah had the same reaction as well.

They were clearly in the same ballroom, but now the place was filled with hundreds of spirits. All of the living people had disappeared.

"How is this even possible?" Sarah asked in amazement.

Annie looked confused. "What? Keeping two dimensions open at the same time and occupying the same space?"

He nodded, though he didn't understand what she had even just said.

"Oh, I'll grant you, it's no simple task. Requires an *enormous* deposit of residual energy. Setting this up took many of us the better part of last week," she said, gesturing around the ballroom. "But we've taken extra precautions this time and the bi-dimensionality should last for the length of the party. In all these years, we've only had one unfortunate incident." She put up one finger for emphasis. "As a matter of fact, it was at the last New Year's Eve Glitter Ball."

Michael's curiosity was peeked. "What happened?"

"Two ghosts got into a terrible fight." She shook her head disapprovingly, tsk-tsking under her breath as she recalled the memory. "The disruption of their energies caused a tear in the veil between the two planes, and a few living guests caught a brief glimpse of this side...including the ghost of Elvis, who was up on stage at the time. Well, as you can imagine, this caused all sorts of chaos and confusion on the living side." She continued shaking her head, but chuckled.

"Luckily, we fixed the tear straight away, the living chalked it up to having had too much champagne, and the night went on uneventfully after that. But it *was* a close one."

Amazing.

Now, as they entered the grand ballroom, he and Sarah took a good look around. The blue walls exactly matched the color of a Tiffany gift box, which went perfectly with its black and white parquet floor. With its polished white woodwork, old-fashioned wall sconces, and antique chandeliers, the room had an air of Southern charm and elegant sophistication.

Annie scanned the crowd. "Let me point out a few of our more special guests. That's Benjamin Harrison," she said gesturing discretely, "our twenty-third U.S. President of the United States. He made Congress Hall his official summer home during his presidency, so he tries to come back and visit whenever he can." Next, she waved her hand in the direction of a man clad in the class-A uniform of a Union Army General. "The man Ben's talking with, that's Ulysses S. Grant, our eighteenth U.S. President. Grant worked closely with President Lincoln to lead the Union Army to victory over the Confederacy during the Civil War. The two of them discuss politics and world affairs every time they see each other." She bent her head low and cupped a hand beside her mouth. "It can get a bit tedious, if you know what I mean."

"Over there we have John Philip Sousa," she said nonchalantly motioning to a bespectacled man with a thick mustache and pointed beard who was wearing another rather ornate military style uniform.

Michael pinched his eyebrows together. "The composer of all the famous marches? What's he doing here?"

"Oh, John loved it here," Annie said fondly. "He visited Congress Hall regularly with the U.S. Marine Band and even composed a march in the hotel's honor. It was named the *Congress Hall March* which he conducted on the lawn here in the summer of 1882. The march is played here every year during the big Fourth of July party and fireworks celebration."

"And last, but not least," Annie said gesturing to a tall, but round man in the center of the room, "that's Thomas H. Hughes, the host of the party and founder of Congress Hall."

"We've heard he only comes back to visit every thirty years," he said. "Why is that?

Annie smiled. "Let me introduce you and he can tell you himself."

After a few brief introductions, Annie said, "Thomas, I'm going to leave these guests in your very capable hands. They'd like to know why you only host the party once every thirty years." With that, she stepped away to speak to a few World War II soldiers sitting at a nearby table.

"Oh, it's simple really," Mr. Hughes said, turning to the two of them. "If we had the ball more frequently, it wouldn't be seen as so special and that would be a *true* folly. And quite frankly, it might get a tad bit depressing."

"How so?" Sarah asked.

"Well…," he said, as if he were choosing his words carefully, "let me put it this way. We all get a bit encouraged when enough time has passed that some of the old spirits have not returned to the party and new faces such as yours have arrived. It gives everyone hope."

He and Sarah exchanged a knowing glance, but said nothing.

"I see you met ol' Annie," Mr. Hughes said with a fondness in his voice. "She left an indelible mark upon Congress Hall and indeed, the town of Cape May. Even with her graceful and genteel nature, she was one of our most stubborn and fierce defenders of Cape May's heritage."

Sarah smiled. "We could see that," she said. "Annie's obviously quite proud of Congress Hall."

"We all are," he replied, as he started shuffle off. "If you'll excuse me, I have some other guests that I simply must greet. The two of you should go enjoy some of the music. Lovely turnout tonight, don't you think?"

Sarah nodded politely to him.

Now, Michael took her hand, and they moved further through the crowd. As usual, he was amazed that the guests seemed to be from several time periods. But all were dressed in their New Year's Eve finery.

On the far side of the ballroom, a big brass band played jazz and swing tunes. He could swear he recognized a few famous musicians up on the stage, like Frank Sinatra and Tommy Dorsey, but he couldn't be sure.

Leaning over to Sarah, he whispered into her mind. "I can hardly believe they're all stuck in the afterlife."

A man next to him must've overheard because he now chimed in, "I don't think all of them are."

"What do you mean?" Sarah asked, shyly.

"Most of them are probably visiting spirits," the man replied.

Michael cast a sideways glance at Sarah. "What's a visiting spirit?" they both asked simultaneously.

"I can't say for sure because I'm not one of them, mind you," he said, lowering his voice to a whisper. "But rumor has it they're spirits who have been to the other side and have been allowed to come back for a visit."

Michael's jaw dropped open and it took him a moment to digest what the man had said. *This might explain at least some of the ghosts I've seen.* "How can you tell the difference?" he asked, curious.

"Technically, you can't. Unless you observe closely." The man paused and leaned over to him dramatically, as if he was going to divulge something super-secret. "The visitors are usually the ones who don't look like they mind being here," the man said with a sly wink. Then he laughed at his own joke. With that, he gave a jovial nod, and floated over to one of the tables to chat with some ladies.

Maybe like Babe Ruth, he thought. *Still visiting by choice.*

Just then, he noticed a small crowd gathered in the far corner of the room. They had formed a wide ring around someone or something he couldn't quite see. He nodded his head in that direction so Sarah would notice too. "What do you think's going on over there?"

"Let's find out," she said, taking his arm once more. "Maybe it's the buffet."

He turned to give her an appropriately snarky grin.

As they reached the circle of ghosts, he caught sight of the man seated at the center of everyone's attention.

With his bushy untrimmed mustache, white floss-like hair wild and uncombed, baggy over-sized clothes, and that unmistakable German accent, Michael recognized him immediately as the father of modern Physics and theory of relativity. *Oh my God, that's Albert Einstein.*

Next to him, Sarah drew in a shocked gasp.

He couldn't blame her. So far he'd seen so many famous and strange ghosts, but it was always still a surprise. One could never be sure just who they were going to bump into in the afterlife.

Einstein was seated behind a banquet table lined with several dozen empty champagne glasses, one of which was lying on its side broken.

A young woman about their age stood in front of Einstein and on the other side of the table, as if she were one of his students. The old professor seemed to be teaching some kind of lesson while puffing away at a tobacco pipe.

Michael peeked under the table and grinned. True to legend, Einstein wore a pair of black dress loafers, but no socks, upon his feet. In school, he'd once read a story about how Einstein stopped wearing socks altogether after deciding that the big toe always ended up making holes. To a genius, this lack of civilization must've made perfect sense.

The woman in front of Einstein pointed to one of the glasses nearest to her. "It is *impossible*, Professor. I'm never going to be able to lift anything," she said flatly. "I've been trying for years. The most I've been able to do is knock a book off a shelf or push a door open a few inches."

Many people in the crowd of ghosts either mumbled or nodded in agreement. Even he and Sarah cast a sidelong glance at one another, for they were in pretty much the same predicament.

"My dear, lady," Einstein replied in his thick German accent, "the only source of knowledge is experience. I can assure you it is not impossible. It is as natural for you now, as breathing was when you were alive. If you use your mind, you will be able to pick up this glass," he said in a patient, but encouraging voice.

The frustrated girl pursed her lips. "But *how*?"

"It is quite simple actually." He stopped to take a few more puffs of his pipe. "Psychokinesis, or movement of the mind, is what allows you to lift, push, or vibrate objects without using a corporeal body. You need to use the principles of nature and your energy to affect these objects on a molecular and subatomic level."

He leaned forward for emphasis.

"Let me demonstrate," he said in a humble yet authoritative way. "If I do not wish to pick up an object, my hand will do exactly as I bid it." With a giant flourish, he swished his hand right through the center of four crystal glasses closest to him.

Not a single glass so much as wiggled.

"However, if I wish to pick up a glass, I have only to concentrate my will and energy upon its particles, secure in the knowledge that I am master over them...and lift the glass." As Einstein said the words, he effortlessly picked up the champagne glass and waved it around for all to see.

This drew gasps and looks of awe from everyone in the crowd, including him and Sarah.

Einstein looked down his nose at the pessimistic girl. "Now, try again."

Once more, the young woman placed her hand under the

bottom of the glass. With a quick movement she swept her hand through the crystal flute, tipping it sideways. The glass broke as it hit the table.

"I can't do it," the girl said, sounding defeated.

"My dearest lady," Einstein said in a fatherly voice, "lifting the glass did not work for you because you still think of your hand as different from the glass. I tell you, your hand is *no* different. Your hand is energy, the glass is mass and energy combined, and they are all one in the same. Indeed, you have more power in your ghostly hand than the glass shall ever have, because your energy is not encumbered by mass. You need only believe that, in order to be able to lift that glass." Using the end of his pipe, he pointed to another champagne glass. "Now, try again."

Once more, she only managed to tip the glass over and it fell to the floor with a crash this time. Einstein must have found this extremely comical for he barked a laugh that sounded similar to a contented baby harp seal.

"Ahhh, I zee your problem now," he said, pointing his pipe directly at her face. "You still believe gravity is in charge of this glass. I can assure you it is not. *You* are in charge of the particles which make up that glass." As he jabbed at the object more emphatically this time he commanded, "Now, *again.*"

The woman contorted her face, as if concentrating harder. This time, her hand closed around the stem and the champagne glass lifted off the table without fail.

"I did it! I did it!" she exclaimed, waving the champagne glass around triumphantly.

Einstein smiled a proud, yet boyish smile. "Bravo, my dear lady, bravo."

"Thank you *so* much," the woman said in wonderment.

Einstein nodded humbly mumbling in perfect German, "Bitte schön." A moment later, a violin materialized next to him which he deftly picked up by its neck. "Now my good people if you don't mind, this is a party and I vould like to play the violin. As he pried himself up from the chair slowly, he added under his breath in perfect French, "Laissez les bons temps rouler."

The minute he stepped away a number of spirits rushed up to the table and began trying to pick up the champagne glasses. Some had immediate success, others did not.

Michael couldn't help it. He was curious as hell. Moreover, he could tell Sarah was as well. "Let's give it a whirl, shall we?"

It took them a few tries, but eventually they both met with success. Once again, the afterlife had revealed secrets that made him feel as if he were a child discovering an unexpected present under the Christmas tree.

"Fantastic," he said. "Now I can cross levitating objects off my bucket list."

Sarah laughed. "I thought a bucket list was only if you hadn't kicked the bucket yet."

"Technically it is," he said with a wide grin, "but I'm also keeping an afterlife post-bucket list, too."

She smiled.

As they now walked towards the dance floor, he noticed about a half dozen gray spirits in the far corner of the room. Some of their expressions were melancholy, while some appeared almost cross, but all of them hung back, just watching the rest of the crowd.

I'm not liking the looks of those wallflowers, he said to Sarah telepathically so only she would hear him. In the back of his mind, he wondered if they could be spirits who might be on the verge of becoming malevolent.

They sure are a lively bunch, he quipped as a joke, though they made him nervous.

Sarah slapped him on the arm, but nodded all the same. *Let's keep our distance.*

The next band had just taken the stage. He and Sarah exchanged a sidelong glance, completely dumbfounded. If he had been shocked by anything he had seen in the afterlife so far, it paled in comparison to this. As the music began, Chuck Berry played guitar, Jimmy Page sat in on drums and Jerry Lee Lewis banged on the electric keyboards while belting out the lyrics to 'Great Balls of Fire'.

Even though most of the spirits were from earlier time periods and had never heard anything like the music of the fifties and sixties, everyone started dancing as if it was the most natural thing in the world for them to do.

He would've given his right leg to have a cell phone right now, so he could get this all on video.

With a squeal Sarah suddenly grabbed his hand, yanking him out on the dance floor. She threw her hands up in the air, enjoying the music, her body twisting this way and that. He'd never been much of a dancer, but with her by his side he could do anything. She made him want to do everything he never got the chance to do.

She was the beautiful never-ending symphony playing inside his soul.

Dancing around the ballroom with her through several songs, he smiled inwardly and thought, *Wow. There she goes again, making me feel more alive than any dead man ever had a right to.*

As the last song ended, the revelers grew unusually quiet and a rush of whispers swept through the room the way an ocean wave might wash over the sand. Every head swiveled toward the direction from which it came, the double entrance doors.

A breathtaking woman dressed in a midnight blue gown of layered lace floated into the room, flanked on either side by what appeared to be her bodyguards—two bare-chested men, ripped with muscles and nearly seven feet tall.

Even though Sarah was by his side, he couldn't help but stare at the mysterious woman and her bizarre entourage. Her presence and poise screamed royalty, but something about her looked familiar.

Then, the puzzle piece clicked into place.

CHAPTER NINE

NEW YEAR

HE ALMOST DIDN'T recognize her without the hippie clothing, or flower in her hair.

She was one of the Elders he'd met at Arthur's Stone in Wales that had read him the Covenant. The one who had told him love was forbidden in the afterlife. His eyes strayed down to his wedding ring as he toyed with the gold band around his finger. *What would she say now?*

As a devilish smile crept across her face, Sarah answered him telepathically. *Why don't we find out?*

Michael took her hand and pushed through the crowd of ghosts towards the woman. Overcome with excitement that he might finally get to question an Elder, he must've approached her too fast. With one swift motion each of the bodyguards thrust up a single hand, hitting him square in the chest with a wave of energy that paralyzed him in his tracks.

"That's far enough," one of them bellowed in a voice so deep, it sounded as if it had originated somewhere near the bottom of the Marianas Trench.

"It's okay," the woman said to both men in a soft, yet dignified way. "Let them come closer."

He and Sarah took a few steps closer, but kept a respectful distance. "I'm Michael Andrews and this is my...," he hesitated and blocked his thoughts in the same breath, "...this is Sarah."

The woman gave him a friendly smile. "I remember you, Michael. And Sarah, it's a pleasure to meet you," she said, extending her hand. "My name is Catherine."

"I remember you," he said in awe, "you're one of the Elders." He tried to read her mind, only to find it still blocked. He had so many questions he didn't know what to ask first.

Before he had the chance, Sarah stepped forward. "What does it mean to be an Elder?" she boldly asked. "Michael told me all about the Covenant. You Elders sure seem to know a lot. What are you...the repository for all wisdom?"

Catherine's eyes went wide and wary. She appeared half-shocked and oddly, half-proud of Sarah for her boldness. "Not quite," she replied in a kind voice. "I...and all the Elders, am merely a conduit for wisdom and truth."

Michael fixed her with a penetrating stare. "And what is the *truth*?"

Catherine hesitated and narrowed her gaze on him, as if contemplating how best to answer. "By now, I'm sure you've figured out this limbo, this afterlife, whatever you wish to call it, is only a waypoint. It is *not* your final destination. Everyone's waypoints will be different...as can be their destination, as well," she said significantly. "Remember, Michael Andrews, everyone has the potential to make it into the light. In death, as in life, it's the choices you make that determine the fate of your soul...for every choice we make causes ripples throughout eternity."

Her eyes drifted down to their entwined hands and

lingered on the gold band around Sarah's ring finger. "I see you chose not to heed every aspect of the Covenant."

Michael tensed, as he took a defensive half-step in front of Sarah. Elder or not, he wasn't going to be intimidated, so he met her gaze full on with defiance. "With all due respect, that's *our* business, not yours."

Catherine's face lit up with a smile which radiated compassion. "Don't worry Michael, I mean you and your wife no harm," she said, shaking her head lightly back and forth in emphasis. "What's done is done, but the two of you will now have to bear the consequences of your actions. The covenant is not meant to punish, so much as it is meant to prevent trouble in the afterlife and in many cases...heartache."

The strength and gravity of her words did not fall lightly upon his shoulders. He looked at Sarah and prayed to God the mysterious woman didn't mean he'd ever come to regret their union. Still filled with mistrust though, so many questions tossed in his mind. Were they in trouble or not for binding their souls? But how could Sarah be in any trouble? She never heard the covenant, so how could she be bound by it? And that raised a valid question in his mind which he now posed to Catherine. "That's another thing," he said, with a sideways glance at Sarah. "How come not everyone gets to hear the covenant?"

"You ask the most intriguing questions, dear one." She said it in a stern tone, but again smiled warmly. "Not everyone *needs* to hear the Covenant."

This perplexed him. "Why not?"

"Let me put it this way, Michael. Those with more power

need more checks and balances," she said, staring deep into his soul. "Whoever brought you before the Council paid you a nice compliment by doing so. They obviously thought you had great power and believed you *needed* to hear the Covenant, so you would use that power wisely."

Immediately, his thoughts drifted to Tom. *Maybe I should thank him for that after all.*

Sarah now chimed in with another question that was burning in his mind, too. "Why do some spirits go into the light right away and some linger much longer?"

Catherine paused. "It's different for everyone," she said, sweeping her arms in a wide arc, "as different as each individual in this room."

Great, she's as skilled as Tom at giving non-answers.

She must've overheard his thoughts, because she stared down her nose at him, much the same way Tom did when he was perturbed with him. "And also...," she said somewhat testily, "many spirits are affected by the magnitude of their emotions at the time of their death and the abruptness of their departure from this life. They must first work through that before they can figure out the rest." She leveled her gaze on the two of them. "I'm sure you can both relate."

They each squirmed under her stare, realizing how much she probably knew.

Now, looking around the room at all the different ghosts, he thought of something else. "If it's true some of these spirits are only visiting, and they've been to the other side and back, then why can't we ask them how they did it?"

"You could...," Catherine replied with a strange intonation, "but it probably wouldn't tell you much."

"Why not?" Sarah asked, looking genuinely confused.

"Because…you'd be asking the wrong question."

"The wrong question?" he said, pinching his eyebrows together. *How to get to heaven is the main question I've been trying to find the answer to since almost day one.*

"Yes, the wrong question" Catherine said firmly. "Instead of asking questions about how someone else got to heaven, you should be asking the questions of *yourself.* For instance, what preconceived notions do I need to discard from my previous life and way of thinking, and what do I need to embrace in this new reality? In other words, what is my new purpose?"

"But how do I figure out this new purpose? And how does Sarah figure out hers?" he asked, unable to keep his frustration in check.

Catherine turned to look at them both with kindness in her eyes. "I know you wish I would give you all the answers, but there is a reason we Elders do not…and cannot," she said, her words full of empathy. "The most profound answers to the most profound questions…come from within *ourselves.*"

That sounds awfully similar to what Tom said to me earlier.

"Think of it this way," Catherine continued. "If a man is sailing a ship, he must concern himself with the oars, the sails, and the ship's wheel. His purpose is clear—to keep the ship afloat and moving towards his destination. But once he reaches the next port and leaves his ship, he must now abandon that purpose and those concerns, and take up the new concerns related to existing on the land—gathering or farming food, a warm and dry shelter from the elements like a roof over his head, maybe a horse for transportation."

He listened intently, but wished the Elder would make her point.

"You've both reached a new port," she said, gesturing at the two of them. "So you're journey isn't over, but your purpose has changed. That's all I can tell you."

He sensed their little game of twenty questions was coming to an end, so he threw one more at the Elder while he still had the chance. "Then why can't we at least ask the visiting spirits what heaven is like?"

"What good would that do you?" she asked rhetorically. "All you would do is waste time pining for a place you can't go until you're ready, or until you're called, instead of figuring out what your new purpose is."

Catherine now reached out to shake each of their hands.

The second her hand touched his, intense warmth roamed up his arm. "One last bit of advice," she said slowly while still holding onto his hand. "We cannot control the direction or strength of the wind, but we can choose whether to go with it or against it, Michael. Remember that."

As Catherine moved through the room, whispers and cautious looks preceded her. Several of the wallflowers he had noticed earlier, shrank back altogether. Clearly unnerved by her presence, some of them even left the room.

"It's almost midnight," Sarah said suddenly.

Sure enough, right on time at ten seconds to midnight the spirits around the room began the countdown, "10, 9, 8, 7, 6, 5, 4, 3, 2, 1...Happy New Year!"

A flood of emotions cascaded through his soul, as he stared into her eyes. "Happy New Year, sweetheart."

With love in her eyes she said, "Happy New Year."

Bending down, he placed his lips on hers in a tender kiss, as the band began to play the traditional song, "Auld Lang Syne".

He pulled away and looked around the room at the other ghosts. Most raised their hands in the air with invisible glasses or empty one's they'd conjured from memory. Some swayed to the music, arm in arm. A few female ghosts cried a little, dabbing their eyes with handkerchiefs.

Sarah's eyes glistened with tears, too.

I am so in love with you, he mouthed.

Instantly, her tears stopped.

And I with you, she replied in her mind, as she clutched him tighter, laying her head against his chest.

"You know," he said, as he swayed with her to the tune, "I don't think I even know what this song means."

"Oh, I know this," she said with a touch of smugness. "There's some uncertainty in its origin, but most say it comes from a Scottish poem by Robert Burns because of a line which says something about wandering many a weary foot since auld lang syne."

"But what does auld lang syne even mean?"

"It roughly translates to times long past or times gone by," she said as a wistful smile crossed her face. "Either way, the song is about remembering friends from the past and not letting them be forgotten."

He looked at her in awe. "I never knew that."

Now, he remembered an old song by Dan Fogelberg

about New Year's Eve that his mom used to play. The lyrics mentioned drinking a toast to innocence and drinking a toast to time. In his mind, he did both, bidding them a bittersweet farewell.

In his heart, he was more than happy to bid farewell to the old year—the year of his untimely death. And look forward to the future, which now included Sarah.

With her at his side, his mood was hopeful.

"It's a New Year," he said to her. "I feel like we need a new game plan. We need to find out what kind of souls we are and I'd like to know what it was my father was trying to tell me."

"So, why don't we try to find him?" Sarah suggested. "You didn't look for him in that many places, only your house and his office, right?"

"Right."

"So, where else do you think he could be?"

Michael racked his brain, flipping through all of the places his father had been in life and think of the most logical place his father might be.

Abruptly, he stopped dancing. "I've got it," he said, snapping his fingers. "My father grew up outside of Boston in a little town called Saugus. That's why my aunt still lives close by that area, near Salem. I don't know why I didn't think of it before. I'm always going back to visit the house I grew up in…why wouldn't my father do the same?"

"He probably would," she agreed. "So I think that's a great idea."

"It's settled then," he said, spinning her around in time with the song. "Tomorrow, we'll leave for Saugus."

"We?"

"Yes, I want you to come with me," he said emphatically. "After what happened to Emily, it's too much of a risk to leave you alone."

She spun around, coming to a stop in his embrace. "Okay, but why tomorrow? Why not right now?"

He leaned in close and whispered in her ear. "Because tonight, I just want you to dance with me."

With a smile and a rush of heat that nearly melted his soul, she placed her lips softly on his in a loving and luscious kiss.

CHAPTER TEN

SAUGUS

NEW YEAR'S DAY arrived cold but sunny, so they planned to leave immediately after dark. Michael wanted to be sure they wouldn't be drained by the daylight, so they would have their maximum energy for travel in case they encountered any demons.

The safest way to get there would be to have Sarah draft along with him. "Are you ready?"

"I think so," she said, taking his hand. "Just drive slowly, okay?"

A smirk crossed his lips, as he planted a gentle kiss upon her cheek. Wrapping his arm tightly around her waist, he pulled her close. As usual, his skin flared with electricity and tingles everywhere their bodies connected. For a moment, he nearly forgot what they were supposed to be doing. He had to force himself to ignore how good she felt, and concentrate on what he remembered of the town of Saugus, Massachusetts.

What seemed like a split-second later, they landed in an idyllic vision of a tiny New England town. A heavy snow had fallen on the rotary, a keystone shaped roundabout across the street from Saugus Town Hall.

"Sorry, I guess I got a bit distracted," he mumbled. "I

missed by a little bit. We're obviously in the center of town."

"That's okay," she chided. "I don't mind. The place looks charming."

Between the New Year's holiday and the heavy snowfall, not many people were out and about. The town had a quiet, peaceful stillness about it.

Sarah now glanced around, taking it all in. To their left, a tall blue spruce and evergreens dotted the green lawn. To their right, stood a tall granite monument of a female figure holding a shield in her right hand, and wearing a helmet with an eagle perched on top. Below the woman, on the left and right sides of the monument, two bronze figures of a sailor and a soldier were mounted on pedestals at the base of the statue.

Sarah reached out to touch the engraving on the monument, so he explained, "This is the Civil War Memorial to honor those in the town that fought in the war."

They both paused a moment to read the inscription:

WHO WENT FORTH TO BATTLE ON LAND AND SEA
FROM 1861-1865 FOR THE
PRESERVATION OF THE UNION
BY THEIR LOYALTY AND DEVOTION THEY HELPED
TO MAINTAIN THE FLAG OF OUR COUNTRY AS THE
EMBLEM OF EQUAL RIGHTS AND NATIONAL UNITY.

"It's a lovely sentiment," she said.

Placing his palm on the small of her back, he said, "Come on, the house is only a few blocks from here."

From the rotary they strolled up Central Street hand in

hand, past the library and the Saugus Town Hall. His grandfather had told him the mostly stone structure had been built back in 1875. With its magnificent Victorian-gothic architecture, its slate-tiled roof, and elevated bell tower with a clock underneath, the building made the center of town look like it belonged in a Norman Rockwell painting.

Sarah was right. He'd forgotten how much Saugus looked like the perfect portrait of small town America. And he'd forgotten how much he missed visiting.

As they turned the corner onto Parker Street, his grandfather's old house came into view halfway down the tree-lined block.

Anticipation zinged through him at the prospect of possibly finding his father. Gliding to a stop out front, he stared at the modest New England Colonial. For a moment, he questioned if he was really at the right house.

"What's wrong?" she asked delicately.

"Nothing, I guess," he replied with a pause, "it just… looks so different." Whoever had bought his grandparent's house had replaced the country blue wood siding with a newer tan aluminum. The windows and doors, which had always been trimmed in white, now sported a dark brown edging.

Taking her hand, he led them up the front porch steps. "Let's go inside and take a look around."

The minute he ghosted through the front door, his mood crashed in a hundred mile-an-hour nose-dive.

All of his grandparent's well-worn, homey furniture had been replaced with modern leather sofas, a flat screen television mounted to the wall, and shiny glass tables. Even worse, someone had painted the living room a hideous pea green color. The well-stocked bookshelves his grandparents always kept had been removed too. Framed pictures with unfamiliar faces sneered at him from the top of the mantle.

"Well, you said your grandmother sold it, right?" she said lightly. "You kind of had to expect that the new owners would change a few things."

"Yeah, I guess…but *nothing* looks the same." A hollow sadness twisted in his gut. "It's like a completely different house."

No matter how hard he tried he couldn't sense even a bit of his family's energy in the house.

"Are you going to check upstairs?"

He gave a dejected headshake. "No, my father hasn't been here."

"How do you know?"

"I just don't feel his energy here at all. I don't feel my grandparent's energy either," he explained. "So, why would he come here? It's like…like all I can feel is the new people that live here."

"Is it the new paint and furniture?"

"Nah, it's more than that. I could've told you someone else lived here even if all that was the same." The disappointment hit him hard. "It's as if the house has a different energy about it, a different feel. Not that it's bad or anything, but it's just…different."

Sarah tried to be helpful. "Maybe you could try summoning your father from here though," she suggested.

For a moment he closed his eyes, calling out to his father from deep within his mind and his soul. Unfortunately, he got the response he expected though. "No, there's no part of any of them left here anymore," he said, shaking his head. "Their energy is gone from this house."

A painful sense of melancholy enveloped him, dragging him under its weight. The energy and memories of this new family were already part of these very walls. He now understood why spirits stayed close to home. A piece of themselves truly was imprinted on every place they went.

How did he know? How was he so sure? Because he could feel their absence now that they were gone. It was as if his family had taken most of their residual energy with them when they finally left.

"I'm so sorry, sweetheart," she said in a tender, heartfelt way.

"It's alright," he said with a shrug of his shoulder. "It was worth a try anyway."

Slowly, he drifted out the back door and into the backyard. He grimaced. Someone had even taken down his favorite rope swing that used to hang from the big oak tree. *Heathens.*

Despondent, he flopped down on the back porch step, leaning his back against one of the railing posts. Sarah rested against one of the posts across from him.

A memory tickled the edges of his consciousness. He tried to brush it away, but like an annoying fly it kept coming back to pester him. On one of their summer visits to see his grandparents, he and his brother had spent hours running under a lawn sprinkler, and around the yard chasing each other with water guns. He could almost feel the sunshine and heat on his back, the refreshing chill of the cold water, the carefree laughter going back and forth between the two of them.

Filled with a profound sadness, he heaved a heavy sigh. Those joyful childhood days already felt like several lifetimes ago. *Have that many years really passed since we were those two little happy-go-lucky brothers?*

She interrupted his thoughts, obviously trying to take his mind off of Chris and his troubles. "If your mom was from New Jersey and your dad was from Massachusetts, then how did the two of them ever meet?"

He gave a half-hearted grin, grateful for the distraction. "Oh, it's actually a cute story really. They met at Boston University. My father and my Aunt Susan both went to BU. My mom was up here visiting a friend from Jersey, who happened to introduce her to my Aunt and a few of her friends. All the girls were walking across campus together on their way to a fraternity party one night, when they spotted my father and a couple of other guys sitting up in a tree."

She opened her eyes wide in shock. "What were they doing up in a tree?"

He smiled as he recalled the story he'd heard his mother lovingly tell so many times before. "What do you think?" he said with a chuckle. "All of them were hammered, of course. My father, being a wise-ass, called down to the group of girls and asked if any of them wanted to be an honorary member of I Phelta Thi."

She nearly choked trying to suppress a giggle. Finally unable to hold it in, she burst out laughing.

He couldn't help it and laughed right along with her.

When they finally collected themselves, she asked, "So what did your mother say?"

He grinned from ear to ear. "Nothing, at first. My Aunt Susan yelled at my father to get outta the tree and stop making an ass out of himself. But when he went to jump down, he lost his balance on the landing and fell right at my mother's feet."

"Oh my God," she said, cracking up some more. "Then what happened?"

"Well...the rest, as they say, is history. My mother said my father looked up at her, and somehow she just knew." He fidgeted with his own wedding ring, before looking her in the eyes again. "And I think it must've been true, because all of their friends said my mom and dad were married at first sight."

Sarah's smile lit up her whole face. "Married at first sight. I like that."

"Yeah, I never really understood what that meant before, but now I think I can relate." Leaning over, he planted his lips on hers, lost in a blissful kiss.

Finally, he pulled away and they both fell into a content silence again.

After a few minutes, she said, "What are you thinking about?"

He knew she could easily have read his mind again, but she must've been trying to be respectful and not pry into his sensitive thoughts. "Oh nothing," he replied, "...just my grandpa. I really miss him too. We were super close. It's hard to explain, but he had these little ways about him." He paused, searching for the right words. "My grandpa was...

funny, and smart, and kind. He cared so much about people and you don't see enough of that these days. For instance, he had this old-fashioned prayer he used to repeat every time he passed a bad car accident."

She cocked her head to the side in curiosity. "What was it?"

He grimaced, trying to recall it. "I don't know if I remember it exactly because he used to kind of mumble it under his breath in front of us little kids, but it went something like this. Be they alive or be they dead, have mercy on their souls, Lord. Much mercy if they're in pain, but even more if they're dead, for surely this day they were not prepared to meet you." He looked into her eyes. "I never really understood that saying at the time, but I think I do now."

She pinched her eyebrows together. "What do you mean?"

"Not only did I die in a car wreck, but I wasn't ready for any of this, were you?"

"No," she answered with an honest sincerity on her face. "You're right. No one probably ever is, but we'll figure it out together."

She leaned forward and he wrapped her in his arms. As always, she was his steady satellite, keeping him sane. *How does she do it?*

After a few minutes, he said, "Well, one thing is for certain. I can't rely on my father's help. Looking for him isn't getting us anywhere. It really is starting to feel like I'm looking for a needle in a haystack. I guess I'm going to have to face facts…I'm not going to be able to find him."

"I'm so sorry, sweetheart," she said, squeezing his hand.

"It's alright. It's my own fault," he said with a pause, "for focusing on the wrong problem. The most important thing right now is figuring out what types of souls we are. I think that's the key to moving on. It's at least the beginning anyway."

"Remember," she said in a lilting tone. "I'm going to stand by you no matter what happens. We're in this together now."

He smiled, just content to have his eyes on her. After a few moments, he took her by the hand, "Come on, let's get going."

Together, they descended the stairs, drifted down the driveway and onto the sidewalk in front of his grandfather's house.

"Where should we go next?" she asked him.

He thought for a moment, but he was fresh out of ideas. "I guess back to the Angel for now," he said with a shrug.

"You know," she said, "I've never been to Boston and we're so close. Do you mind if we go back through the city?"

"Not at all," he said, perking up. "That sounds like fun. I can show you all the places my parents used to take us when we came up here for a visit. There's literally tons of stuff to see all over the city."

Suddenly, a troubled looked crossed her face.

He quickly stepped closer to her and put his arm around her waist. "What's the matter, Hon?"

"I don't know," she said haltingly, "but I just got the strangest feeling. As if...as if you've said that to me before…you know, like déjà vu." She trembled, as if she'd caught a chill. "But you couldn't have. Could you?"

At this point, he thought, *there are so many mysteries about the afterlife. Nothing would surprise me.*

CHAPTER ELEVEN

BOSTON

AS THEY FLEW south from the tiny town of Saugus, Michael kept Route 1 in his sights below, sticking close to that highway so he wouldn't get them lost. When they reached the Chelsea area, he veered hard left at the Tobin Bridge which goes over the Mystic River. He was careful to fly as closely as he could over the narrow bridges, so the water wouldn't drain their energy.

On a whim, he took them over Logan Airport just for fun. Sarah got a real kick out of flying alongside of an American Airlines 777 as it was taking off. With the roar of the plane's engines filling their ears, they skirted directly under the belly of the wide airplane.

He had to admit he got a charge out of it himself. *What a rush*, he thought, *better than a breakaway drive across the court.*

"Thank you," she said in a sweet voice.

"For what?"

"You've shown me how very lucky we are," she replied.

"How so?"

"Because I can guarandamntee you no one gets to fly next to an airplane while they're alive."

He smiled.

After that, he pulled a wide arc and headed toward the center of Boston. Approaching the North End of the city, he pointed out several important buildings and landmarks to her. There was so much to explore here, he wasn't sure where she wanted to begin.

He motioned to a brick church with a tall white steeple, rising out of the center of other modern buildings and skyscrapers, completely out of place amongst its neighbors. "Over there is the Old North Church. The start of Paul Revere's famous ride."

"Oh, yes. I remember. One if by land, two if by sea," she said in a giddy voice. "The British are coming. The British are coming."

He touched down on Beacon Street in front of the Massachusetts State House with its gleaming gold dome. The heavy snow earlier in the day had turned the entire city into something out of Narnia. Every tree, every branch, every bush coated in a thick flocking of snow.

"We could head east," he suggested. "That will take us past the Granary Park Burying Grounds and the Kings Castle Burying Grounds, two of the oldest cemeteries in Boston. Some famous people are buried there, but the snow's pretty high so it might be difficult to see the headstones."

Sarah screwed up her face and shook her head. "Oh no, the last thing I want to see is a bunch of old graves," she said emphatically. "Let's hang among the living tonight. Besides, it looks like many of the resident ghosts are coming out for a night on the town anyway."

As she pointed across the way, he followed her gaze. A steady stream of spirits seemed to be crossing Park Street and making their way towards them. Many dressed in sixteenth, seventeenth, and eighteenth century finery.

"Okay, then. Let's walk around Boston Common instead." He gestured toward the tree-lined park directly across from the State House. "It's like Boston's version of Central Park."

"It definitely seems like the place to be tonight," she commented.

They strolled hand in hand across Beacon Street into Boston Commons until they came to the nearly fifty foot tall Christmas tree which had been decorated with thousands of tiny multicolored lights. Most of the surrounding trees were adorned with twinkling white lights.

From there they headed toward the ice skating rink on Frog Pond. Dozens of skaters, both alive and dead, twirled about the ice enjoying the winter wonderland. Occasionally they passed right through each other, but who was to notice in the chilly night air?

They watched from the sidelines for a few minutes.

"You know, the best part about this is we don't even need skates." He took hold of both of Sarah's hands and pulled her toward the ice. "Do you know how to skate?"

"Oh, a little," she said with a wicked grin. As soon as her feet were out over the ice, she took control and playfully swung him around until he spun a few feet away. She then completed a perfect spin, ending in a perfect pirouette. He pulled her up and brought her lips to his. For a moment or two, he was lost in her kiss.

The skating was exhilarating, but after a while the contact with the ice grew tiring. "My legs are beginning to feel heavier than two pylons," he remarked.

"I wonder why," she mused, "but mine are too."

He considered this for a minute. "I guess we are still over water, if you think about it…even if it is frozen."

Leaving the skating rink behind, they now crossed Charles Street. Large white globes topped the posts of a suspension bridge for pedestrians, which hung from one side of the shoreline and over the middle of the mostly frozen lagoon. Forty foot tall snow-covered weeping willows lined the shore surrounding the lagoon. With their greenery gone for the winter, their large, protective domed canopies became fluttering ropes of glittering ice and snow. Their ethereal, flowing effect nothing short of breath-taking.

"They must've put the swan boats away for the season," he said, a bit disappointed that he couldn't show them to her.

"That's okay. This is so lovely," she said. "It's like something out of a dream."

As they continued on through the park, the two of them drifted in between the enormous round evergreen bushes that resembled giant gumdrops with icing on top. Wrapped in white lights, the bushes glowed under the newly fallen snow.

Up ahead, spotlights illuminated both the statue of George Washington atop a prancing horse, and the Arlington Street gate—the ornate entrance to the commons, an elaborate wrought-iron gate draped with evergreen boughs and adorned for the holidays with a red-ribboned wreath below a large disk for the great seal of the city of Boston.

Glancing around, he noticed that most of the living had retired and gone home. "It must be getting late," he said.

"Do you want to see if we can still catch a show or see a ballet? We could go over to the theatre district. It's really close by."

Her eyes lit up. "Sounds wonderful."

"You know what," he suggested, "we can take a quick tour through the Bay Village area on our way there. I bet you didn't know this, but Bay Village is the birthplace of the famous American poet and short story writer Edgar Allan Poe."

"No, I didn't know that," she said, sounding surprised. "When I think of Poe I always think of Baltimore, Maryland."

"That's because he died there and I think he's buried there, too. But he was actually born in a house right here in Boston," he explained. "I think in 1809 if I remember correctly. I've read all about him. His parents were well-known actors in Boston's first theater."

"Ohhh, I loved his writing," Sarah gushed with admiration. "The Tell-Tale Heart, The Pit and the Pendulum, every one of them are great stories. And I always thought The Raven was the most haunting poem ever." She turned to him with hopeful eyes. "Can we go see his house? You never know, we might run into his ghost."

Michael laughed. "Nah," he said, shaking his head, "unfortunately the house isn't there anymore and there's been so much new construction, even the street where it sat is gone too. He didn't live there long anyway, less than a year I think. But that's why they dedicated a section of streets and renamed them Edgar Allan Poe Square. I went there once with my Aunt Susan. There's a bunch of Poe themed shops and a really cool statue of him beside a flying raven. I think you'd like it."

"So let's go see it," she said enthusiastically. "Where is it?"

"Around here somewhere." Michael looked left and right from the corner where they now stood, trying to recall the way. Finally, he gave up. "You know what, I don't remember exactly, but Bay Village isn't that big. I think if we walk up Arlington and cut in on one of the side streets we should be able to find Poe Square."

After a few minutes of walking, it seemed as if they were lost.

He stopped to try and get his bearings. When he realized he had no clue, he frowned. He was tempted to fly over Bay Village in order to find it, but he preferred to do things the 'normal' way for once. He took her hand in his again. "Here, let's try going up Piedmont. We should come across the statue and the shops sooner or later."

Contentedly he strolled side by side with her up the street. Until, seemingly from out of nowhere, a penny dropped from the thin air and rolled past his foot. The coin appeared to have been tossed from behind him, but when he turned around no one was there. He had no idea where the penny had come from.

Out of random curiosity, he and Sarah followed the shiny coin's path. It rolled forward several feet before coming to a stop on the sidewalk in front of some luxury condominiums.

She reached down to carefully pick up the coin, which had come to rest on top of a brass plaque embedded in the sidewalk. "Huh, it's a brand new penny," she said in wonder, "but the date on it is 1942."

Michael pointed to the brass plaque at their feet. "What do you think this is all about?"

Sarah furrowed her brow. "It looks kind of like a blueprint, maybe it's some sort of dedication for the building?" she speculated.

He read the main inscription on the top and bottom of the plaque out loud, "The Cocoanut Grove, November 28th, 1942, Phoenix out of the Ashes."

Sarah started to read the rest, "Erected by Bay Village Neighborhood Association, 1993. In memory of—"

But she never got the chance to finish, for two ghosts suddenly materialized directly in front of them.

The young man and woman looked to be about their age and held hands as if they were also a couple. They were dressed in old-fashioned clothes—the man, clad in a brown suit and vest with a casual top hat, and the woman, wearing a pink chiffon party dress.

"My name is Daniel," the man said, giving them a warm, friendly smile.

"And my name is Ruth," the woman said in a kindly way. "We can tell you all about the Cocoanut Grove."

Daniel extended his hand to Michael. "There's something important here that we need to show both of you."

"Something you will need to learn and remember later on," Ruth said in a soothing, yet serious voice, as she took Sarah's hand gently in her own.

Sarah glanced at Michael questioningly, but before he could do anything, Daniel grabbed his arm.

Powerless to stop him, the spirit invaded his consciousness.

Michael struggled to break free, but the man's hold on his mind was strong. Stronger than anything he'd ever felt. Even stronger than the inmate who had briefly hijacked his mind at Eastern State Penitentiary.

As before, memory and reality melded together, until he was firmly and unwillingly plunged into the past.

CHAPTER TWELVE

LESSON

THE NEXT INSTANT, he was standing beneath the tall, theater-style marquis of the famous Cocoanut Grove. Stepping off Piedmont Street, he strolled under the arched stone portico and entered through the Grove's signature revolving door. He now stood in the grand foyer, Ruth's delicate hand entwined with his.

They had waited months for this chance to come to the Cocoanut Grove. In all of Boston, this was the place to see, and be seen. The most elegant and exclusive supper club in the city, modeled after the famous nightclub of the same name which was part of the Ambassador Hotel in Los Angeles.

Daniel's stomach trembled with anxious anticipation, as he fingered the small box in his jacket pocket. Tonight was going to be a special night. A very special night. *After tonight, nothing will ever be the same.*

He took off his hat and nervously unbuttoned his topcoat. "Are you hungry, Sweetheart?"

Ruth slipped off her wool coat, laid it over his outstretched arm, and smoothed down the folds of her poofy pink chiffon dress. "No, Darling," she replied sweetly. "I already had supper before you picked me up."

As they nudged their way through the crowd of people to the coat check room, a bit of guilt nagged at him for not being able to pick her up until eight thirty. He had wanted to get here earlier, treat her to dinner, make a real night of it. Now, the place was already packed with hundreds and hundreds of patrons. "Sorry, I came so late and all."

"It's perfectly okay." She squeezed his hand affectionately. "I know you had to work. I don't mind."

Daniel strolled over to the crowd waiting near the coat check room, but so many people had clogged the line. He certainly didn't want to wait all night just to put their coats away. He turned to a cigarette girl standing off to the side of the entrance to the ballroom. Her bright-yellow blonde hair stood out in stark contrast to her black and red uniform. She held open a display case of the popular smokes and her nametag read, *Claire*. "Excuse me, Miss. Can you tell me if there's another coatroom?"

"Sure is, Sunshine." She motioned to a dimly lit hallway off to the left of the main coat check area. "If you go through that corridor there and stay to the left you'll get to it eventually."

"Thank you, Miss."

Eventually, they found the second coat check room and deposited their coats along with Ruth's handbag. Turning around though, they found the way they had come impossibly blocked with a fresh line of guests.

Daniel gestured to another narrow hallway off to their right. "Here, let's go this way."

Weaving their way through a series of twisting and

confusing corridors, they finally emerged at the edge of the main ball room.

"Holy mackerel! This place sure is a maze." He chuckled. "I'm not sure we're ever going to be able to find where we left our coats again."

Ruth laughed. "Oh, who cares? I'm just so happy to be here."

Her excited smile melted his heart. *That's all I want to do for the rest of my life…make her happy.*

They stepped into the ballroom now, their gaze sweeping about the room to take it all in. The large dance floor took up the middle of the room, surrounded by dozens and dozens of tables along the outer walls. Six pillars, three on each side, were decorated to look like tropical palm trees, with enormous paper fronds extending way out over the tables and the main dance floor. The way they naturally bent and swayed, they looked as real as if they had been uprooted from an island and planted in the club.

"My goodness," Ruth remarked in awe. "It really does look like something straight out of Casablanca."

Daniel gestured toward the ceiling above their heads. "I've even heard the roof above the dance floor can be electrically rolled back so everyone can see the night sky and dance under the stars."

"That's *amazing*," she said, craning her head to look up. "But I hope they don't do that tonight. It's much too cold."

He laughed.

The band had just taken the stage at the far end of the ballroom and started another set. Daniel recognized the song as "In The Mood" by Glenn Miller, one of Ruth's favorites.

"Would you care to dance?"

Her eyes lit up. "Of course," she shouted over the din.

Within seconds, they found themselves swallowed up into the rollicking crowd on the dance floor, whirling and twirling about to the glorious sounds of swing.

After a few minutes, Daniel slowed down to catch his breath. "So, what do you think of the place?"

"Oh, it's so grand...," she said, breathless herself, "and everyone is dressed so elegantly. I feel like we *are* in Hollywood and I'm Ginger Rogers."

His stomach quivered with happiness. That was exactly how he wanted her to feel on their special night. He leaned in to whisper in her ear, "I think you're prettier than Ginger Rogers."

As the band began to play a slow song, Ruth blushed and laid her head on his chest, so close her perfume had him instantly intoxicated.

The crowd now thickened, so they shifted closer to the far side of the dance floor to have some more space. Daniel glanced over at the area called the Terrace, an exclusive section of tables meant for the most important and famous guests of the restaurant, elevated off the main floor of the ball room and edged with wrought iron railings to complete the separation. A friend had encouraged him to keep his eyes peeled for celebrities. It was obvious why the special guests got to sit up there—the elevation on the terrace allowed prime views of the ballroom and floor show. And most importantly, it put the VIPs on display for all to see.

"Look, Sweetheart." He pointed to a rather suave, well-dressed man seated at a table on the Terrace, surrounded by a crowd of equally ritzy men and women who seemed to be doting on the man, laughing and smiling at his every word. "I'm fairly sure that's Buck Jones."

Ruth went wide-eyed. "Not the actor from all the cowboy movies?"

"One and the same," he said, enjoying her stunned reaction. "Did you know he's starred in more than two hundred films?"

"No foolin'?" she asked in a whisper. "Wow, I don't think I've ever been in the same place as a hotshot celebrity before."

"Of course you have, Darling," he said, raising an eyebrow at her. "You've been with me."

She slapped him on the chest. "Oh, you're a *pistol*, that's what you are."

All evening patrons drifted back and forth between the basement and the dining room upstairs, but as the night went on, he noticed more and more people heading down to the Melody Lounge. A friend had told him the basement lounge was much smaller than the upstairs, only big enough for about a couple hundred people—more dimly lit, more intimate, more romantic. The perfect place for what he had planned. He glanced at his wristwatch, *10:00. Where had the time gone?* He had better get to the business of the evening before he lost his nerve.

With his hand on her back, he ushered Ruth off the dance floor and pointed to the stairs off to the right side of the revolving entrance doors. "Let's head down to the Melody Lounge," he suggested.

"Oh yes, *let's*," Ruth said excitedly. "There's so much to see here. I don't want to miss a *thing*."

He took her hand in his and led the way. "My father said they've been adding on and adding on to this place like crazy because it keeps growing in popularity."

"I can see why," she replied.

The stairs were so narrow, barely four feet wide across he guessed, that he had to let go of her hand so they could walk single file. Leading her down he said, "We'll have to check out the new Broadway Lounge after this."

Once they reached the bottom, he took a quick glance around the packed room. *Forget two hundred. There must be at least twice that many people crammed down here tonight.* Customers surrounding the bar were at least four deep waiting for drinks.

The décor was similar to upstairs—tropical palm trees with tiny twinkling lights in the corners, and tables lining the surrounding walls.

Ruth pointed to the center of the room. "Look, the stage even moves."

Sure enough, she was right. A young woman had just started playing the piano, which sat on a slowly revolving circular stage in the middle of an octagonal dance floor. One soft spotlight beamed down upon her as she sang.

He scanned the dimly lit room searching for an open table or private spot to retreat to, but it was difficult to see much. The only light came from the spotlight on the ceiling above aimed at the stage, a few cocoanut covered lights in the palm trees, and a bit of bluish-white neon lighting that lined the underside of the bar.

"Oh listen," Ruth exclaimed. "It's that new hit by Bing

Crosby, White Christmas. I just love this song. I wonder who the singer is though…"

"Her name's Goody Goodelle, I saw it on the marquee outside," he said. "She sure does have a swell voice, doesn't she?"

Ruth nodded enthusiastically. She gestured over their heads. "And look at all the pretty, blue satin draped from the ceiling."

"I've heard it's supposed to make you feel like you're sitting beneath a star-filled night sky."

As he watched Ruth's smiling face taking it all in, he also noticed a sailor and his date enjoying the privacy under one of the artificial palm trees in a particularly dark corner. He sort of wished they had gotten that spot first. It would've been perfect.

Guiding Ruth by the arm, he led her as close as they could get to the darkened corner. Luckily, they found two chairs that had been vacated, so they shared one side of a table with a Marine and his date on the other. It wasn't ideal but the lounge was so over-crowded, this would have to do.

Just then, the busboy passed them and walked over to the corner where the sailor sat kissing his date. "Bartender says I gotta plug the light back in," the teen said in a shy voice.

"Sure, whatever," the sailor replied with a grin.

Daniel didn't envy the poor kid, who looked mortified to interrupt in the first place. Now the situation was only getting more embarrassing as the busboy fumbled and struggled to fit the light bulb back into the fake coconut husk.

Striking a match so he could see better, the busboy finally

found the socket and replaced the light bulb, which flickered for a second then came back on. The young man blew out the match and dropped it to the floor, crushing it under his shoe to make sure it was out.

Now that the funny spectacle was over, Daniel turned his attention back to Ruth. He looked down at her lips. He'd waited long enough. *Maybe now's the time to pop the question?* With his heart pounding in his throat, he opened his mouth to say the words he'd been rehearsing in his mind all week.

But a commotion in the corner interrupted him again.

"Quick, get some water!" someone shouted.

"Hey, the palm tree's on fire!" came another cry.

Daniel's jaw snapped shut, as he whipped his head around. Sure enough, a swirl of bluish flame and oddly colored smoke seemed to dance just above the top palm fronds close to the ceiling and in front of an air conditioning vent.

In a flash, one of the paper leaves caught fire. Then the next. And the next.

The bartender ran from behind the bar with a towel and began swatting at the flames. He and the busboy batted at the tree, trying to pull the fake branches down and extinguish the fire, but a shower of sparks flew every which way. Other employees now came to their aid throwing pitchers of water at the tree. For a few brief moments, the scene was almost comedic and a few people around them chuckled in amusement.

Until, the satin fabric above the tree started to smoke and burn.

A split-second later, a larger ball of orange and blue fire exploded out of the corner and roared across the fabric covered ceiling. The flames spread so quickly there was barely time to think, barely time to move, barely time to act.

Men and women pushed out of their chairs and started to shout, as the hot fabric melted off the ceiling, dripping down on them, burning their skin, hair and clothes.

He jumped to his feet, at the same moment Ruth and others screamed in panic.

The Marine next to him hopped up on a chair, furiously slashing at the dark fabric with a pocket knife to cut off the fire's path and stop it from spreading. Another tall man tried to help him, but it was no use.

The monstrous fire just kept coming, roaring across the ceiling in bursts, claiming everything in its path.

The fire was spreading with unholy speed.

Daniel glanced up to see dozens of wooden slats now exposed beneath the fabric.

We're going to be trapped inside a tinderbox.

He yanked Ruth by the hand and off her chair.

It was pandemonium. They and the other panicked patrons scrambled around tables and overturned chairs, racing towards the narrow stairwell that lead upstairs.

His mind now thundered with panic. *My God, only one way out. There's only one way out.*

As they neared the stairs, he glanced back. The room was already an inferno, the entire ceiling now a rolling sheet of blue and orange flame, coming in waves.

And the fire was racing towards them.

Something was also very wrong with the air. He tried to

draw a breath, but the noxious, acrid smoke assaulted his nose and seared his lungs.

No air, there's no air!

They were among the first to reach the stairs, but the panicked crowd pushed at their backs. With the last bit of breath he could muster, he screamed to Ruth. "Don't let go of me! Grab the back of my jacket!"

Horrified, he realized the low hanging fabric continued above their heads and all the way up the stairwell, which had now become a chimney for the fire sucked towards the updraft.

It was now a mad frenzy to escape, as several people yanked and pulled to get past them.

Ruth went down.

He yelled at her to get up, pulling hard on her arm.

Screaming men and women trampled her, others fell on top of her. He had only seconds to get her up or she would be done for. In only a matter of moments, the bottom of the stairs was quickly becoming a tangle of bodies. The heat of the fire already intense and unbearable.

Gathering all his strength, he threw one of the people off of her and yanked on her arm again. She broke free, scrambling to her feet.

In a blind panic they were pushed up the narrow stairs by the moving crowd, stepping on and over people. The raging fire within inches of their heads. The flames already feeding and sucking on the only oxygen left in the room. He struggled for breath and could hear Ruth gasping and choking behind him too.

His clothes caught fire.

Ungodly pain seared his skin, but it was nothing compared to the all-consuming thought that swelled in his head, choking out all other rational thought, *we're going to die!*

Reaching the top, he spotted the emergency exit immediately to their left.

A man was already trying desperately to open it, as people gathered behind him and began pushing.

Everyone was screaming, "Open it! Open the door!"

"I think it's bolted shut!" the frantic man yelled back. Over and over, he yanked violently at the door handle in vain.

As heart-wrenching as it was to turn around with an exit so close, something told Daniel to go the other way. *They aren't going to get that door open.*

Grabbing Ruth's hand again, he suddenly darted to the right, screaming at her, "Hold on to me! We have to find another way out!"

Blinded by the thick black smoke, he remembered with growing dread the maze they had come through upstairs, and realized he would have to navigate them through it.

Everyone who had been downstairs and had made it up before them was now pushing through the revolving door at the front of the lobby. But with no air, and the smoke and fire at their backs, they were panicking, pushing from both sides.

To his great horror, the door jammed.

Very quickly people started to crush against the doors, screaming and clawing. Fighting for their lives.

Someone grabbed Ruth from behind, throwing her out of the way. She stumbled and fell backward.

Terrified that Ruth might be trampled to death, he quickly yanked her up off the floor.

That's all it took. Others jumped in the gap, forcing them backward and into the entrance of the main dining room.

Finally, he emerged in the dining room with the fire and Ruth right behind him. A sigh of half-relief escaped his lips. Stunned guests stared at the commotion in the foyer, wondering what was going on.

A split second later, the fire burst through the wall behind the Caricature Bar, giving them their answer.

Without warning, the lights went out.

The entire ballroom now plunged into a terrifying nightmare of darkness.

Immediately, a cacophony of noise—piercing screams, people yelling, glasses and dishes breaking, tables and chairs sliding, overturning—threatened to overwhelm his sense of direction.

As the fire invaded the main ballroom, the only light now came from the violent blue and orange flames on the walls and over their heads. The fire jumped from palm tree to palm tree, climbing the walls, consuming the fabric, devouring everything in its path. In some places fireballs seemed to be rolling freely through the air, attached to nothing at all.

Hell! We're in the very pits of hell!

Paralyzing terror seized them both. Ruth's nails dig into his arm. "Don't lose me!" she pleaded with a desperate scream.

He plunged forward though he couldn't see.

People shoved this way and that, bumping into him.

Screaming, they were all screaming.

Ruth couldn't take the flames on her clothes and hair any longer. She let go of him, ran to the right, dropped to the floor and rolled back and forth for a few precious seconds to extinguish the flames.

He dove to help her, but stumbled because it was so dark.

Now closer to the floor, he found it a tiny bit easier to breathe. As he gulped a few precious breathes of air, a hand grabbed his coat from behind.

The smoke thinned for a moment, so he stood up and turned around to say something to Ruth. He thought she was right there.

His heart nearly seized in his chest.

Claire, the blonde cigarette girl now clung to his jacket.

When had he lost Ruth?

He looked behind him, trying desperately to see through the dense, black smoke but another cloud of it closed in again, thicker than before.

People grabbed and pushed at him from every direction, forcing him forward.

It was hopeless. He'd never be able to find her.

Unable to take a clear breath, his chest seized as his lungs cried out for air.

He had only two choices. *Keep moving forward, or die in this inferno.*

With his heart and his soul tearing in two, he made an unthinkable decision.

And left his beloved Ruth behind.

Tears sprang to his eyes, as he lunged forward through the darkness and choking smoke.

Though he couldn't see, with each footfall, he knew.

He was surely stepping on and over bodies.

He couldn't see Claire any longer either.

A huge fireball roared past on his left, and he caught a brief glimpse of a woman completely engulfed in flames. Her screams ripping apart his soul. He wished he could help her, but there was nothing he could do. Nothing anyone could do. It was every man and woman for themselves.

The death and horror surrounding him threatened to overwhelm him, but an insane will to survive drove his body forward through the all-consuming blackness.

He struggled to think, struggled to move, struggled to breathe.

Finally, he reached the back of the dining room. Only twelve or so more feet to a door someone had found.

He sprinted forward, blind with panic, lungs seared, heart pounding.

Just as his hand touched the door, a crush of bodies shoved him up against it.

I'm going to die. I'm going to die.

Suddenly, a fireman's ax broke through the flimsy plaster of an adjacent wall. Along with another man, he now rammed his body full force into the wedge-size hole, tumbling out onto the wet pavement.

Shouting, screaming and sirens filled the night air.

Instinct drove him to run around to the front of the building. He prayed they had gotten the revolving doors open.

He still couldn't breathe, but he wanted to help. Maybe he could get an ax and go back in for Ruth.

When he got near the entrance, his heart sank.

Singed survivors stumbled around, dazed by the unimaginable horror. Discarded bodies lay everywhere like dressed up mannequins.

A few lucky souls climbed down from the upper floors and the roof on fire ladders placed against the side of the building.

Soldiers and firefighters pounded with axes on the revolving glass doors. But it was no use. Packed with bodies, the doors wouldn't budge. So many young people trapped inside. Through the smoke and the glass he could see the bodies stacked four, five and six high.

Everyone could see them, but there was nothing anyone could do.

One of the fireman started speaking to him, but his words sounded as if he were submerged under water. *Something about going to the hospital.*

Before he could even respond, the fireman and a Navy sailor grabbed him under his shoulders, and ushered him into a waiting taxi.

At first he tried to protest, but then he collapsed onto the seat in the back of the vehicle. The driver in the front kept glancing in his rearview mirror, talking fast, rattling off questions.

Nothing registered.

His calves stung and he glanced down, expecting to still be on fire. Instead, he found the bottom of his pants shredded, with deep claw marks gouged into his skin beneath, grim evidence of the final desperate moments of so many poor souls.

Out of sheer habit, he glanced at his wristwatch. *My God.*

It's only 10:30. Near as he could tell, the fire had started around 10:15. All that destruction and death had occurred in only fifteen minutes. *Only fifteen minutes.*

The kind stranger said they were on their way to Boston General Hospital.

When they arrived, he quickly thanked him and began a frantic search for Ruth. Perhaps somehow she had managed to get out. He clung to that hope, he had to…or he feared he might go mad. Over and over again he prayed in his head, *please dear God, let her be okay. Please let my Ruth be okay.*

A crowd of people clogged the receiving area of the hospital, which had been pitched into complete bedlam. Medical staff darted about, clearly swamped with critical arrivals, the dead, the dying and the injured. Though overwhelmed, they were doing their best to keep order and tend to those who needed it most. Worried family members had descended upon the hospital in droves, as news of the fire must have spread across the city. Their anxious questions and anguished cries filled his ears, as he forced his way through the cramped hallways. In a blind panic he scanned each of the treatment rooms, but he couldn't find his Ruth.

As one of the nurses hustled by with a clipboard in her hands, he snatched her by the arm. "Excuse me, Miss. Is there a list of the survivors?" Desperately, he searched her face for the truth. "Any sort of list? I'm looking for my…fiancée." Overcome with emotion, he nearly choked on the word.

She looked up at him with tear-filled, tormented eyes.

"No. I'm sorry, Sir. There isn't yet. Most of the patients, they can't speak...they can't even tell us their names." She hesitated, her hands shaking. "Some of the men had their identification in their pockets, but the ladies...," she looked down at the floor, "...they don't have their purses or any belongings, so we can't tell who is who yet. I'm so sorry," she repeated, her words full of pity. Motioning helplessly at the lifeless bodies still lying side by side on the floor, she added, "If you haven't found her yet in one of the treatment rooms, you're welcome to look for her here. But please, stick to this corridor and the one to your left. The others—"

Daniel quickly nodded, so she wouldn't have to finish what she clearly didn't want to say, *the others won't be recognizable.* Coughing and trembling, he slowly shuffled down the hall, scrutinizing all the faces. Many were about the same age as he and Ruth, in their late teens, early twenties, thirties at most. Young men and women, arms folded on their chests, dressed like porcelain dolls in their best suits and party dresses, still and peaceful, as if they were merely sleeping. Other than some black soot and scorch marks around their mouths and noses, many looked as if they might wake up at any moment. Most of the bodies were hardly burned. Several had a large black M scrawled on their forehead. He knew what that meant. They'd been given morphine to comfort them in their final, dying moments.

Daniel fingered the jewelry box still in his pocket, as he remembered his thought from earlier that evening, *after tonight nothing will ever be the same.*

Turning the corner into the next corridor, he froze in horror. At the far end, lay a girl in a pale pink dress.

He couldn't breathe as he ran down the hall past the other bodies, screaming a silent prayer in his head.

When he reached the girl with the pink chiffon dress, he glimpsed Ruth's angelic face. Like all the others, she looked as if she had simply fallen asleep.

He tried to take a step closer, but his legs refused to move. He tried to draw a breath, but his lungs wouldn't respond. He tried to cry out, but the words wouldn't come.

The room spun, as he collapsed next to her body.

A milli-second later, Michael finally gathered enough energy and expelled Daniel from his mind.

With the pain of the hideous, tragic memories still fresh, his strength waned and his knees buckled. Sucking in a ragged phantom breath, he blinked twice and looked around. He was back on the street corner in front of the condominiums once again. No more fire, no more bodies, no more burned out shell of a building. No more grief and pain. He shook his head for a second to help him regain his focus and untangle memory from reality. Quickly, he wiped spectral tears from his cheek.

Before he could fully recover, Sarah grabbed onto him, clinging tightly to his neck. "It was awful," she sobbed into his chest. "Just awful."

Only at that moment did he realize she had been drawn into the past along with him. *She must have felt the agony of the fire and experienced that poor girl's horrific death.* Anger roiled within him, but as calmly as he could, he gave her shoulders a reassuring squeeze and let her go.

Raising his hands, he rounded on Daniel, preparing to

strike a blow. "You put my *wife* through that horror show too?" he screamed at him. "How *dare* you?"

Fearlessly, Ruth stepped in his path to protect Daniel. "*I* put her through it," she said in a bold tone of utter defiance.

Michael hesitated, uncertain what to do. *Damn it! I can not hit a woman!*

Ruth turned her kind, sweet face to Sarah. "We're sorry we had to put you both through those terrible memories, but it was the only way to show you, the only way to make you truly learn."

He stole one more dagger-like stare at Daniel before saying, "Look lady, I have no idea what your deal is, but we're outta here."

Ruth grabbed him by the arm, her touch oddly warm. "No, you *must* listen," she pleaded. "I am a Messenger, you see."

That stopped him cold. Still, he thought, *she better have some damned good answers.* "So why did you show us all this horror?" he demanded.

"Because we were told to," Daniel said pointedly. "You both had a lesson to learn. Please give us a chance to explain."

Ruth glanced at Sarah, and then back at him. "Four hundred and ninety-two souls perished in the fire at the Cocoanut Grove that night," she said in a somber voice. "Including me."

"Hundreds more were injured," Daniel added.

"Wait a minute," Michael interjected, sticking an accusatory finger in his face. "That's right. You didn't even die in that fire."

"No, I didn't," Daniel replied with a solemn shake of his head. "But I lived it. And I lost the love of my life." He squeezed Ruth's hand. "And afterwards, like everyone else, all I could do was pick up the pieces from that terrible, tragic night. Like so many others, I collapsed after the fact from unseen burns to my lungs. It took me weeks to recover, but I was one of the lucky ones. I survived and went on to live a long, relatively happy life until I died at the age of sixty-two." He glanced at Ruth with tender eyes, as if she was still his best friend. "More importantly, in the months following the fire, I was part of a group of people who testified before Congress about what we witnessed...the jammed revolving door, the barred exits, the locked doors, the over-capacity crowd, the toxic smoke, the flammable materials."

Ruth now turned and pleaded with Sarah. "Don't you see? What you both needed to learn is that in one tragic night, that fire changed lives."

Michael gave her a horrified look. *How can she say that as if it's a* good *thing?* "Yes, for the bad!" he yelled emphatically.

"True," Ruth said to him, "but also for the good. Because of that one fire, over the decades countless lives have actually been *saved.*"

Sarah stepped closer to him and he protectively wrapped his arms around her. "What do you mean?" she asked in barely a whisper.

"As a direct result of that tragedy, many safety standards and fire codes were reformed first in Massachusetts and then, across the country," Daniel explained. "Better fire laws were enacted for public places banning flammable decorations, inward-swinging exit doors, and requiring exit signs to be visible at all times, meaning that exit signs have to have independent sources of electricity, and be easily readable in even the thickest smoke. Every time you see a red exit sign lit up, it is because of Cocoanut Grove," he said with a solemn pause.

Michael now realized, *I've never given those signs more than a moment's thought.*

Daniel now continued. "The new fire laws also made sure that there would *never* be a tragedy with a revolving door again," he said in the strongest terms. "Those kinds of doors must now either be flanked by at least one normal, outward-swinging door, or be able to fold flat in a panic situation. No emergency exits are ever allowed to be chained or bolted shut in any way," he added, as he jabbed emphatically at the palm of his hand. "Nearly every fire law on the books and being enforced today…is a result of this tragic fire."

"And that's not all," Ruth said. "The Boston doctors and hospitals had never dealt with a medical emergency on such a massive scale before that night. Out of sheer necessity, many medical advancements also came about as a result of the fire—in the treatment of burn victims, the widespread use of penicillin, the treatment of grief, and the use of a blood bank just to name a few."

"That's all peachy," he said, not even trying to conceal the sarcasm in his voice, "but what about all those poor souls who died? What about them? Was *that* fair?"

Ruth pushed right up to him, jutting her finger straight at his face. "Don't talk to me about fair. I was one of them and

I was only *nineteen*," she replied in a stern, yet steady voice. "But I've come to learn, the seed of triumph is often planted by tragedy. That fire was a catalyst for change. Sometimes sacrifices are necessary to affect a greater good."

Well, she shut me down. Shut me right down.

He thought about something Lincoln had said, *God uses many human instrumentalities to affect His purposes.*

Obviously this strong woman didn't mind being one of those instrumentalities. Hell, she even seemed proud of her sacrifice. Despite his annoyance, an admiration for this brave, young woman rose up within him.

Sarah's curiosity must have gotten the best of her. "Who told you to teach us this lesson?"

"You know," Ruth replied, pointing back and forth between the two of them. "You both know." Gently, she tapped him on his chest right over his heart. "The answer lies in here."

Sarah glanced up at him with a knowing look.

He was stunned. "But how did they even know we were here…in Boston?"

"They always know where you are, Michael," Ruth replied in a reassuring way.

Daniel gave him a definite nod. "Always."

Ruth now turned her gentle, apologetic eyes to the two of them. "We really are sorry the memories were so painful," she said sincerely, "but it was the only way to show you, the only way to make you truly learn."

"One last thing," Daniel said. "Keep doing what you're doing, both of you. You may not believe this, but you *are* moving in the right direction."

Michael froze, and so did Sarah alongside him. "How do you know that?"

Daniel smiled. "It's my job to know. I'm a Navigator. I can sense if souls are, or are not, on the correct course," he replied, "and though you may not be able to see it, you *are* on the right track." He put a reassuring hand on Michael's shoulder. "You *will* find your way. And so will Sarah."

As Michael mumbled a quick thank you, he turned to gauge her reaction.

She nodded, but still looked shaken. "I just want to go home."

CHAPTER THIRTEEN

VALENTINE'S DAY

THE LAST FEW weeks had been a lover's dream. No distractions, no pressures, no responsibilities to get in the way of their bliss. After the terrifying experience of meeting the ghosts from the Cocoanut Grove fire, they both needed some time to decompress.

Occasionally, worries of demons, his father's mysterious warning and their harrowing experience at the Cocoanut Grove would creep back into his thoughts, but having Sarah by his side helped to calm most of his fears and anxieties.

And what better place for two ghosts to spend their time but an old-fashioned bed and breakfast by the ocean. No wonder so many couples came here for their honeymoon or a romantic getaway. The Angel of the Sea was little by little capturing a piece of his soul.

All he wanted to do was walk like lovers do, talk like lovers do, kiss like lovers do. But they had to be careful. The slightest brush against her still gave him an almost electric shock. Over time, he learned how to be able to hold her for a long time without their energies slipping together, but it was difficult to maintain. If their touch started feeling too good, he would feel that pull, that unearthly magnetism. He definitely had gotten better at controlling himself around her, but he still had to be cautious.

As usual, he had no idea how time had managed to pass so fast. It was impossible to miss that it was Valentine's Day. The owners of the Angel of the Sea had truly outdone themselves, with the downstairs of the bed and breakfast decked out in bouquets of lush red roses, yards of glittering red tulle, and lacey paper cupid decorations.

The sun was out, but a storm far offshore was quickly driving clouds inland. So for now, they stayed in the shade sitting side by side on the wicker bench on one of the verandas. Besides their attic, it was the only place to get a little privacy right now. Every room in the majestic bed and breakfast was booked, so with the Angel brimming with guests there weren't too many places they could hang out without literally bumping into the living every other minute. They could always stay in their attic of course, but how many hours could two young ghosts linger in a dusty, old attic without getting terminally bored?

Furthermore, the ocean views from the porches were simply spectacular. The haunting call of the seagulls, the sound of the rolling surf, and the crash of the waves hitting the beach a short distance away caressed his soul.

Sarah leaned back, nuzzling against him until he wrapped his arms around her. "It's our first Valentine's Day together," she said with a contented sigh.

He slid her red hair aside to kiss her lightly on the cheek. "You're right. It is." He tightened his arms, letting out a happy sigh of his own. "We should do something special."

"Like what?"

He thought for a moment. "Did you ever get to see much of the Jersey Shore?"

She shook her head. "No, I hadn't been in the States very long before...the accident," she said regretfully, "and I was always so busy working at the Christian Admiral Hotel that I never had the chance to see much else besides a few places around Cape May."

"That's a shame," he said. "Even though my grandmother had the beach house in Seaside, we used to visit all the shore points. Once I got my driver's license my friends and I would come down to the shore every chance we could. In the summer, most of the basketball games for the Shore League were somewhere in South Jersey. So I would go to a game in the morning or afternoon, shower at my grandma's or a friend's beach house, and then we'd hop back on the Parkway and head either North or South to wind up at one of the shore towns. Didn't matter which one...Seaside, LBI, Belmar, Ocean City, Wildwood...just as long as we were somewhere down here. In fact, we were planning on going down to Wildwood for Senior Week right after graduation."

Tilting her head inquisitively, Sarah giggled. "What on earth is Senior Week? It sounds like something involving elderly people."

He laughed out loud. "No, no, no. It's a week-long out-of-control party for seniors, that's what we call kids who are graduating from secondary school in the US. I keep forgetting you went to school in Ireland," he said with a grin. "All the seniors come to the Jersey Shore and rent a big house with their friends to celebrate graduation. It's tradition."

"Ohhh," she said with a chuckle, "then it sounds like fun."

"Yeah," he said with a tinge of regret, "except I never got to go. I'd only been looking forward to it my entire life." He had to get ahold of himself. He didn't want to ruin his first Valentine's Day with her by being sad, but a touch of bitterness nagged at him. Suddenly struck by a great idea, he jumped up from the chair. "Hey, you know what I'd like to do?" he said excitedly.

She stood up from the bench, looking genuinely curious. "What?"

"Let's get out of town for a little while," he suggested. "Have you ever been to Wildwood Boardwalk?"

"No." She shook her head sullenly. "I know it's not far away from here, but I never did have a chance to go there before—"

He wrapped his arms around her and kissed her deeply, so she wouldn't have to finish that sentence. When he finally pulled back he said, "Then, I'd love to show it to you."

He offered her his arm so she could draft with him.

She hooked her arm around his, but said firmly, "Now take it easy, not too fast. We've only drafted a few times and it still gives me a touch of vertigo."

Within seconds, they landed on Cresse Avenue and Beach Avenue near the archway which marks the southern end of Wildwood Boardwalk.

He searched her face to see how she had fared with the drafting. "Are you alright?"

"Yes, I'm fine, but I'm not sure I'll ever get used to that," she said touching her forehead. "It makes my head spin a wee bit."

The wind-battered boardwalk and surrounding streets

were deserted, not a soul to be seen, alive or dead. The blistering cold was definitely keeping the living away and he guessed maybe the dead had better things to do than haunt an empty boardwalk in the off-season.

He couldn't blame the living for staying away. On a day like this, the wind down here so close to the ocean could whip a person's cheeks raw in five minutes or less. A Nor'easter was definitely brewing offshore.

As they floated up onto the boardwalk he said, "Thank God the tram car isn't running."

She scrunched up her pretty nose in the cutest way imaginable. "What's the tram car?"

"It's this linked chain of bright yellow and blue open air cars on wheels, which runs up and down the boardwalk along that path," he said, pointing out the cement paving along the middle of the right and left sides of the boards. "They have at least two sets of them that operate kinda like a trackless train service. And of course, they paste advertisements on every square inch of the cars. The tram car loops around from one end of the boardwalk to the other, stopping to pick up and drop off passengers all along the boards." He shrugged. "I guess it's necessary because it saves people from having to walk the length of the boardwalk, which is over three miles."

"So what's wrong with that?"

He laughed out loud just thinking about it. "Well, because it has to run straight through the crowds on the boardwalk, the tram car has this annoying recording that repeats over and over again." He pinched his nose and mimicked the audio in a horrible, nasally voice, *"Watch* the tram car please, *watch* the tram car please, *watch* the tram car please, *watch* the—"

"Oh my God, stop!" She put her hands over her ears. "I get it. I get it," she said, laughing.

He paused for a long minute, lost in a memory. He was four years old and his father held him tightly as he rode the tram car for the first time. Next to him, his mother gripped the handle of the umbrella stroller where his baby brother lay blissfully asleep.

But as easily as a puff of smoke vanishes with a gust of wind, the memory was gone.

All those years ago, a simple ride on the tram car with his family had seemed so nondescript, so inconsequential, so insignificant. Since then, he had learned something though, *you never know the true value of a moment until it becomes a memory you wish you could jump back into and relive again.*

When he looked back at Sarah, she was staring at him with a knowing grin. "You really do miss the tram car, don't you," she said with a tiny nod.

He rolled his eyes and shook his head begrudgingly. "I can't believe I'm gonna say this...but yeah, I do."

As they meandered hand in hand down the boardwalk, they reached the parking lot rotunda near the Convention Center. Sarah got a kick out of the enormous, colorfully painted beach balls and iconic towering letters of the Wildwood sign.

"Every year, my mother and father would take pictures of me and Chris near the big sign. Always in the same spots too. Near the 'W' and the 'I' so that they could prove how much we'd grown."

"What a nice tradition," she said sweetly.

He rolled his eyes. "Yeah you'd think so, unless you're a ten year old boy who can't stand being made a spectacle of while your parents make funny faces at you to get you to smile."

She giggled. "I see your point."

As they strolled along the boards, his melancholy started creeping back on him. "It's kind of nice having the boardwalk all to ourselves...but there's also a certain loneliness, too. Some might say it's like a ghost town around here," he said awkwardly, pointing to the gray accordion storm-gates pulled down over all the stores, shops, restaurants, and stands.

She clung to his arm and gave him a reassuring squeeze. "Just remember we're not alone in this afterlife anymore... we have each other."

He smiled, giving her a peck on the cheek. *She always knows just what to say to make me feel better.*

Eventually they came to the first ride pier that extended off the boardwalk and out over the sand at a ninety degree angle—The Adventure Pier. On the corner at the entrance to the pier, he spied the good old Kohr's stand. Like everything else, closed for the season of course, but none the less a time-honored tradition.

"Best soft serve ice cream on the boardwalk," he told her.

"Of course it is," she said with a devilish grin. "You would know."

He turned to give her an annoyed look. "Very funny, don't make me spank you."

"How do you know I wouldn't like that?" she asked boldly.

He smiled, saying to her in his mind, *just so you know, I'm making a mental note of that for later.*

Instantly, she blushed.

Next, on their left, they passed the classic V-shape structure of the Slingshot thrill ride that swings riders way high up in the air on bungee cords. And on their right, The Great White, a sprawling wooden-steel hybrid roller coaster that he'd been on countless times.

"I loved roller coasters," he said, pointing it out to her.

"Me too," she said. "Except the ones that went upside-down."

He nearly laughed out loud at that. Suddenly, a wild notion seized his very core. He flew up onto the platform where the lower tracks began, and started to walk up the steep hundred foot incline leading to the coaster's first big drop. He could've flown all the way to the top of course, but that would've defeated the purpose.

"Where on earth are you going?" she called up to him.

"As a kid, I always used to dream about what it would be like to climb this," he shouted back, as he waved an arm at her. "Come on."

Once they made it the top of the first big hill, he clasped her hand and they let themselves drop as if they were riding in one of the cars. Since gravity didn't really affect them, they were slightly cheating of course, but he didn't care. It was still fun to pretend.

When they hit the bottom, they plucked their way along the next bunch of thin track, back up the next slope and then followed around the bend to the far edge of the coaster at the very end where the pier extended out over the ocean.

Standing there victorious, he grinned as if he were the guy who had just reached the top of Mt. Everest for the first time. He couldn't help it.

He was now perched at the very top of a roller coaster track over a hundred feet in the air. *How many people can say they've done that?*

Taking Sarah by the hand, he made her step onto the adjacent track directly in front of him. He placed his body against hers, wrapping his arms around her in a tight embrace while they both stared out at the raging sea. The wind from the storm had whipped the frothing surf into a frenzy. Below them, the waves crashed and splashed into the wide, wooden pilings that held up the pier.

From up here, the horizon seemed to stretch on to infinity. The view was nothing short of spectacular, the power, fury and majesty of the ocean mesmerizing. They could see up and down the beach for miles. A pleasant smile crept across his lips, while inwardly his soul screamed, *I'm the king of the world.*

Her eyes roamed over his face. "This place means a lot to you...doesn't it?"

"More than you can ever know." He squeezed her hand, trying his best to put it into words for her. "This place isn't like anywhere else in the world. It's hard to explain but...," he paused searching for the right words, "...growing up in Jersey, you knew the ocean held beauty, the boardwalk held magic, and beach sand got stuck in your soul." He smiled at how silly that sounded, but all the same he now knew it was true. "It's difficult to describe…," he mumbled under his breath.

She touched his cheek, smiling. "I think you just did a pretty good job of it, Love."

The haunting cry of some passing seagulls caught his attention and he turned his gaze skyward. The foam-white birds played with the wind, banking and flying with its force, moving higher and higher with it, never against. This reminded him of a favorite book he'd read in seventh grade, *Jonathan Livingston Seagull*. The words of Catherine the Elder were also on his mind, *you can either go with the wind or against it.*

But which was he doing? He could never really be sure.

With the light fading and twilight approaching, the gray sky gave way to a perfect ombré sunset of peach, orange, pink, lavender and purple.

Slowly, he stretched Sarah's arms out as if she had wings, pressing his cheek against hers.

"Michael," she said in a breathless, overly dramatic way, "it's like I'm flying!"

He abruptly turned his head, so he could look her straight in the eyes. "Wait a minute, you *saw* Titanic?"

She giggled, as she playfully bopped him on the nose with the tip of her finger. "I watched it on TV in the parlor at the Angel of the Sea one night, you silly goose." Leaning into him, her words, a warm seductive tickle in his ear, she whispered, "Now's the part when you're supposed to kiss me."

She didn't have to say it twice. The next instant, he spun her around. His lips brushed hers and he kissed her deeply, his tongue tasting, probing, loving her. He slid his hand around the back of her neck and pulled her closer.

He wanted more. So much more.

As he pulled away, she gave a tiny moan.

DiCaprio didn't have scratch on him.

He paused only long enough to say, "Happy Valentine's Day, Sweetheart. Sorry I couldn't get you a real present."

Her eyes met his with such passion, he feared the heat and energy moving through them might ignite the wooden track beneath their feet. "This is the best present you could've ever given me," she said lovingly.

His mouth closed over hers again. Lost in the heat of her aura, his hands roamed over her back as she clung to him.

Gently, she took a break to push him away. "I think we should get down now."

"Why, are you afraid of heights?" No sooner had he asked the question than he remembered, *Oh my God, that's right. She fell to her death. How the hell could I have been so insensitive and idiotic?*

"No, silly, that's not it," she said, shaking her head. "It's just that I'm pretty sure those two people down there think we're spying on them." She chuckled. "And I think they want their privacy."

Following her gaze, he spotted a ghostly couple below them lying side by side on the sand a short distance away. He grimaced. "Oh, alright we can get down."

As they left the first pier and continued down the boardwalk, Michael pointed to one of the closed restaurants with its gray metal gate pulled down. Hanging up above, a sign with large, bright yellow letters spelled, MACK'S.

"Best pizza on the boardwalk, hands down," he declared. "Makes me hungry just thinking about it."

She shook her head, but smiled. "No, it *doesn't*. That's not possible and you know it." She laughed, teasingly. "You're simply obsessed with food."

He laughed because he knew she was right.

Next, they came to the middle ride pier, passing Jumbo's restaurant and Mariner's Arcade. The Ferris wheel on Mariner's Pier—or the Giant Wheel as it was called—was lit up with thousands of white and purple LED lights along the outward spokes with a flashing red heart in the center, all the lights synchronized to beat and throb like a real, beating heart. Beating and throbbing, beating and throbbing, the heart in the center changing color from orange to red.

"That's a nice touch for Valentine's Day," she remarked.

As they continued meandering down the boardwalk, they passed the Douglass Fudge store with its signature red and green striped awning. "Best fudge on the boardwalk," he declared.

"Again with the food!" she said, sounding exasperated. "You're going to drive yourself crazy you know."

Finally, they came to the last ride pier—the Surfside Pier. They turned in, walking past all the rides buttoned up for the winter.

A wide smiled crossed his face. "You see that circular kiddie ride over there," he said motioning, "the one that's covered up with that round, green tarp."

"Yes," she replied.

"During the season, they have these small boats for kids to ride in. The highlight is floating around really slowly in a circle and ringing the little bell on the front. Super exciting stuff," he said with a laugh. "I hate to admit this, but my mom said that was the first ride I ever went on as a kid."

"Why are you ashamed to admit that?

"I don't know…," he said with a shrug. "It's just not very manly I guess. Kinda wussy actually."

"Well, I think that's the sweetest thing I've ever heard," she said with a wide grin. "I can just picture you…smiling as you tugged on your little bell."

He rolled his eyes. "Come on," he said, strolling a few paces away. "There's a waterpark on both piers, but this is where all the best water slides are. Have you ever been on a water slide?" When Sarah didn't answer him right away, he turned to see what was wrong.

She had apparently stopped in front of Dante's Dungeon, an indoor roller coaster meant to be a scary, horror ride. The exterior resembled a castle with its gray brick and two high towers, each with a three headed Cerberus popping out. Michael had been on the ride more times than he could count. With its hairpin turns in the dark, funky strobe lights and fake screams, he always thought the attraction was pretty tame by most standards.

As a kid though, he found its most terrifying feature was easily on the outside—the façade's centerpiece—a ginormous devil complete with a forty foot wing span, horns, fangs and glowing red eyes.

And it was those red eyes Sarah was now staring at with a most peculiar, disturbed expression on her otherwise beautiful face.

He quickly glided back over to her. "Kinda silly, isn't it?

The devil even shoots white smoke from its nose every so often. A lot different than the real thing, huh?"

She took a long moment to answer. "I suppose...but I don't like it all the same. There's something about it that...makes me feel uneasy." She shuddered. "In fact, I hate to say this but can we go? I've had a strange feeling ever since we saw the Ferris wheel on the last pier."

He hoped she wasn't disappointed with the boardwalk. "Yeah, it's not the same when everything's shut down for the winter."

She took his hand and smiled. "The day was perfect," she said in a sweet voice. "The boardwalk is lovely...even magical."

As they strolled back in the direction of Cape May, he said, "I'm glad you think so. But I'll still have to bring you back when everything opens for business again on Memorial Day Weekend. This place is a lot different then. Wildwood is a bit too lonely in the off season when it's so deserted."

They had just passed Douglass Fudge again when all of a sudden her face took on this faraway, spellbound look. "Oh, but it's not deserted," she said in a wistful voice. "Can't you feel it?" She let go of his hand and gestured in a wide circle all around them. "This place holds hundreds...no *thousands*...of memories, feelings and emotions."

She darted to one of the benches overlooking the ocean and gripped the railing as if in a trance. "Someone proposed to his girlfriend right here on this spot...and she made his whole life when she said yes."

Suddenly, she floated a few feet to their left. "Over here, a little boy ran too fast with an ice cream cone, fell and scraped his knees on the concrete. His mother comforted him and gave him a kiss he'll remember till the day he dies." She took off again, this time flying down the boardwalk.

He tried to say something, but she was acting so strangely, talking and moving so fast, it was all he could do to keep up with her.

She flew two blocks before sliding to a stop in front of a shuttered restaurant. "And further down this way," she rambled, "someone else found the courage to tell her family to let her go...because she was done with the tests, done with the chemo treatments, done with fighting the cancer. She just wanted to enjoy the time she had left with them." For a brief moment, Sarah turned to him with sad, phantom tears streaming down her face.

He reached out to her, but she flew to the railing which faced the edge of the beach. "And on this bench, a woman's water broke as the first pains of labor hit. She turned to her husband with a faint smile to say it was time, while he stared at her like a deer in the headlights."

Once more, she zoomed to the side of a building near one of the ramps leading onto the boards. She closed her eyes, touched a hand to the brick, clutching her chest with her other hand. "Over here, a man leaned up against this wall, short of breath," she said with a gasp, "...he felt a heart attack coming on and the police had to call an ambulance."

By the terror-struck look on her face and the raw emotions flowing out of her, he could tell she was experiencing the last desperate, heart-thumping moments of a dying man.

But before he could even ask her what in the world she

was talking about, she collapsed on the boardwalk as if struck by an unseen blow.

Petrified, he rushed to her side. "Sarah! Sarah!"

Placing his arms under hers, he scooped her up into his lap. With his help, she gradually regained her energy and rose to her feet. "Are you alright?"

"Yes, I think so," she said, sounding weak. "What the hell happened to me?"

He shook his head, rife with concern. "I have *no* clue."

"I don't know what came over me." She leaned on him, her arms and legs trembling. "It was like...like I could see and feel all of it...the good, the bad, and in between...but all at once. And it was...overwhelming."

He wrapped his arms around her and held her tightly until she stopped shaking. He had no idea what to make of it, but her odd behavior unsettled him as much as it did her.

As he brushed away a stray tear at the corner of her eye, an odd thought pinged around in his mind. *She said she could* see *all of it*. "Sarah, do you think..."

"I...I don't know," she replied slowly, her voice still unsteady. "I guess it's possible, but that wouldn't make any sense. Seers would see the future, right? That was the past I was seeing and feeling."

"What if it wasn't?" He couldn't get the peculiar, faraway expression she'd had on her face during her episode out of his head. It was as if she'd been watching a movie only she could see.

She raised her eyes to his, clearly disturbed by this idea. "If that's true, then what does it mean? What do I do about what I saw?"

"I don't know, but let's get out of here," he said, kissing her lightly on the forehead. "That's enough of the boardwalk." He smiled and touched her cheek, trying to allay her fears. "I'd love to show you Diamond Beach on our way back anyway."

She scrunched up her forehead. "Why's it called Diamond Beach?"

"I'll show you," he said with a happy grin.

CHAPTER FOURTEEN

DIAMOND BEACH

BY NOW, THE hour was getting late. Night had fallen and some of the clouds from earlier in the day had moved on, exposing the moon and the celestial tapestry of the heavens.

Against the star-studded sky they flew until they reached Diamond Beach. They touched down on a sandy beach covered in millions of shiny pebbles. Bathed in the moonlight the small, round stones sparkled, making this stretch of coastline appear as if it were a riverbed of twinkling diamonds.

Concentrating hard, he reached down and carefully lifted one of the clear, smooth pebbles with his ghostly fingers and placed it in her outstretched hand. "This is a Cape May Diamond."

She rolled the tiny stone around in her palm. "They sure look like diamonds."

He nodded, as he lay back on the sand and propped himself up on his elbow. "My grandfather used to say that people had been searching for Cape May Diamonds since at least the early 1800s. Somehow word of the gems spread throughout the trade routes. But the joke was on them because they aren't real diamonds at all." He held one up again to look through it. "See, they're actually clear quartz crystals that wash ashore as smooth, polished rocks because they travel all the way down the Delaware River. And since the river spills out right at the little hook created by Cape May Point, they say that's why the diamonds get caught here."

"They're exquisite," she declared.

As usual, the innocent wonder in her eyes made every moment magnificent. He slid closer to her and placed an arm on her waist. "Not nearly as exquisite as you."

She smiled.

He didn't understand how it was even possible, especially since they were ghosts and shouldn't be able to change, but in his eyes she grew more beautiful by the minute.

That magnetic attraction took over again, pulling them together.

Michael couldn't help himself. He was drawn to her the way a child is drawn to the cookie jar. She was sweet, irresistible, and deliciously forbidden.

His body folded into hers, as if they were made for each other. Instantly, his lips found hers, his tongue playing gently in her mouth.

As her fingers roamed over his body, a warm tingling sensation settled into his skin.

Slowly and teasingly his lips moved down her throat and between her breasts.

Leaning up against him, she gave a sudden moan, her hands tugging at his hair as she tried to push him onto his back.

The heat and electricity flowing between them was so glorious and so intense, that the sudden blast of cold came as a shock. *Cold?*

It took a moment for his mind to register before he realized what had descended upon them.

By the time he recognized the threat, he didn't have enough warning to react.

Or to protect Sarah.

Seemingly out of nowhere, a bolt of energy shot from the darkness near the dunes.

He tried to roll over on top of her in time, but the blast hit her directly in the back.

"No!" he screamed in terror.

Her limp body fell against his, as she turned her face to look up at him.

For one brief moment, he saw the shock and anguish reflected in her tear-filled eyes.

And for a second heart-wrenching time, all he could do was watch as his beloved's soul vanished in his arms.

A raw fury blazed through him, as he thrust his hands up in retaliation.

Without even thinking about the consequences, he sent a volley of blasts into the dunes setting them ablaze.

But whoever or whatever had hit Sarah was gone.

CHAPTER FIFTEEN

BIRTHDAY

HALF HIS SOUL had been ripped away.

And along with it, half his sanity.

Days and weeks might have passed at the Angel of the Sea. Michael had no way of knowing. And he was far from caring. Once again, he completely blamed himself for Sarah being the collateral damage in an attack meant solely for him.

He spent hour after hour, day after day, flying from room to room, floor to floor, searching for her. But there was no sign of her anywhere.

Consequently, he spent every minute terrified out of his mind that he might never see her again.

Tom patiently kept him company through most of it, but occasionally he got the usual faraway look on his face and left for short periods of time.

Now, as Michael relentlessly paced the floor of the parlor, the guests had just sat down to afternoon tea in the dining room. The staff had set the table with half a dozen silver trays of delicious-looking cakes, cookies, and pastries.

Shortly afterwards, they served the wine and antipasto— an assortment of fine meats, cheeses, olives and savory treats—along with warm breads and crackers. There was even an inviting crock of vegetarian chili that he would've given his right leg to try.

But of course, even if he could eat, he would've had no appetite whatsoever despite the hollow feeling at the pit of his stomach.

Presently, Tom floated through the heavy wooden entrance door of the Angel and into the room. He didn't even bother asking if Sarah had come back yet, since a blind man could easily see the distraught look on his face. He sighed heavily. "Michael, you knew something like this might happen—" his mentor began.

Cutting Tom off before he could even get started, he yelled at the top of his lungs, "Please spare me the I-told-you-so! This is not helping!"

Rude or not, he stalked out on the porch, clenching and unclenching his fists. He really couldn't take another one of Tom's lectures or he might really blow his stack.

Behind him, he heard a footstep.

He whirled around ready to verbally assault Tom.

Instead, he was staring at Sarah's lovely, but confused face. She slowly turned her hand over and over, obviously very disturbed by the fact that she could see through it. "Where am I?" she whispered in a frightened voice.

All he wanted to do was take her in his arms, but he resisted, realizing this might scare her. He needed to handle this situation with the utmost care. "You're at the Angel of the Sea in Cape May," he answered in a gentle tone.

Her next question confirmed his worst suspicions. "What happened to me?" she asked, her words full of anguish.

Oh my God, it's worse than I thought. She doesn't

remember a thing, not even her own death. Agonizing over how best to tell her, he broke the news as delicately as he could. "You died here...a long time ago," he replied with caution. "Your spirit has been here ever since."

Her face dropped, as she must've known he was being truthful. After a long pause she asked timidly, "Who are you?"

His heart tore in two, as he glanced down at his wedding ring, then back to her beautiful face. "I met you here after I died...and we fell in love."

Nothing. No trace of recollection. No love in her eyes.

If anything, a bit of shock registered on her face. He had thought maybe telling her would jog her memory into motion, but he certainly hadn't meant to frighten her.

"Can you give me a few moments?" she asked softly. "I...I think I'd like to be alone." Her words said she was being polite, while her eyes were like that of a lost child.

Crushed and utterly lost himself, he drifted back inside the Angel of the Sea.

Finally, almost an hour later, Sarah ghosted through the front door and into the parlor.

With his heart breaking he stood stock still, not knowing what to say.

"Oh, Michael," she cried, rushing over to him.

Relief flooded through every inch of his ghostly body, as he wrapped his arms around her in a bone-crushing embrace. Over and over he hungrily kissed her lips, ever so grateful to have her back in his arms.

She sobbed in between each of his kisses. "Somehow I knew in my heart that I should know who you were, but everything was fuzzy and I couldn't remember anything for sure."

"Shhh, shhh, it's okay," he whispered, trying to calm her down. "It's over now. You're home."

A few hours later while Sarah was laying down upstairs resting, he and Tom went for a stroll along the beach. He wanted to be able to talk to Tom about what happened, but he didn't want it to upset her again, so this was the perfect opportunity.

Step by step, he again recounted for Tom everything that had happened on Diamond Beach weeks before. Now that he had more time to think about it with a clear head, one thing about the incident especially didn't sit right with him. "I don't understand why the demons would hit Sarah and then vanish."

Tom was quiet for a long time, staring at the moon which had just risen in the night sky. "Tough to say," he replied lightly.

"It doesn't make any sense."

"No," Tom said. "I guess it doesn't."

Boy, he sure is a man of few words this evening. Normally, he had gotten used to Tom having more than enough words of wisdom to share. Feeling half-guilty and half-annoyed, he fell silent.

After a while, Tom broke the uncomfortable silence. "What else is bothering you?"

A knot of tension wormed its way through his insides. Talking to Tom usually made him feel better, but for some reason it didn't tonight. "We've had so many close calls," he said, full of worry.

"And?"

"I guess it just makes me wonder…how many chances are we gonna get?"

Tom now turned to him fully. "What do you mean?"

"It took weeks for Sarah to come back this time. And it took twice as long as last time for her to remember me once she was back." His leg began to shake nervously, just thinking about it. "What if the third time is the charm for her, and she forgets me altogether?" he said, looking him straight in the eyes. "Or worse yet, doesn't ever come back?"

Unfortunately, his mentor had no answer for him.

• • •

Michael and Sarah usually spent the early morning hours in the parlor, before the sun came up and the guests started moving about.

Restless for some reason, he had come down first today. He loved the early morning stillness of the Angel of the Sea before everyone awoke. His favorite thing to do was to sit on the porch outside, just gazing at the ocean across the street and watching the waves.

Sarah had lingered upstairs for a moment or two while she made her usual morning rounds and checked in on the guests. It was one of her old habits, so he left her to it.

A few minutes later, she came rushing down from the second floor and into the parlor.

"I thought I saw some dark shadows through a window upstairs," she said hurriedly, twisting her hands. "They were moving around the back of the house near the bike racks."

Steeling his courage, he began to draw in energy from every source in the room. "I'll take a look. Go back up to the bedroom and stay there until I tell you it's safe to come out," he commanded.

Without another word, she darted back up the staircase.

Preparing to defend Sarah and the Angel of the Sea, he flew outside circling the perimeter of the house, but no demons seemed to be in sight. Oddly, he didn't sense their evil presence either. After two or three more passes he decided all was well and there was no threat.

Ghosting back into Sarah's bedroom, he skidded to a sudden stop.

Tom, Matt, and his sister Emily were seated on chairs around the room. Sarah sat on the bed next to a triple-decker chocolate birthday cake.

All at once they yelled, "Surprise!"

"Happy birthday, Sweetheart. Sorry we had to fool you like that," Sarah said with a giggle. "But even with each of us helping, it's a little hard to levitate a chocolate cake all the way from the dining room up here without you seeing. Hard enough to do it without the guests seeing it, too. Thank goodness there were no early risers around this morning."

He smiled at their harmless deception. *It's March 16th already?* He had completely forgotten about his birthday. After all, what was the point of celebrating that now?

Emily giggled. "I wonder what they're going to think downstairs when they realize an entire cake has gone missing."

"Sorry we couldn't put a number nineteen on it," Sarah said.

Michael gave her a devilish grin. "You're not going to sing are you?"

"Of course we're going to sing," she exclaimed, clapping her hands.

Carefully, he lit the candles by gathering a bit of energy on the ends of his fingertips. "Okay but just remember, when your birthday rolls around, I can't be responsible for how badly I'm going to sing for you."

Sarah counted to three, and all at once his friends began crooning 'Happy Birthday'.

The moment turned out to be an unexpectedly poignant reminder of birthdays past. He hadn't anticipated how hard it would hit him. The feeling kind of snuck up on him and he was glad when they were done singing. He would've felt like a complete sap if he had teared up in front of his friends.

Sucking in a ghostly breath just for show, while tapping some minimal energy, he stirred the air enough to blow out the candles. The four of them clapped and cheered.

He now turned to Sarah with a smile. "You know, I don't think I even know when your birthday is."

"June tenth," she replied. "But you're not allowed to get me back for the awful singing if that's what you're thinking."

June tenth. So close to the date of his own death.

Sarah must've picked up on his thoughts. "Are you okay?" she asked in a small voice.

"I was thinking about the day I died," he said plainly.

Her hand flew over top of his. "Oh, Michael. *Don't.*"

"No, it's *okay*," he said, squeezing her hand tenderly in reassurance. "I was thinking how it was a lot like today.

Such a ripe spring day just...dripping with possibilities, you know. So *much* like today that I was thinking this feels as good as being alive." He looked around at all of his friends and smiled.

Sarah wrapped her arms around him in a warm embrace.

He could've stayed like that all day except for the fact that Tom, Matt and Emily were now staring at them uncomfortably.

"Now what?" Emily asked, pointing to the cake. "What should we do with it? It's not like we can eat it."

"I think we should gravity test it by throwing it out the window," Matt suggested with a snicker.

Sarah laughed. "That's a great idea. Everyone's probably awake by now, so it would be impossible to carry it down the stairs without being seen now anyway." She clapped her hands again excitedly. "Oooh, I can't wait to see the look on the gardener's face when he discovers it in the rose bushes. I can only hope we'll be there to see it the moment he finds it."

"No, no, no," Michael interjected, "that would be a waste of a perfectly good cake. And you know how I feel about cake. Let's leave it for the guests."

"Oh, alright," Sarah said with a begrudging grin. "But it'll still be awesome when they wonder how it got up here and into a locked room. That outta keep them guessing. Now, we have the whole day to do whatever we want," she said with enthusiasm. "So what do you want to do?"

He thought for a moment. "Hey, I know," he said with a twinge of excitement. "I never got to try gambling since I never made it to twenty-one. All I know about gambling or the casinos is what I saw in movies, or what my mother told me about them. She didn't gamble much, but she used to go for fun once a year with my Aunt Susan. So, why don't we go to Atlantic City?"

"That's a great idea," Matt chimed in. "I always wanted to see what the casinos were like and never got the chance either."

"None of us did," Emily added lightly. "We all died too young."

Tom stood up from his chair. "I can get us there the fastest. I used to go all the time," he admitted in a somewhat sheepish manner. "Drinking and gambling unfortunately went hand in hand for me, and the casinos always served free booze."

"Are we going to draft then?" Emily asked him.

"No, I've never tried to draft before with more than one or two spirits in tow. Too much of a chance that the connection could get broken," Tom replied. "Someone could get left behind. I think it's best if we all fly on our own."

Michael rubbed his hands together in anticipation. "I don't care how we get there, just lead the way."

Leaving the cake behind in the room for the staff and the guests to enjoy, they went out to the second story veranda.

A light rain fell upon the porch roof with a steady pitter-patter. Tom leaped off first and the rest of them followed. Michael gripped Sarah's hand as they sped out of town, following the Garden State Parkway below as a guide.

He would never get sick of flying. It was always such a thrill. If there were any perks at all in the afterlife, his two favorites had to be the invisibility and the flying.

Within minutes they zoomed past the famous Steel Pier

and had landed in front of Boardwalk Hall, the historic convention center on the boardwalk in Atlantic City. As he well knew, the regal hall with its iconic stone columns topped with arches had been the home to the Miss America pageant most of the years since its inception in 1921. The venue for the pageant changed a few times, but eventually returned to Boardwalk Hall. But he had never set eyes on the place before this.

Impressed with the building, he read the inscription across the top out loud. "A permanent monument conceived as a tribute to the ideals of Atlantic City, built by its citizens and dedicated to recreation, social progress and industrial achievements."

"A lot of great history made within that building's walls," Tom said with appreciation. "I bet you didn't know that Boardwalk Hall contains the world's largest musical instrument, the 'Poseidon', a pipe organ consisting of over 33,000 pipes and eight chambers."

"No, I never knew that," he said. The others readily agreed they hadn't known either.

"In addition to the Miss America pageant, over the years Boardwalk Hall has also been home to many a sporting event—boxing, soccer, basketball, ice hockey, tennis and even football," Tom said. "Many a music star has performed within her hallowed halls including the Beatles, Rolling Stones, Beyoncé...even rock legend and Jersey native Bruce Springsteen along with his E Street Band."

"Can we go inside?" Emily asked.

"Only for a few minutes," Tom suggested. "We don't want to run into Enoch Johnson."

Michael looked at him inquisitively. "Who's that?"

Tom expression turned to one of disdain. "He was the political 'boss' of Atlantic City from about 1910 until his imprisonment in 1941," he explained. "Best to stay away from him. He wasn't a very nice man while he was alive and he's not very different now. You'll know him if you see him, because he still wears a long raccoon fur coat with a fresh red carnation in his lapel."

As they ghosted through the front doors and into the hall, Michael was amazed at the sheer size of the place, which resembled an enormous airplane hangar with rows of seating on each of three sides. On the fourth side stretched an almost three hundred foot wide stage draped with an ornate fire curtain depicting a sailing ship. He tilted his head back to look up. *That rounded ceiling has to be at least 100 feet high*, he thought to himself.

"One hundred and thirty-seven feet to be exact," Tom corrected him.

"Where's the organ?" Sarah asked.

"It's so large, the pipes are concealed in the ceiling and the walls," Tom replied. "One of these days we'll have to come back and take a listen. They're still renovating it, but when it's played you've never heard anything more powerful in your life. Here, come see the main console."

Tom led them over to a ten foot tall, semi-circular booth made of rich, dark wood and gold lamé which sat on the right side of the stage. Inside, a wooden player's bench sat in the middle surrounded by more keys, buttons, and pedals than Michael had ever seen in his life. It was as if someone had taken half a dozen organs or more, and melded them all together in one large keyboard.

"This is 'Poseidon'," Tom said with an air of admiration, "its console is the largest in the world."

"That's amazing," Sarah commented.

Just as she said that, the organ began to play, filling the enormous hall with such a loud, rich, melodic sound that every one of their jaws popped open in shock.

Not a single key on the organ moved.

"One or more of the spirits here must be projecting their memories of the organ music," Tom explained.

"Aren't the living outside going to be able to hear that?" Matt asked.

"No, probably not," Tom replied. "That's meant for us to hear. Someone wants us to know they're here."

No sooner had he finished, than a hundred or more spirits seemed to materialize out of nowhere. In the center of the darkened hall, they began to ballroom dance about its large open floor, many dressed in eighteenth and early nineteenth century garb.

Michael and his friends all watched for a few moments, mesmerized.

Then, as abruptly as their performance started, they all disappeared.

"How strange," Emily said.

"Yes," Tom readily agreed. "Which is probably why we should take our leave and head over to the casinos."

This was fine with Michael, because he was anxious to try his hand at gambling anyway.

Drifting back out onto the boardwalk, he now noticed how crowded it was. Even though it was mid-March, many of the living still enjoyed strolling along the boardwalk bundled up against the cold. Unbeknownst to them, ghosts of all kinds strolled here and there along the boardwalk right beside them in small groups. Michael wondered if some of them had maybe just come out of Boardwalk Hall.

As the clouds rolled away, the sun began to peek through, so many of the not-so-departed souls abandoned the boardwalk and went into the nearest casino.

Michael and his friends followed suit, ducking into Caesars.

As they drifted down the corridor, they passed each of the stores plying their luxury wares—expensive jewelry and watches, fancy suits and accessories, and of course, the latest haute couture.

Makes perfect sense. Lay temptation out before them, so it'll entice them to gamble more.

Finally, they entered the main casino floor with the slot machines all singing the siren song of money—chachachaching, chachachaching, chachachaching. Even though he knew it was only recordings making the sound to simulate money falling, it still made his phantom heart race.

At first glance, the brightly lit machines with comical graphics made it look as if they had walked into Mariner's Arcade in Wildwood.

He turned to his friends. "Is it my imagination, or does this place look like nothing more than an elaborate arcade for adults?"

"That's exactly what it is," Tom replied, grinning. "Except the money gets eaten up even faster in these machines."

Michael thought of how fast he blew through his money

when he played at the arcades down at the boardwalk. *Damn, a place like this could be downright dangerous.*

To make matters worse, waiters and waitresses walked around with free beverages on trays, most of them alcoholic and meant to keep the gamblers in their seats and gambling. *Smart, ply them with liquor.*

A slot machine called Heavenly Riches now caught his eye. "Hey look," he said to Sarah finding it quite ironic, "I thought you couldn't take it with you."

She and Emily both giggled.

For a few minutes, they stood behind an elderly woman and watched her play. She had just fed the slot machine another fifty dollar bill. The counter on the machine displayed over a thousand credits.

"Wait a minute," Matt said as he noticed the denomination, "this is a dollar machine, isn't it?"

"Yes," Tom said with a nod. "It's a lot of money, but you'll see people spend a lot more than that in this place. Sometimes it can be heart-breaking when you can tell they really don't have it to spend either. But they're enjoying themselves, I guess."

Sarah turned to him, her eyes gleaming with gambling-fever. "So where should we start?"

Michael's knee bounced eagerly as he thought it over. "Every time I saw one in a movie or on TV, I always thought the roulette wheel looked kinda fun." He pointed to a set of tables on the right side of the room. "I think they're over there."

"Oh, let's go," Emily exclaimed. "I always wanted to play roulette too, but I never got the chance."

"Do any of you even know what roulette means?" Tom chimed in.

They all shook their heads in unison.

"I didn't think so," Tom said with a roll of his eyes. "In French, it means little wheel. Let's go over and I'll give you all a quick lesson. The first rule of gambling is to never play a game unless you completely understand how it's played and know all of its rules."

They glided over to the first table with a shiny roulette wheel. Two young girls stood by deciding how to place their next bets. Judging by the way they were struggling to figure it out, they were obviously also rookie gamblers. The fake tiara and sash the red-head was wearing with a big '21' on it, kind of gave it away, too.

"To determine a winner, the croupier," Tom said, indicating the gentleman in a suit standing behind the table, "spins the wheel in one direction, then spins the white ball in the opposite direction around a tilted circular track running along the circumference of the wheel. Eventually, the ball loses momentum and falls onto the wheel and into one of the thirty-eight colored and numbered pockets on the wheel. There are thirty-six black and red spaces, with two special green ones." Tom waved his hand over the table. "This burgundy cloth covered betting area is called the layout. In this case it's an American style layout, not French. The principle difference being that it includes not only one green zero, but also a green double zero. Of course, since those are the hardest spots to land on, they also pay out the most. But for beginners, the simplest bet is to just pick a color, either red or black."

"Let's see if I would've been any good at gambling," Michael said mischievously. Leaning forward, he projected into the girl's mind in a whisper, *choose red*.

"I think I'll try red this time," the girl said to her friend, as she placed her bet.

With a quick flick of his wrist, the croupier spun the wheel again. They all watched in rapt anticipation as the white ball spun with a clicking sound around and around.

And landed on black.

"Well, I guess that settles that," he said with a smile, "gambling probably wouldn't have been for me."

Next, they glided over to the nearby gaming tables.

A middle-aged man at the end of one of the craps table was drinking, swaying, sweating and barely able to stand. He must've been trying to impress his date because he kept placing bets larger than any of the other gamblers.

They watched him play for a few minutes, but it really wasn't much fun to watch because he was losing so badly.

"I may not know much about dice games, but I don't need to," Michael said. "This guy's drunk as hell and losing his shirt. I'm gonna do this guy a big favor." Picking up a black chip off the top of the guy's stack, he made it levitate a quarter inch in the air for a second, until the man noticed his own hand wasn't touching it. Then he let the chip slowly drift back down on top of the others.

The man stared dumbfounded at his fingers, as if he might be seeing double or hallucinating. He leaned over to the girl next to him, stumbling sideways in the process. "You know what. I think that's enough for me," he mumbled, accidentally spitting in her ear. "I'm gonna cash out before I losemyshirt." His last few words came out in one continuous slur.

They all busted up laughing.

Next, they strolled over to the money wheel. Except for the different denominations of money pasted near the wheel's pegs, it looked no different than one of the wheels on the boardwalk where you can win candy and stuffed animals.

He found this incredibly comical. *More proof that casinos are nothing more than arcades for adults who never grew up.*

A mother and daughter stood nearby with their hands folded, practically praying to win. "That's the last of our spending money," the mother said.

"Well, let's just hope we still have some luck, Mom," the daughter replied. "I wanted you to enjoy your birthday and going home as two big losers won't be any fun at all." They placed a twenty dollar chip on the ten dollar spot.

As the money wheel spun round and round, Michael gently nudged it at the right time, so it would keep spinning for one more peg and hit their denomination.

Of course, as soon as they won they jumped up and down hugging each other in celebration.

Sarah smiled at him and he shrugged. "It's her birthday too, so I had to help her out."

Just as the words left his mouth, he froze.

If he hadn't already been dead, the sight would've surely stopped his heart.

Two men had entered the casino floor with bombs strapped to their upper bodies, each one running headlong into the middle of a crowd of people near the money wheel.

It all happened so fast.

There was barely any time to react.

"Don't move!" Tom commanded, looking straight at him.

But as Michael reached out to push one of the men backwards, the bombs detonated in a deafening explosion of glass and metal splintering, sending shrapnel flying into victims.

For a moment, the energy of the blast even disrupted all of their auras.

He and Sarah's spectral forms wavered and then took shape again. A distorted sound like echoing static filled his head, as if someone had struck an oversized tuning fork on his skull. He grabbed his head, squeezing his eyelids shut until he regained his balance.

When the smoke cleared, a ghastly sight surrounded him.

At least thirty people lay scattered about, bleeding, suffering, dying.

Others picked themselves up off the floor, shuffling around in a daze or trying to help those more wounded.

Still others were obviously already dead. Their spirits stood next to their dismembered bodies with confused expressions on their faces.

Michael turned to Sarah to see if she was alright.

He never made it to turn completely around before the room took on a dazzling, ethereal glow. A magnificent column of light shone down from above, spilling through the ceiling as if the roof had been peeled back by some Divine hand.

Immediately, an intense warmth and greater peace such as he had never known swelled within him. As before, an indescribably beautiful music filled the space, louder and clearer than the last time he heard it.

The very sound and melody made his soul ache.

This time, he was much closer to the light. If he could stretch out his arm, his fingers would be able to reach it. He longed to touch its glorious rays.

Except, he couldn't move an inch. Again unable to reach the light, all he could do was listen and watch as each soul rose up into its brilliance, becoming forever part of it.

A single tear now rolled down his cheek, though he hadn't realized he was crying.

As best as he could, he swiveled his head around to glance at the others. Matt stood frozen mid-step facing the light, but his eyes seemed to be staring off to his right.

Paralyzed also, Tom was slightly behind him and to his left.

As before, the light began to withdraw back into itself, as the last few souls ascended skyward.

And one of them was Emily. Her face a perfect picture of peaceful bliss.

In his periphery, Michael now caught sight of Sarah.

A few stray beams of light fell directly upon her.

His chest constricted in panic as he swallowed hard, glancing at the illuminated ceiling and then back at her face.

She slid a small step forward, before she caught herself and stopped.

But that was all he needed to see. With painful precision, the truth sliced straight through his ghostly heart, the pain so sharp his knees threatened to crumple beneath him.

As the column of light finally faded from their sight, Sarah's eyes met his.

And she couldn't hide the truth.

Not from him.

She had been faking it. She hadn't been pinned to the spot like the rest of them.

The light would've taken her.

She could've gone.

CHAPTER SIXTEEN

CHRIS

THE VERY SECOND he could move again, he rushed to her side.

Grabbing her by the shoulders, he franticly shook her as he tried his best to understand what he'd seen. "Why'd you *do* that, Sarah? Why'd you do that?" He yelled in desperation. "You've waited so long!"

Her eyes spilled with tears as she collapsed into his arms, clinging to him and sobbing into his chest. "I couldn't go, Michael. I just couldn't go."

"That was so stupid! So stupid, Sarah!" As he kissed her face, her lips, her hair, a tempest of emotions threatened to shred his soul to pieces—love, frustration, relief, even anger. "You could've gone. You could've gone into the light. They wanted you to go!"

She stubbornly shook her head back and forth. "Not without you. I'm not going without you," she protested through sobs, throwing her arms around him once more.

It took at least another minute before he realized he'd been yelling at her. He couldn't help it though. His worst fear had come to pass—clearly his love had kept her bound to earth for longer than she was intended to be.

Inside, he was screaming at himself as much as he was her.

Gently, he caressed her cheek in an effort to say he was sorry. His mouth found hers, and he kissed her over and over again with every last ounce of his energy.

"I didn't want to go," she cried in between his kisses. "I want to stay with you."

Tormented by guilt, he slowly pulled away.

Now, he finally took a second to look around them. Once again, he found it difficult to understand why God would allow such violence and tragedy. The floor was covered with debris and bodies. Already, many brave people were assisting the injured. As horrible as he felt for the victims, there was nothing they could do and this was the last thing Sarah needed to see at this moment.

In a somber tone, he said to his friends, "Let's go back."

Within minutes, they had touched down on the porch of the Angel of the Sea.

Ghosting into the parlor, Sarah collapsed onto the sofa. "They may be ready for me to go, but I'm not ready," she mumbled sheepishly. "I'll go when *I'm* ready."

"I can't believe you could've gone, Sarah," he replied in a harsher tone than he wanted to. But he just couldn't help it. He paced back and forth, back and forth like a panther, barely skimming the carpet. He didn't know what to say. This was one of the few times he'd ever been truly angry with her. He remembered the last time, when they had disagreed about the importance of moving on, and he made the rash and inexcusable decision to leave her on the beach.

Now, dueling emotions tore him apart once again. On one hand, he was furious with her for not going into the light. On the other hand, he could selfishly kiss the ground she walked on that she was still there by his side.

It took a moment, but he managed to steady himself and regain control. His voice softened, as he knelt down beside her. He gently took her by the shoulders and forced her to meet his gaze. "What if you don't get another chance?"

She turned her tear-streaked face up at him, her eyes pleading for understanding. "I'm sorry," she whispered. "I couldn't do it. Not without you."

He took a deep breath and nodded, folding her tightly in his arms once more. "We'll get another chance," he said, kissing the top of her head. "I know we will." He cast his eyes heavenward as he said it, in a plea that came from the deepest recesses of his soul. If a look could be a prayer, he had just said a thousand prayers. And if he were honest with himself, to some extent, he was also daring heaven to cross him.

Eventually he remembered they weren't alone. Like it or not, his friends had witnessed every second of their fight.

Now, he turned to Matt. "I'm so sorry," he said from the bottom of his heart. "I saw Emily go. Are you upset?"

Matt shook his head emphatically. "No, why should I be? I'm happy for her." He smiled and gave a slight nod of approval. "I told her ahead of time to go if the light ever came. Told her I'd be furious if she didn't."

Michael couldn't help but notice Tom had been unusually quiet. In fact, the tension in the room was unmistakable.

"What's eating you?"

Tom always did a pretty good job of blocking his thoughts from him, but he couldn't hide his emotions from him. Michael could sense them a mile away. And right now, regret, tension and worry were rolling off of him in waves.

"Nothing," Tom replied. "Just been kind of a long day."

Michael half expected him to bug out like he usually did, but neither he, nor Matt left.

After the carnage they had seen, it seemed as if they were all seeking solace from one another. For what seemed like an eternity, the four of them sat on the porch of the Angel in silence, as the sun melted into the ocean, painting ribbons of bright pastel color across a twilight sky.

Obviously, no one knew quite what to say. People had tragically died. The celestial light had come and gone, yet again. Now where did that leave them?

After a while, he reached out and entwined Sarah's hand in his. He didn't even try to hide his troubled thoughts and feelings from her. If anything, he needed her now more than ever. *The light would've taken you...but not me.* He whispered to her with his mind. *Why you? Why Emily? Why all those other people?*

Why not me?

The heavenly Hoover machine had failed him, yet again. His only consolation...the light hadn't taken Tom or Matt either.

But why?

She looked up at him with apologetic eyes, and gave a sorrowful shrug. *I'm so sorry, Sweetheart. I just don't know.*

As the last rays of sunlight dipped below the horizon and the pinpoints of stars began to shine, Sarah's lilting voice broke the tension. "Michael, it's still your birthday. Why don't you go home to see your family…" she said with hesitation, "…to make sure they're doing okay."

He was hardly in the mood for another painful family reunion. "What for? So I can only get more aggravated with them?" His words came out much testier than he intended.

Sarah cocked her head to the side, showing her disappointment with him. "Michael…you haven't been home to see your family since Christmas," she said in a gentle, yet forceful way. "And I bet having to miss you on your birthday…was probably a bit rough for them."

He looked into her compassionate eyes and knew she was right. His first birthday since his death had most likely hit them hard.

"Okay, fine," he replied begrudgingly. "Let's go."

She shook her head. "No, I think I'd rather stay here if you don't mind." She saw him grimace and added quickly, "Don't worry. I'll be safe here without you. There's been no sign of trouble for at least a little while and the demons have never found us here yet."

"Yeah, well…let's hope they never do," he said with a frown. "Are you sure you don't wanna come with me?"

"I'll be *fine*," she reassured him. "You go ahead."

Michael instantly picked up on what she wasn't saying. He knew her too well. She needed a little space after their fight.

Maybe he did too.

Still, he wasn't crazy about her being at the Angel by herself. "Someone has to stay with you," he said firmly. "I'm not leaving you alone."

"I'll stay with her," Matt chimed in. "As much as I'm glad Emily went into the light and whatever comes next, I'm not gonna lie…this first night without her is gonna be tough."

"I can stay for a while, too," Tom added.

As Michael listened to the two of them offering their help, a chilling thought zinged across his mind and he blocked it just in time. *Can I really trust either one of them to be here alone with Sarah?*

Unfortunately, the answer he came up with was a resounding, *No.*

Even if his mistrust was completely unfounded, at least if Matt and Tom both stayed with her, it would provide some sort of checks and balances.

One can keep an eye on the other.

So, as casually as he could he said, "Thanks, guys. That would be great. I really appreciate you keeping her safe while I'm gone."

"I shouldn't be too long," he said to Sarah. Gently, kissing her on the lips, he telegraphed to her, *I'm sorry I yelled at you. I love you.*

A faint smile of forgiveness crossed her lips. *I love you, too,* she said. *There's never a need to be sorry.*

Closing his eyes, he concentrated on his memory of home. Within seconds, he stood in front of his house on Fieldpoint Drive. No cars were in the driveway, so everyone must have been out.

He'd been hoping maybe things had gotten better, but the next thing that caught his eye didn't exactly give him a warm, fuzzy feeling. One of the banisters on the porch railing lay cracked and broken in the grass in front of the house.

Not a good sign.

Once he ghosted through the front door, nothing much had changed inside either. Still the same mess he had seen the last time. Maybe even a bit worse. The place was such a disaster, it was difficult to tell.

One thing he couldn't help but notice—the stack of unopened bills on the credenza had grown to twice its normal size, with most of them now in bright yellow envelopes and stamped 'overdue'. When he reached the kitchen he figured out why. On the table, a crumpled set of pink termination papers sat next to another empty whiskey bottle and a list of potential job contacts that was never finished. Apparently, his mother had been fired from her job at the real estate agency.

With a heavy sigh he glanced at the clock on the wall, *10:45 pm.* He wondered where she could be at this hour. The answer hit him straight in the gut, with all the unpleasantness of a sucker punch to the liver.

The bottle was empty. *She's probably out at the liquor store or a bar.*

Not that it mattered much anymore, but he also vaguely wondered where the hell his brother was so late on a school night.

He didn't have too long to wonder. For a few seconds later, his brother's car pulled into the driveway. Chris got out, but he was by himself.

This ticked him off. *He's only got his permit. He's not even supposed to be driving on his own yet.*

His brother came in through the back door, tossed his keys on the kitchen counter and stalked right past him— clothes dirty, hair disheveled, eyes red-rimmed and bloodshot. To call him a train wreck would've been a gross understatement.

Even more worrisome, the sense of tension, fear and panic radiating off of him.

But who, or what, was Chris so afraid of?

He tried to read his brother's mind, but it was such a jumbled mess he couldn't make sense of the multiple disjointed thoughts flying about his addled brain. Something about meeting someone, something about wanting it to be out in the open...

Baffled, he followed his brother back outside. Chris kept glancing at his phone, as he nervously paced the sidewalk in front of the house. Whoever he was meeting had him more anxious than a groom on his wedding day.

Could he be meeting a girl?

Out of the corner of his eye, Michael caught Mr. Jasinski spying from behind the curtain of his living room window. Something about the worried look on his neighbor's face sent a jagged chill up his ghostly spine.

He had barely recovered, when out of nowhere Tom suddenly materialized right next to him. After almost jumping out of his own aura, he said, "What the hell are you doing here?"

Tom shrugged his shoulders nonchalantly. "Thought you might want some company. So, what's going on?"

He could care less that Tom was there, but what really perturbed him was that he had left Sarah alone with Matt. *So much for my checks and balances.* "I have no idea yet," he replied in a short tone, "that's why I'm watching."

There really wasn't time to argue with him though, as barely a moment later his attention was drawn to two guys who drove up in a brand new, white pickup truck. He had never seen either of the men before, but they seemed to know his brother. They gave a slight wave of acknowledgment to Chris and parked sideways blocking the end of the driveway.

As they slid out of the truck, Michael took a good look at them—one was about thirty years old, tall and stocky with a swath of tattoos up his arms, including a new one on his right forearm that he couldn't keep from scratching. The other guy was younger, maybe mid-twenties, and resembled a sickly mouse—short, skinny and twitchy.

Tattoo wasted no time in getting down to business. "You have the money you owe us?"

The minute he heard what the dirtbag said, his skin began to crawl. *So, that's what this is all about. Chris' thriving drug business. Great. Just great.* Filled with disgust, he could barely watch. And now he was even more embarrassed that Tom was watching.

The anxiety and fear rolled off Chris in waves. "Things are tight, Man. My mom lost her job and she's getting suspicious," he tried to explain. "It's easier for her to tell now when there's money missing."

Tattoo wasn't having any of it. He charged at Chris, getting right up in his face. "I don't give a *shit*," he spat out. "Justin said you'd have the money tonight." He poked at his chest threateningly. "You're into us for like four G's, you little piece of shit, and we've given you all the time we're gonna give."

His brother nodded slightly, as he began fishing for something in the front pocket of his sweatshirt.

But while Chris was looking down, Twitchy jerked his hand from the back of his jeans and pointed the barrel of a hand gun straight at his brother.

Oh my God, he thinks Chris is pulling a gun!

He had only seconds to act.

Raising his hands, he prepared to deliver a blow to the shooter's hand.

All of a sudden, Tom grabbed his forearm with such force that Michael was almost knocked from his feet.

"You can't!" Tom yelled, clutching his arm in a death grip. "If you interfere, you could make things much worse."

"Get off me!" Michael screamed, struggling.

Chris never even looked up. "I've got s—"

Before his brother could finish his sentence, two short pops came from Twitchy's direction.

As Tom let go of Michael's arm, Chris' face went slack and he looked down in confusion to watch the curled up wad of cash drop near his feet and roll away towards the curb.

Michael froze in horror at the blood stain blossoming across the front of his brother's t-shirt.

Almost in slow motion, Chris' body crumpled forward.

"No!" He rushed towards his brother but he couldn't stop his fall. With a loud smack, Chris landed face down on the asphalt.

Michael knelt down beside him, wishing there was

something, anything he could do. *My brother, my baby brother. Jesus God, no.*

"What the hell did you do that for?" he now screamed at Tom. "How could you do that?"

Meanwhile, Tattoo jumped back a foot, yelling much the same at his cohort, "What did you do that for, Man?"

"It's not my fault! I didn't mean to shoot!" Twitchy yelled, his panic-stricken face finally registering what he had done. "I thought he was pulling a gun!"

Tattoo reached for the cash in the street. "Let's get the eff' outta here," he shouted, grabbing Twitchy by the arm.

The loud wail of sirens and the screech of tires startled Michael out of his shock.

A police cruiser now slid into position to block off the truck's getaway. Red, white and blue lights bounced off the front of the houses up and down the street.

The two drug dealers dove behind their truck, while Twitchy's arm thrashed wildly, a rapid staccato round of pops filling the air.

Luckily, all the shots completely missed any of the officers who had now ducked behind their own vehicles. One of them grabbed a small, black radio pinned to his chest, rapidly shooting out orders. "County 12, Officer 317 requesting backup. Multiple suspects. Shots fired."

Garbled voices squawked from the police car's radio in response. "All units, all units. Multiple shots fired. Fieldpoint Drive and Deer Trail."

The officers gave them one last chance. "Put down your weapons! Put down your weapons!" One of them shouted over the hood of a squad car. "Or we *will* shoot you!"

The answer came in the form of two more rapid bursts of gunfire from Tattoo, who had now also pulled a gun. He panicked and tried to open the passenger side door as the officers opened fire, but he was hit first, his body bouncing off the side of the truck and slumping to the ground.

Twitchy stood up and tried to throw his hands up in the air, but he must've forgotten he still held the gun.

The two officers yelled for him to put it down, but when he didn't they had no choice but to shoot him. One bullet hit his elbow, another hit his abdomen, as he let out a ferocious wail, collapsing in a heap.

Now that both suspects were on the ground, the officers moved in to secure the scene. One of them shouted into his radio, "Suspects are down. Three victims. Safe for EMS!"

All Michael could do was look down at the color draining from his brother's face, the light leaving his eyes. Shaking, he turned helplessly to the police close by and pleaded, "Help him. Help him, please."

Within minutes, the blare of sirens filled the air as multiple flashing lights rounded the corner. Three ambulances followed by two more police cars.

The emergency vehicles screeched to a stop beside the first police cruiser and two EMS techs jumped out from the front cab of the one closest to Michael.

Immediately, they went to work on his now unconscious brother.

All he could do was stand there and watch in horror, as the paramedics tried to stem the flow of blood from his brother's chest and shoulder.

After a few brief moments of applying trauma dressing

and pressure to his brother's wounds, one of them got on his radio, "To County from Branchburg 74 BLS 4, we have an approximately seventeen year old male with a GSW to the upper right arm and right chest. Blood pressure is 80 over 40, pulse is 140. Patient is hypotensive."

The response was immediate. "County to 74 BLS 4 trauma alert has been sent to Somerset Medical Center. What's your ETA?"

"To County from Branchburg 74 BLS 4, ETA eight minutes," the paramedic quickly answered.

Eight minutes. Michael dared to glance at his brother's face. With his eyes shut and his face a milky-gray, he already had the look of a dead man.

With his eyes full of deep remorse and concern, Tom slowly approached.

Michael didn't even give him the chance to make excuses. Shaking with fury, he jumped to his feet, firing off a burst of energy straight at him. *Back off!*

Tom swiftly flew to his left, narrowly avoiding the blow.

Michael couldn't care less. He'd deal with him later.

Now, he turned his attention back to Chris, as the two paramedics carefully shifted his brother's limp body onto a gurney.

Following the paramedics into the ambulance, he screamed back at Tom, "Don't you *dare* follow me!"

On the way to the hospital, he sat mere inches from the techs working on his brother.

Now, trembling overtook him, as the words tumbled from his mouth uncontrollably. "Please Lord, please. I know I have no right to ask this because I've had my moments of doubt here, but please, please save my little brother." His voice faltered. "I don't want him to die, not this young, not like this." His lips trembled to the point where he almost couldn't speak, but he kept going. "He's all my mother has. And he has his whole life to live yet." He folded his hands in prayer, but shook them like an angry fist at heaven. "You *robbed* me of a chance at life, *please* don't rob him too. *Please.*"

Spectral tears streamed down his face now, but he hardly cared. He dropped to his knees right beside his brother laying lifeless on the gurney. "Please. I know I doubted you and I'm not gonna lie...I do wonder why you let these terrible things happen to good people. And I know I have no right to ask. I know that. But I believe. I *do* believe you're up there now." He bowed his head, pleading. "Help my brother. Save him. Please *save* him."

As usual, he heard no response from anyone.

CHAPTER SEVENTEEN

HOSPITAL

THIS AMBULANCE RIDE seemed to take even longer than a thousand years. Especially since all he could do was sit by helplessly and watch as the paramedics tried unsuccessfully to staunch the bleeding. The sight of blood never bothered him before, but this time was different.

This time it was his one and only baby brother.

And judging by the way one of the techs was hurriedly talking into his radio and working feverishly on him, something was very wrong.

Time warped and slowed as the paramedic's words faded from his hearing. As if trapped in a thick bubble he caught phrases here and there—something about entry and exit points uncertain, something about an artery rupturing, the patient being critical.

Once the ambulance arrived at the hospital, the paramedics delivered him straight into the ER, and into the waiting arms of the nurses and surgeons of the trauma team. He admired how calm and collected they were while they assessed his brother's injuries.

Within ten minutes they had triaged his wounds, run a cat scan, an ultrasound, and drawn blood. After that, they rushed Chris into an operating room.

He didn't have the heart to follow, at least not yet. Knowing all too well what would happen next, he decided to wait in the ER for his mother to arrive.

He sat on one of the unoccupied chairs over by the water cooler in the far corner, his eyes glued to the front entrance. As stranger after stranger straggled or was wheeled in, he thought about all the different reasons that had brought each of them here tonight. A middle-aged man experiencing severe chest pain, an unresponsive teen girl who had overdosed, a pregnant woman crying in a wheelchair, obviously having some kind of unforeseen pregnancy complication. Once again, he was reminded how life could change in an instant, and how there's simply no way to prepare for that. He wondered how many lives would be forever changed tonight. How many lives would never be the same? Would his brother's be one of them?

Thankfully, waiting for his mother didn't take as long as he thought it might. The glass revolving door rotated once more and he caught sight of her, leaning on Mr. Jasinski's arm. His kindly old neighbor must've driven her to the hospital after seeing what had happened. It couldn't be a coincidence that the police had gotten there so fast. His neighbor must've seen what was going on and called the police even before the shots were fired.

Now, his mother tilted up her face.

My God.

If he hadn't known it was his mother, he might not have recognized her. With her eyes a bloodshot mess, her cheeks gaunt, her body trembling, and her mind a distraught jumble, he took one look and knew for certain, *if my brother dies, this will be the final straw that shatters her completely.*

He flew to her side, wishing he could be the one to hold her up. "I'm so sorry, Mom," he murmured, as a fresh flow of tears sprang from his eyes. "I'm so sorry I couldn't help him. I tried." As he choked out the words, vivid images of how Tom had prevented him from helping his brother flashed before his eyes, and a rush of white hot anger swelled through him such as he had never felt in his life.

When this is over, *I am going to make him pay for this.*

For now though, his main concern was his own family and getting them through this ordeal. He wasn't going to leave the hospital or his mother's side, until he knew if his brother would be okay.

Only problem was waiting for word about his brother became excruciating. He kept glancing at the clock, but for once, time didn't seem to be moving at all.

Finally, when staying with his distraught mother became too difficult, he wandered down the corridor and followed the signs to the OR.

It didn't take him long before he found the right hallway. As he had now grown so accustomed to doing, he walked straight through the locked double doors meant to guard against unauthorized entry.

Moments like this made him appreciate his lack of earthly limitations.

A nurse pushing a cart darted through a set of double doors on the right-hand side. On a hunch, he followed her.

He swallowed hard and forced his leg to stop shaking.

The operating room was abuzz with activity. His brother lay on a steel table under bright, white lights, while two surgeons worked on his open shoulder and chest. Apparently, they had already removed one bullet, but were in the midst of deciding if a second bullet should remain inside his body or not. Their expressions were grave as they exchanged directives and opinions, doing their level best to save his brother and fix the mess created by the bullets.

He knew very little about medicine or surgery, but it sure as hell seemed like the team was going through an awful lot of blood. The nurse hung a new bag every few minutes. When she called for three more units of blood a short time later, his suspicions seemed to be confirmed.

Even without being a doctor, he knew the truth. *My brother is obviously walking that fine, ethereal line between life and death.*

For what seemed like forever he watched his brother's surgery, but then he noticed the clock on the wall.

Only thirty minutes have gone by?

How was that even possible?

Now, he regretted every petty fight they'd ever had. Over his brother borrowing his car, his phone charger, his clothes, his sneakers. Chris getting into fights, not doing his homework, not helping around the house with the chores. Everything they had ever argued about, it all seemed so insignificant now. He wished he could tell him he was sorry. He wished he could take it all back.

He just didn't want to do it with his brother as a ghost.

Minute by minute, it was killing him to simply stand by and watch, impotent. The least he could do was encourage the doctors to try their hardest, do their very best, and not give up on him. Gliding over to the younger-looking of the two surgeons, he carefully projected his thoughts into the man's mind, *he's too young, you've got to save him.*

A beat passed while he gauged the doctor's reaction.

Unfortunately, his idea backfired in the worst way. His words rattled the doctor whose once confident and steady hands now visibly shook.

Great. I guess I should've kept my mouth shut.

In fact the longer he stood near, the worse the operation seemed to be going. An older nurse dropped an instrument as she tried to hand it to one of the surgeons. Another nurse lost track of something he had put down on a tray and couldn't find it right away when it needed to be picked up again. The surgeons' hands increasingly trembled. Everyone seemed more tense and strained by the minute.

Somehow, the panicky vibes he must've been sending off were clearly affecting the emotions of the surgical staff, making them even more nervous.

It took a near-monumental effort to pull himself away, but if his presence was going to further jeopardize his brother's life, then he was going to have to leave.

Besides, if he watched even one more minute, his soul might tear in two.

With one last painful glance at his brother's face, he ghosted through the nearest wall and into the adjacent operating room.

The middle-aged man who had been brought into the ER earlier now lay on the table with his chest cavity wide open.

From what the doctor was telling his staff, the man had several suspected blockages and had been scheduled for tests later that week, but apparently his body decided for him that time had run out.

As he watched the surgeon's careful hands work on the man's heart, he thought about how he could've been a cardiologist. He couldn't help but stare.

Maybe I would've been a great heart surgeon after all.

After a while, it seemed as if the surgery was winding down. "Good job everyone," the young surgeon said, confident their work was done, "let's close him up."

"Wait a minute," the surgical nurse suddenly cut in, "his heart rate's dropping rapidly."

A split second later, the long beep of the monitor flat-lining sent a phantom chill up his spine.

"He's crashing," another nurse blurted, as her hands flew automatically to a nearby crash cart to get what was necessary.

"I need one milligram epinephrine," the doctor called out to his team. He had barely finished his sentence when the first nurse placed a syringe in his hand and he administered the dose. A second, male nurse grabbed the paddles and placed them directly on the man's open heart. The other doctors and nurses calmly took a step back as the nurse yelled, "Clear!"

The shock jolted the man's body up off the table.

But it didn't work.

His vital signs were still flat-lining.

Unexpectedly, the spirit of the man now sat up looking calm, but extremely confused. He touched his face and his torso, much the same way he himself had done in those first few moments when he realized he was dead. The man swung his legs over the gurney, stood up and slowly walked over.

The stranger leveled his eyes on him, pleading for the truth. "Am I dead?"

"I think so...," he said gently, adding at the last moment in a hopeful tone, "for the moment anyway."

The man nodded gravely. "I should've gotten on the treadmill more often, laid off the sweets," he mumbled mostly to himself, his words laced with remorse.

For the first time, the man now seemed to truly register his presence. "Hey, who are you?" he asked, scrunching up his face. "Do I know you?"

He shook his head. "Nah, I'm only a...visitor passing through."

"Oh," the man responded with a tremor in his voice. Obviously, the truth had hit him, and he realized he was talking to another ghost.

They passed the next few minutes in an awkward silence, watching the doctors and nurses. He had no idea how to console another man who had just lost his life. *How do I tell him it's going to be okay, when I'm still struggling through this myself?*

The man turned to look back at the surgical staff working feverishly to revive his expired corpse. "I have five kids you know. This'll be hard on them...and my wife."

A sharp stab pierced his insides as he remembered the almost unbearable pain his father's death had caused his family. Fighting to keep his expression neutral, he nodded solemnly at the man, but said nothing. He didn't want to give him any false words of encouragement.

Suddenly, the man looked at him with wide, hopeful eyes. "Do you think I could go back?"

The man's question threw him for a loop. Something about the way he said it made it sound for all the world as if he were asking his permission.

If he is, then he's giving me way too much credit.

Still, he didn't want to discourage the man. Maybe his situation would be different. "Yeah, I think so," he said lightly. "You should go ahead and try."

"I will," the man said decisively, and with a very determined look on his face he made his way back onto the gurney, hovered over his corpse for a moment, then laid down. At the very moment his energy melted back into his body, the ER technicians picked up his heartbeat on the monitors again. The machine beeped in perfect rhythm once again.

"He's back," one of the nurses declared in relief. "We have normal sinus rhythm, his heart rate and blood pressure are stabilizing, he's 110 over 60."

"Good, let's button him up quickly before we have any more trouble," the doctor added with an air of confidence.

Michael frowned. He'd tried the same thing when he died and yet it hadn't worked. It took a mere second for the naked truth to hit him with the force of a meteor from the heavens. *I wasn't meant to go back, but clearly…this man was.*

Despondent as he was, he smiled a little thinking of how happy the man's family was going to be. He hoped the man's health troubles would be behind him, and a bright future ahead of him. He'd like to think he'd helped, if only in some small way.

He wasn't sure if the man would hear him or not, but he couldn't help himself. Before he left the room he said out loud, "You've been given a great gift, Mister. Better use it wisely."

. . .

By the time Michael came out of the operating room the stranger had been in, he couldn't find his brother. The operating room where Chris' surgery took place was now empty and dark.

Panic now set in.

Had they taken him to recovery, or to the morgue? Would he run into his brother's ghost at any minute?

There was only one way to find out.

As fast as he could he flew back to the ER waiting room.

Thankfully, barely a minute later one of the surgeons he had seen in the operating room—a tall, older man wearing glasses and a white coat—came out of the double doors and over to his mother. With one glance the doctor must've assessed her frail state, so he delivered the news without delay. "Mrs. Andrews, my name is Doctor Grayson," he said, extending his hand for a quick hand shake. "Your son is out of surgery. He's in ICU and his condition has stabilized."

Michael was never so relieved in his life and he looked up to the ceiling, mouthing *thank you, thank you,* over and over.

As the doctor's words registered, his mother dipped her head and began to weep into her hands. Mr. Jasinski gently patted her shoulder to comfort her.

For a moment, Michael forgot himself and also put his hand on his mother's shoulder. He couldn't help it. She shook so violently already, his cold touch wasn't going to make a damned bit of difference.

The doctor gave his mother a moment to collect herself before he continued.

Given the grave expression on the man's face, the other shoe was about to drop. "While your son is stabilized, his condition is still serious. One of the bullets hit him in the top of the chest here," he said, pointing to the approximate spot. "The other shattered the rotor cuff in his shoulder and compromised an artery. We managed to repair as much of the damage as we could and stop the bleeding. But your son's lost a great deal of blood. His right lung has also collapsed and he isn't breathing on his own." He looked her straight in the eyes to make sure she understood the gravity of the situation. "We've put your son in a medically induced coma to give him the best chance of healing. You'll be able to see him in a few minutes, but we wanted to give you some time to digest all of this first."

"Please tell me straight," his mother pleaded with the doctor, her words coming out strained and raspy. "Is my son going to die?"

Obviously used to answering impossibly tough questions day in and day out, the seasoned physician didn't even flinch. "If your son can make it through the next forty-eight hours without any serious complications, he'll have a good chance."

A coma? A chance? The doctor's prognosis staggered him for a moment. It didn't take a genius to read between the lines.

Chris' life was hanging in the balance. By a thread.

My baby brother is in a coma...and he may die. His mind reeled. *This can't be happening. It just can't be happening.*

His mother's reaction hit him hardest, like a prize fighter dealt a devastating second blow to the chin right after a killer jab to the throat. She collapsed under the weight of the news, leaning into Mr. Jasinski's shoulder and sobbing.

More than ever, Michael wanted to be the one to comfort her, but he knew it was useless to try.

No matter what though, he would always be eternally grateful to his faithful neighbor for being there for his family. *If it wasn't for him, my brother might have been dead on arrival like I was. And my mother would have no one right now.*

Despite being appreciative of that, he turned a disappointed gaze up to heaven and demanded answers. *Why are you doing all this to my family? Why?*

Without a response, the tears threatened to fall again. But he bit back the bitterness and took a steadying breath instead. Tears served no purpose right now.

Once he collected his wits, he flew off into the corridor from which the doctor had emerged, searching room to room, until he found his little brother. Crossing over the threshold into the Intensive Care Unit, he halted in his tracks unable to go even a step further.

Chris lay in a bed surrounded by more medical devices and contraptions than he had ever seen. A clear, thick tube was stuck down his throat and a mask was taped over his mouth and nose. Small white pads and electrodes had been glued to his chest. Dozens more wires connected him to beeping machines. Multiple IVs stuck out of both arms. His brother honestly resembled some kind of half-human, half-cyborg.

One tentative step at a time, he made his way over to his Chris' bedside. His brother's face was pale. So very pale.

Gently, Michael touched his hand. He knew what touching the living should feel like, but his brother's hand radiated cold, as if most of the life had already drained out of him.

"I'm here, bro," he croaked out. "I don't know if you can hear me, but if you can, I want you to listen to me. You have to live," he said forcefully. "You have to live, okay. You *have* to fight. Life is worth living," he said, wiping away more phantom tears, "and mom needs you. I need you. I need to know that one of us got their chance. No one will be angry with you about all that other stuff. It doesn't matter what you did." He hung his head, as more tears trickled down his cheeks. "You need to come back so you have a chance to make things right. I want you to get that second chance."

A few minutes later Dr. Grayson led his mother into the room.

When she saw Chris, she had much the same reaction to seeing him in the hospital bed. Her jaw dropped and her hand flew to cover her mouth, as she choked back another small sob. Mr. Jasinski helped her into a chair near the bed and took a seat beside her.

Mary started to say something to the doctor, but the door opened again.

Two of the officers on scene during the shooting stepped into the room.

His body tensed, as the harsh reality smacked his consciousness. *Oh my God, I completely forgot. On top of everything else, Chris is in one metric buttload of trouble.*

Luckily, before the two cops could say a single word, the doctor cut them off with a stern look. "Not now," he said, sharply.

"With all due respect, we're going to have to talk to your patient at some point," the one officer said in no uncertain terms. "We've got two dead suspects and a whole lotta questions."

Dr. Grayson shook his head 'no' with more emphasis this time. "I understand that, Officer," he said evenly. "But this patient isn't capable right now. So, you're going to have to wait. He's not going anywhere anytime soon." He looked him straight in the eye, making it perfectly clear he didn't want to have to say anymore. This wasn't up for debate.

"Fine," the officer conceded with a slight nod. "We'll be waiting outside. We need some information from you too, Doc." He turned to Mary. "Ma'am we hope your son will be okay," he said gently, "but just so you know…based upon the cash we found and the drugs we found in the house and in his car, when your son wakes up he's most likely going to be arrested."

It nearly killed him all over again to see his mother's head droop forward in shame. She gave a little nod. "I understand," she mumbled, almost incoherently.

Mr. Jasinski let out a heavy sigh and rose from his chair. "Officer, I'm the one that called you. I saw everything from my window. I can talk with you now if you'd like."

"That would be fine, Sir. We'll see you out in the hall."

Once they all left, Mary finally got to ask her question. "Dr. Grayson…what was that you said before…about my son's shoulder?"

The doctor delivered his prognosis. "Like I said, our first concern was to close off the artery and stop the bleeding. But the bones in his upper arm and shoulder, here and here," he said pointing, "were shattered by three bullets. We've done the best we can to repair the damage for now, but your son's most likely going to require further surgery somewhere down the line to increase the mobility in his arm. His right arm's definitely going to need a lot of rehabilitation, but in time he should regain limited use."

Limited use? The two words clanged around in Michael's head.

His mother's eyes went wide. "He loves baseball," she said in a zombie-like whisper, "he…he pitches."

The doctor gave a slight grimace. "Let's take things one step at a time," he said, urging patience. "We can worry about his arm after he's cleared these other hurdles." His words certainly sounded optimistic on the surface, but Michael had the advantage of being able to read his mind.

And he heard all he needed to know.

He has his doubts whether Chris is going to pull through. And even if he does, he'll definitely never pitch again.

At that moment, the blind fury welling up inside of him

grew too much to contain and he flew out of the hospital headed towards his house.

As he reduced himself down to a small glowing orb, one thought blazed crystal clear in his mind.

I am going to destroy *Tom.*

CHAPTER EIGHTEEN

FIGHT

WITHIN SECONDS, MICHAEL had orbed back to his house on Fieldpoint Drive. He stood in the driveway, uncertain if Tom was still there. By now it must have been about four in the morning. A sparkling frost coated the grass, all the houses were dark, and the entire neighborhood was blissfully asleep. No emergency vehicles. No yellow police tape. No sign of the chaos that had unfolded hours earlier.

As he came around to the front of the house, he stopped short.

Tom was casually sitting on the porch steps, as if simply enjoying the night air.

This just added insult to injury as far as he was concerned. Even from this distance, Tom no doubt sensed the fury rolling off of him in tsunami-like waves. And it wouldn't require even half the IQ of Steven Hawking to figure out that the murderous look on his face spelled trouble.

And yet, he's calm as a freakin' cucumber.

"How's your brother doing?" Tom asked him in a tentative tone.

Michael ground his teeth together. "His life's hanging by a thread, thanks to you." His words came out menacing and low, almost a growl. "And even if my brother lives, he's never going to be able to pitch again."

Tom glanced away, avoiding his gaze. "I'm very sorry, M—"

Michael cut him off with a warning shot, a weak blast of energy that didn't quite reach the stairs. "Shut up, you evil son of a bitch!" he screamed. "You're not sorry." His body shook with rage, as he stood there clenching and unclenching his fists. "How could you have let this happen? Why couldn't you just get out of my way and let me help my brother?"

Tom stood up and stepped onto the sidewalk to face him. "You weren't supposed to interfere," he said flatly. "Neither one of us were supposed to interfere. I know it's going to be hard for you to understand, but I…"

"Bullshit!" he yelled, cutting him off again. "I know you could've saved him! I've seen you do it before with the little girl outside Yankee stadium and the boy in the fire! And even if *you* didn't want to do anything, you had no right to stop *me* from saving him!"

"You don't understand," Tom implored with outstretched hands. "I only did what I had to do!"

Michael couldn't stand to hear another word he said, couldn't stand the sight of him another second. All the frustration, all the fear, all the mistrust of the past several months overwhelmed him and he spread his arms wide to draw in energy from his surroundings.

Suddenly, a street lamp to his left blew out, the glass showering down in tiny jagged shards.

Michael shook his head back and forth slowly,

menacingly, as he advanced on his so-called Protector. "My father warned me not to trust you...but I didn't listen..."

Seeing what he was doing, Tom halted mid-step and raised his hand up in a gesture of caution. "Stop it, Michael. You don't know what you're doing," he warned. "You don't want to do this. Listen to me..."

"I'm through listening to you!" His voice rose at least three octaves, as he sent a powerful surge of energy hurtling toward his mentor.

Tom jumped out of the way, the bolt missing him by mere inches and nearly setting the porch steps ablaze.

This only served to rile him up more. If only Tom would just stop trying to talk him out of attacking and fight back. He wanted the satisfaction of kicking his ass. Now, he moved to the middle of the street, firing off another huge jolt of energy.

Yet again, Tom slid out of the way barely in time. "I don't want to fight you. We're not supposed to fight each other." Even so, he raised his hands, apparently getting ready to defend himself if need be. "You don't understand," he insisted, obviously still attempting diplomacy. "I only did what I had to do!"

"Bullshit! You had no right to get in my way!" On that last word, he thrust another powerful jolt of energy at Tom.

This time his mentor spun to his left, firing off a quick round of shots as he tumbled through the air.

"Come on, you can do better than that," he mocked, expertly dodging each one of the bursts. Drawing more energy from around him, he now sent a volley of mega-bursts surging straight at Tom.

In a blur, his mentor darted several feet to the left, all of the shots completely missing him. He finally seemed incensed. "Stop this right now!" he yelled. "You *must* listen to me!"

"The hell I will! My little brother may *die* because of you!" he screamed, thrusting his hands out repeatedly for half a dozen long bursts.

The flashes of energy zinged past Tom's head, a few of them ricocheting off the pavement.

Now, shot for shot, they aggressively answered each other. Flying back and forth across the road, they traded blows so rapidly that sparks gathered in the air around them.

As quick as Tom was, Michael made sure he was quicker. Still, Tom's effort was impressive. "You fight pretty well for an old guy," he quipped. "Too well, in fact. Makes me think even more that you're hiding something."

"I don't want to fight you at all," Tom countered in an angry tone. "But you're forcing me to defend myself. Now stand down, Son."

"Don't call me that!" he yelled, sending a blast barreling towards his chest. "I am *not* your son!"

Tom spun away in the nick of time, but then turned to face him. His eyes looked genuinely hurt, but Michael now knew it to be an act. "Give me a chance to explain—"

"What? So you can tell me more lies, more half-truths?" He fired off another burst, this time at Tom's head. "My father was right about you! He said not to trust you and I shouldn't have!"

Tom ducked, firing off a shot that grazed his forearm.

White-hot pain radiated downward paralyzing his fingertips, and for a second he couldn't move his hand to return fire. "You missed, Old Man."

"I missed on purpose," Tom retorted. "I. Don't. Want. To. Hurt. You." He drew out every word, while firing off six bolts in a row, his best salvo yet.

Michael expertly dodged each incoming shot one after the other. "Well, that's funny cause I *really* wanna hurt you," he snarled. In rapid succession he sent several more blasts rocketing towards Tom.

This time, all Tom did was flick his hands left and right, knocking the blasts off course and sending them surging into a nearby wall and tree. Bricks and bark exploded in a cloud of dust on either side of him.

For a moment, Michael was shaken. He had no idea how Tom had managed to deflect his shots.

"Oooh, very Jedi," he said facetiously. He wasn't going to give Tom the satisfaction and he wasn't going to give up so easily. "Fine, why don't we do this the old-fashioned way then."

With all the force he could muster, Michael set his jaw and prepared to lunge at him.

But he never got the chance.

"Enough!" Tom yelled in a voice so deep and so threatening—the sound reverberated through Michael's soul with the strength and power of a wrecking ball, knocking him off his feet and sending him sprawling on the ground. At the same moment, a brilliant flash blinded him, forcing him to cover his face and squeeze his eyes shut against the bright and searing light.

Slowly, he rose to his feet. When he opened his eyes again, he couldn't believe what he saw.

Standing before him was not the man he knew. Not his mentor. Not Tom. The face was still familiar. Yes. But nothing else about him was the same.

A glowing being nine feet tall hovered in front of him, draped in an opalescent-white robe and holding up a sword of powerful, blinding light into the air. The enormous blade crackled and sparked, radiating heat and energy, as if he had snatched an actual lightning bolt straight from the heavens.

The effect was so confusing, so troubling, so humbling, that it instantly dropped Michael to his knees.

He bowed his head and tried to remember a prayer. Any prayer. A part of a prayer.

But his mind went totally blank.

He couldn't be sure if Tom was about to smite him or not, but one thing he knew for certain, *I'm in the presence of an angel.*

A. Very. Pissed. Off. Angel.

CHAPTER NINETEEN

RISE

WHY HAD IT never occurred to him? Why hadn't he seen it before? Of course Tom was an angel—it all made perfect sense now.

How Tom had come to him that night on the beach, at the very moment he was at his lowest and needed him most.

How knowing he was.

How powerful.

Bathed in the warmth of Tom's radiant light, Michael trembled. "So you're an angel," he said, his words full of respect and awe. Cautiously, he raised his head up a few inches to look into his mentor's eyes.

Tom merely nodded, but did not answer.

The silence felt damning. With his stomach in tense knots, he wriggled under the angel's unflinching stare.

In response, Tom placed a fatherly hand on the top of his head and whispered reassuringly with his mind, *do not be afraid.*

As the energy and power of the angel's touch radiated through him, he shuddered with relief.

When Tom finally did speak, he said the last thing in this world Michael could've ever expected.

"Rise," the angel commanded in a low baritone, much like that of the Elder's guards. His voice seemed to unnaturally boom and echo off the houses.

He slowly rose to his feet, acutely aware of his mentor's piercing gaze.

"For it is I...who should kneel before you." With that, Tom respectfully bent down in front of him and bowed his head.

The only thing that dropped faster was Michael's own jaw.

"I...I don't understand," he stammered. "What are you talking about? You're the one holding the...the sword of... *doom* or whatever."

Tom raised his head to look at him and cracked a lopsided grin. "This is a truncheon of light and truth. And once you learn to command it and use it, yours will be ten times as powerful as mine. You're a Warrior angel, Michael." He said with a proud smile. "More powerful than I could ever dream to be. Descendant of Saint Michael the Archangel. Defender of Truth. Soldier for Righteousness. Warrior for Heaven itself." Again, he bowed his head low. "And I am your humble servant...sworn to protect you while you were learning your purpose. And sworn to *continue* protecting you while you're still in training."

If he'd had any actual air in his lungs, it would've been crushed right out of him.

His mind spun. This was a lot to process, and that was putting it mildly. He swallowed hard, trying to digest Tom's words.

So many questions clamored around his mind. *Could it*

really be true? Was he really an angel in training? And even if he was, what did it even mean to be a Warrior? What was he supposed to do? What was expected of him?

After a stunned moment or two, he finally collected himself. "Well...," he said, gesturing with his outstretched palm, "please stand up. You're *freaking* me out." He tried to keep the awkwardness out of voice, but failed miserably.

Tom rose to his full height, which was intimidating to say the least.

On second thought, he wished he hadn't asked his mentor to stand up again. He had no clue how to speak to him when he was nine feet tall and throwing off more light than the beacon on a lighthouse. The best he could come up with was, "nice sword," which came out sounding cheekier than he had intended.

Tom grinned. "It's much more than a sword. Although it looks like one, it's very different. A sword is manmade, as are guns, bombs, grenades and other weapons. Those things can injure or kill both the good and the bad alike. But this," he said, holding the blade aloft, "*this* is an instrument of the Divine, forged of purest truth and light. This weapon can only smite evil." He extended the glowing sword out in front of his body. "Go ahead, touch it."

Trusting no harm would come to him, he ran his fingertips along the sharp, luminescent edge of the blade. He marveled at the sensation, as a pleasant warmth tingled through his hand and traveled up his arm.

"See, it won't hurt you because you're a good and pure soul." Tom looked him straight in the eye. "However, should it meet with an evil entity, its judgment is swift and final."

He stared at the blade in awe. "Why is it glowing as if it's radioactive?"

In obvious admiration, Tom twirled the sword round and round in his hand. "The weapon's illumination has been called angelic white fire. But it's not actually fire at all." He paused, as if awestruck himself. "I've been told it's a piece of the very fabric of heaven," he said, his words filled with deep reverence and respect. "It's made of the goodness and light that dwells within each of us." Tom turned to him with a piercing gaze. "Have you ever heard the expression, it's always darkest before the dawn?"

He scrunched up his eyes. "Of course, I have."

"Do you know why that is?"

He'd never really thought about it all that much before, so he answered with honesty. "No. Not really."

"Because light is gathering behind the darkness...and the darkness tries to fight back and extinguish the light," Tom said significantly. "You and I, Michael...we are the light."

His words filled him with strength and hope. He'd waited all this time for something good to come out of his death. But a question still simmered deep in his soul. "Why didn't you tell me before that I was a Warrior?"

"Because I wasn't positive until now," he said frankly. "I was fairly sure you had more power than I did that first time we were in the parking lot and you tried to use your energy. But every time I even tried to tell you my suspicions, I was prevented. No matter how hard I tried, the words just wouldn't come out. Even after you fought all those demons so well at the school," he explained. "I took that to mean I wasn't supposed to tell you, and you were only supposed to know when you were ready. And obviously now you're ready."

Ready? He was anything but ready. In shock was more like it. "So, I'm an angel," he half-mumbled. Even though he said the words he still didn't quite believe it.

"Not exactly," Tom answered. "You're still an angel-in-training and so am I."

"Wait a minute…you look like that," he said, gesturing up and down at him, "…and you're still in *training*? In case you haven't noticed, you have a full length glow-a-thon going on."

Tom gave a hearty laugh. "That's the first time this has happened to this degree. That's how I knew we had reached some sort of milestone. But I think I can tone all this down if you wish." Closing his eyes briefly, he seemed to exhale energy.

And just like that, Tom appeared normal again. "I can't exactly control when my full power is unleashed. And the sword only comes forth when I need it most. But you're so strong that when you challenged me like that, my power had no choice but to reveal itself."

He scrunched up his brow, partly in confusion, partly in embarrassment. "What do you mean, I'm so strong?"

Tom's face flushed with an odd look of pride. "Always remember this, Michael…once you have your own sword, you will have the power to create light in the darkest of places. Warriors are among the strongest, most powerful angels at heaven's disposal," he said. "That's why the devil fears their powers the most and seeks to turn as many as possible over to evil. He's preparing for the final battle between heaven and hell."

He now recalled what Vassago had said, *I must turn you or destroy you.*

"And some Warrior angels are more powerful than others," Tom added. "You, Michael, are one of the most powerful Warrior angels heaven has seen in a very long time. I believe that's why the devil marked you and wants you so badly. That's why I not only had to protect you, but I had to test you."

He read between the lines of what Tom was saying. "So I was right all along...," he exclaimed at the revelation, "you did lead me into battle with the demons!"

"No, not intentionally." Tom shook his head back and forth. "I only directed you where I was told to. But each time we encountered trouble, I became more and more convinced that you must be a Warrior angel. And I was right."

"So, what happens now?"

"Boy, you really don't have any patience do you?" he said, sounding annoyed. "Well, that depends."

"On what?"

Tom peered down his nose at him. "How stubborn you are and how long it takes you to learn the rest of what you need to learn."

He scowled. "So, if you're an angel and you've been to heaven, then you must be a visiting spirit?"

"No, I never lied to you," Tom said, emphatically. "I haven't been to heaven any more than you have. I'm still waiting for the light to come for me, same as you."

"But if you haven't been to heaven, then how do you know all this?"

"It's like I've told you before...indistinct voices. But it's not really a voice either." Tom looked down at the ground, obviously struggling with the best way to explain. Finally, he said, "Nothing is ever actually said or spoken. It's more like subconscious thoughts. You just...*know*."

With a fresh surge of anger, he suddenly remembered why they'd been fighting. He remembered that Tom had stopped him from helping his brother. And he remembered that Chris was now lying in a hospital bed dying because of it. "Wait a minute," he said suspiciously, "if you *are* an angel-in-training, why do you sometimes dole out help and other times withhold it?"

Tom heaved a heavy sigh. "We're not supposed to interfere in every situation. Sometimes we can actually make things much worse by interfering. I know it's going to be hard for you to understand since it's your brother, but I only did what I *had* to do."

He figured it was probably pointless to argue with him, but his heart still ached. He wanted to completely forgive him for what he'd done, but it sure as hell wasn't going to be easy. "What about my brother though?" he asked in barely a whisper. "Do you know if he's going to live or die?"

"I'm sorry," Tom said in a most sincere way, "but I don't know the answer to that."

An awkward silence wedged itself between them, as neither one knew what to say to the other. Finally, his friend broke the tension. "I know you've had a hard time coming to grips with your own death, Michael. But now I can finally say something to you that I've wanted to say for a very long time."

"What's that?"

"I want you to think about something," he said, his eyes piercing straight through his soul. "Did it ever occur to you that those that are taken from this life early...might have been needed elsewhere?"

He stared at him, a bit thrown by the question. "What do you mean?"

"I mean quite simply, that those souls were needed on a different front," he said in a deep and meaningful way. "They were called to a higher purpose."

As Tom's words sunk in, they lifted the yoke of grief he had carried since the day of his death. While the weight left his soul, he recalled what Lincoln had said, *it does not matter if you fulfill your destiny on one side of the veil or the other. We are all here for a purpose.*

Only one thing still bothered him though. "If that's true, then why do some souls seem to go right into the light...while others like me and you, have to wait?" This was the same question he had asked Catherine the Elder.

Tom's expression seemed to cloud over. "I don't know," he replied a bit tersely. "Maybe they're just more ready than others. Maybe they don't have anything to learn, or anything holding them back. As I told you before, I'm sure it's as different for each person as their own fingerprints."

After a long pause, Tom continued. "But the truth is...when they're ready and if they're worthy, every soul eventually becomes some sort of angel after they die. Either a Protector, Messenger, Navigator, Seer, or Warrior. Each one with different responsibilities and duties."

Every soul has a purpose.

So kicking demon ass was going to be his job, his purpose.

He could live with that.

• • •

Once again it had been another long, strange night. After saying a quick goodbye to Tom, he couldn't wait to get home to Sarah and tell her all that had happened. Becoming a tiny ball of light, he orbed and within minutes he was back at the Angel of the Sea.

The early rising guests would be waking up anytime now. He found Sarah in the dining room, where the staff scurried around setting up for breakfast.

She was seated in a red velvet chair at the head of one of the tables, looking catatonic and forlorn. Matt sat next to her, holding her hand.

Which would've been no big deal.

Except his eyes were glued to her lips as he stroked her hand with his thumb.

It was all just a bit too much and a beat too long for his liking.

Sarah didn't seem as if she was paying Matt any attention at all. Busy staring down at the table, she finally raised her head up when she heard his ghostly footsteps.

The moment she laid eyes on him she leapt to her feet and flew to his side. Throwing her arms around him, she exclaimed in relief, "Michael! Thank God. I was so worried you might've been attacked again." Her voice shook. "It was all I could do to stay put and not go searching for you."

Matt turned to him, looking all too proud of himself. "I wouldn't let her, Mate."

Michael paid him no attention.

Instead, he melted into the comfort of Sarah's arms the way a man might slide into his favorite easy-chair after coming home from a long day at work. She was his rock. His anchor. Right now all he wanted to do was shut out the world, let his cares drift away, and hold her for all eternity.

And he was just about to start telling her everything, when he remembered his father's warning. Instantly, he slammed his mind shut, tighter than a jail cell door. *On second thought, I don't want Matt to know anything about what happened.* "Would you mind giving us some privacy?" he asked him, not even caring if it came off as rude.

Sarah must've have picked up on his defensive signals. "Thanks for staying with me," she said to Matt in a polite tone, but clearly imparting this was his invitation to leave.

Looking a little perturbed, Matt rose to his feet. "No problem." He nodded. "Catch you guys later. Raising his hand in a wave, he slowly faded away.

Once Matt was gone, Michael turned his attention back to Sarah. "I wasn't attacked," he mumbled feebly.

Her sad eyes rose up to meet his. "Then what happened?" she whispered, as she nuzzled next to his cheek. "Why were you gone so long? I was beginning to think maybe you were staying away because you were still angry with me."

He'd forgotten all about their little fight. In the grand

scheme of everything that had happened tonight, it seemed infinitely insignificant. And yet, he regretted that fight more than anything. Lifting her chin, he kissed her gently on the lips, as if she were a priceless piece of fine porcelain. "I could never be angry with you for more than five earthly seconds," he said, drawing out each word with utmost sincerity.

She smiled for a moment, but her troubled eyes searched his face for answers. "Then what happened?"

So full of emotion, it took him at least a minute before he could gather his thoughts and respond. There was so much to tell her, but where should he even begin?

He knew she would be nearly as upset as he was, so he tried to break the news about his brother as delicately as he could. "Chris got himself into deep trouble with some drug dealers. One of them pulled a gun and…"

Her hand flew up to cover her mouth. "Oh, no," she gasped, "Is he…?"

Michael shook his head. "No, he's not dead." The words were harder to say than he thought they'd be. "But he is in a coma."

Immediately, she threw her arms around his neck and pulled him close. "Oh, Michael. I'm so sorry about your brother," she said in a soothing voice. "I hope he'll be okay."

He bit the side of his cheek, trying to steady his emotions. "Me too."

All of a sudden, she pulled back from his embrace with the most peculiar expression on her face. "Something's different about you."

Can she already sense something?

"Yeah, about that...," he said, leading her into the parlor and patting the burgundy tufted sofa, "I think you'd better sit down."

And with that, he began to tell her everything that had happened overnight. About the shooting, about his kind neighbor helping out, about his epic fight with Tom. Finally, he told her all about Tom's incredible revelation.

When he was finished he said, "So, I guess I'm an angel-in-training." Even though he said the words, they didn't still seem real yet. "A Warrior angel to be exact."

Sarah sat wide-eyed and utterly stunned.

He didn't quite know what to make of her reaction. "So...what do you think of everything Tom told me? Do you think it's true?"

Her whole face lit up with a smile that radiated pure joy, as she jumped up from the couch and threw her arms around him. "I didn't need to see a halo," she whispered into his lips. "I already knew you were an angel. My angel."

Tenderly, he kissed her with every ounce of passion in his soul.

When he finished, he gently cupped her cheek. "I love you so much."

"I love you too." She smiled, but it didn't reach her eyes. After a few seconds she pulled away and fell silent.

"What's wrong?" he asked, concerned.

"Nothing." She hesitated. "It's wonderful that you know what kind of soul you are," she said in a lilting voice. "And I...I know it sounds selfish," she stammered, "but...I still wonder what type I am."

You're always so honest with your feelings. He lifted her

delicate hands and kissed them hard. "That's not selfish at all. I completely understand. You've been waiting for answers a helluva lot longer than I have." He looked her deeply in the eyes, desperately hoping to allay her fears and insecurities. "But I have no doubt, you're more of an angel than anyone I've ever met in my life. You'll know your purpose soon. I just know it."

Smiling wide, she laid her head against his shoulder. "So what are you supposed to do now?"

"You know," he said, honestly, "I'm not really sure."

CHAPTER TWENTY

RECONCILIATION

EVERY DAY FOR the next week and a half, Michael and Sarah left the Angel of the Sea to visit his brother in the hospital. They spent hours talking to Chris, keeping him company, and encouraging him to get better. Michael tried projecting all his good thoughts, fond memories, and deepest feelings into his brother's mind, hoping it might be beneficial for his healing.

Through it all, his mother rarely left Chris' side. She talked to him, read to him, even played his favorite music on a small speaker by his bedside. The kind of music he used to listen to before he got involved with drugs.

Many times, Michael listened to his mother's thoughts. She was praying for a good outcome, blaming herself, but also promising to never drink another drop of alcohol if her son would only pull through. More than once she broke down. More than once she had to admit to the nurses and doctors why she so badly had the shakes.

As heartbreaking as it was to see her in so much pain, he just couldn't tear himself away. Thank God he had Sarah by his side so he didn't fall apart.

Unfortunately, Branchburg police paid a few visits too.

They were a constant reminder that his brother was going to be in a world of trouble when he awoke.

If he awoke.

A steady stream of friends and neighbors stopped by as well. Mr. Jasinski was there at least every other day. His Aunt Susan even pledged to come down from Massachusetts, as soon as she could get away.

All of their help was a slim comfort for his mother but he was grateful she was getting some support, despite the circumstances which he had no doubt everyone knew by now.

Late in the evening on the ninth day or so, Tom also popped in to check on his brother's progress.

Hesitantly stepping in the room, he acknowledged both Michael and Sarah with a slight wave. The silence stretched on as he stood near the doorway, his face creased with obvious concern. "How is he?"

"The same as yesterday," Michael said with a dejected sigh, "and the day before that, and the day before that." Immediately he regretted his negative attitude and added, "But the nurses and doctors keep saying they remain hopeful. His vital signs are getting stronger and more stable, so that's something I guess."

After visiting for several awkward minutes, Tom turned to him and said, "Care to take a little break and walk with me?"

He nodded. It had been quite a while since he'd left his brother's hospital room anyway.

As they walked around the courtyard outside, he now cornered Tom. "Isn't there anything you can do? Put in a good word or something?" He was pretty sure he knew what the answer would be, but he had to try.

Tom shook his head regretfully. "I'm so sorry, Michael. But it doesn't work that way. I'm sure you've already asked for your brother to pull through in a much more heartfelt way than I ever could. The fact of the matter is…what is meant to happen, will happen."

He couldn't hide his disappointment. "I just can't believe my brother will never be able to play baseball again." The hollowness in the pit of his stomach was almost unbearable. "It seems so unfair."

"I'm sure it does," Tom replied. "But I want you to think about something. Your brother made choices of his own free will and those actions had consequences."

"Yeah, terrible consequences," he lamented. "He'll never play baseball again."

Tom fell silent for several minutes. "Perhaps…but maybe some other consequences neither you nor I could have foreseen." At the same moment, he got that usual inexplicable look on his face, as if listening to something far off in the distance. "Maybe this will prove my point," he said in a low voice. "I believe your brother is awake. Let's go back in. There's something you need to see."

His eyes went wide at the news, as his phantom heart skipped a beat. Instantly, he flew back into the hospital. He didn't even wait for Tom to follow.

By the time he reached the ICU, he knew it was true.

His brother's eyes were open. He'd awoken from his coma and the breathing tube had been removed. Nurses and doctors now moved around him, administering different medicines and assessing his condition.

Tears welled up in his eyes. As he watched them help his brother regain a foothold in this world, his emotions overwhelmed him. Once again, he looked up to heaven, mouthing thank you, thank you, over and over again. Unsteady on his feet, he plopped down in a vacant chair nearby.

Sarah stood next to him and placed a gentle hand upon his shoulder.

With the nurses and doctors looking on, his mother held Chris' hand, tears streaming down her face. "You're all I have now," she cried softly. "I can't lose you too."

"All we have is each other, Mom," Chris murmured in a raspy, strained voice. He still looked pale as a ghost and very weak, as a few tears trickled down his face too. "I'm so sorry…so sorry."

"Shhh," his mother whispered. "that's not important now. What's important is that you keep getting better."

Chris nodded slightly, as best he could. "I'm gonna need help getting off the stuff," he now whimpered through more tears.

His mother clutched his hand tighter. "I know sweetheart, and so will I…but we'll do it together. One way or another, I'll get my old job back at the real estate office and get back on the health insurance. That will help."

Michael couldn't have asked for a better miracle.

Now, with Tom and Sarah looking on, he hung his head and cried.

CHAPTER TWENTY-ONE

CLOSE

SOMEHOW, THE WEEKS since his brother's shooting seemed to peel away at an astounding rate. His brother stayed in the hospital for two more weeks recovering. After that, he was transferred to a center for more specialized care and rehabilitation.

Through all of it, he and Sarah continued their daily visits. Day after day, they watched as Chris grew stronger. His recuperation was no picnic, but he was getting there.

Finally, almost nine weeks after his brother was shot, Michael learned that Chris would finally be going home on the following Tuesday.

That afternoon, while overhearing the doctor talk about his brother's discharge, Michael was surprised to learn it was already Memorial Day weekend. He'd been so preoccupied with his brother's recovery that the end of May seemed to have arrived in a flash.

But with the holiday came the warm, sunny weather and the promise of hope for a better future. He and Sarah stayed inside the Angel of the Sea most of Saturday taking a break from the hospital and just enjoying each other's company. Later that night after it got dark, they planned on going to Wildwood Boardwalk to see the fireworks and other holiday weekend festivities as he had promised her.

For now though, it had been his idea to borrow a deck of playing cards from the basket in the parlor. Levitating objects right behind the backs of the guests and staff was quickly becoming one of his favorite hobbies.

Sarah threw down the three of clubs, drew another card from the pile and inserted it into her hand. "Gin," she said with a triumphant smile.

Michael frowned as he gathered up the cards to shuffle and deal again. *She's getting way too good at this game.*

"Careful," she said. "I can hear you, remember?"

He shifted in his chair pretending to grumble, but grinned back at her anyway. The two of them had spent a few days arranging the old furniture in the attic to their liking. This old table and chairs at which they now sat had been the most difficult, but eventually the two of them managed to lift it enough and slide it into place. He could only imagine what the guests and staff thought of all the noise coming from the otherwise 'unoccupied' attic. No one even came up to check what was going on. They were probably way too scared, which was both hilarious and pathetic at the same time. He had decided some time ago that, for the most part, the living really do choose to ignore the dead.

A silly thought scampered through his mind. If anyone living walked up the attic stairs at that very moment, they would see playing cards held up by unseen hands, and floating through the air back and forth across the table. He had to admit, the possibility of that happening was absolutely tantalizing. *Sure wouldn't be able to ignore us then*, he grinned to himself.

"Stop stalling," she said playfully. "I want to beat you again."

He was about to shoot a clever comeback in her direction when the sound of music drifting in from outside interrupted him.

Walking over to the window, he put his ghostly hands on the wooden frame, closed his eyes so he could concentrate and pushed with all his might. Slowly, the glass pane rose a few inches, enough to let them hear the music more clearly.

"It's Jerry again," he said, peering out the window. The old gardener was playing a radio and pruning the shrubs while Mitch Ryder and the Detroit Wheels belted out catchy lyrics about a devil wearing a blue dress.

"He definitely shares your taste in music." She laughed, which to his ears was a musical sound in its own right.

"Everybody loves classic rock from the 1960's," he declared. "This stuff never gets old." He picked her up from the chair, swinging her around in time to the music. As the two of them danced like crazy around the attic, he couldn't help but wonder, *what would I do without her laughter, her company, her love in this afterlife?* The answer, he knew right away. He would be utterly and completely lost.

He now understood how the love between two married people could deepen over time. With each passing day he grew more and more in love with her.

The next song was a slow one by Percy Sledge, "When A Man Loves A Woman." He grabbed her hand, swung her around and then caught her in his arms. He held her close, connecting with her, feeling her warmth.

She makes music play like a symphony in my soul.

Pulling her up against him, he placed his lips on hers in a never-ending kiss. Her tongue played on his, the way a bow might play beautiful music on a violin.

Gently laying her down on the rug, he slowly eased his body over hers, letting the glorious electro-magnetic pull take over.

As he let out a small moan, her eyes met his with such passion he was sure they were going to set the wooden boards of the attic on fire.

He pressed his lips to hers once more, as the boundary between their energies grew perilously thin again.

At that very moment he made up his mind. *We deserve to be happy.*

He wasn't going to stop himself this time.

Until…an unpleasant sensation rolled through his ghostly form.

The atmosphere hung heavy with evil. He was able to sense the foul presence now the way a seasoned farmer might sense a rise in the humidity or barometric pressure.

And he was just as ready for the storm.

Demons. And their close.

Sarah pulled away from him with a frightened look on her face. His thought had been so loud he may as well have shouted it at her.

"I feel it, too," she said, her voice quaking. "This is the first time, but I definitely feel it too."

His body coiled with tension, ready to spring into action. "We have to get out of here. I won't let them come here, not to this place." Over time, he'd become as attached to the Angel of the Sea as Sarah. Truly, he had fallen in love with the old-fashioned bed and breakfast. In his heart and mind the Angel had come to symbolize everything pure, innocent and romantic that was left in this world. It was their home, their sanctuary. He couldn't allow evil to descend upon it. He wouldn't let that happen. Not on his watch.

Grabbing her hand, he flew out of the side of the attic which faced the ocean.

Immediately, they were flanked by a tangle of demons, flying swift and close on their tails.

His spine prickled with cold.

Tongues of ice-fire licked at his back, the evil threatening to seep right into his soul.

There was barely any time to think.

They could head for the wreck of the Atlantus like they had before. It was well past the time for the flag ceremony on Sunset Beach, but he worried people might still be hanging around. Besides, that hadn't gone so well the last time.

So if he couldn't head south, and he couldn't head west into the populated town, that only left one option.

Northward up the coast he sped, hoping the demons would follow so he could draw them away from the Angel.

For better or for worse, they did.

CHAPTER TWENTY-TWO

WILDWOOD

AS THE TWO of them flew over the beach, he snatched a quick glimpse over his shoulder.

What he saw nearly made him tumble out of the sky.

Vassago and at least a half dozen other vampires led a writhing, spinning black horde. Black tendrils of pure evil energy stretched towards them only a few feet away.

Up ahead, the many lights of Wildwood Boardwalk shone like a welcoming beacon in the night. Hopefully, they could find some refuge within its brightly lit amusements.

Like a razor-sharp talon, fear for Sarah clawed at his insides.

"We have to get away from the water," she yelled. "It's slowing us down."

She was right. As fast as he thought they had been flying, they had only flown ten miles and barely reached the beginning of the boardwalk.

Gripping her hand, he banked hard left, and flew low, almost skimming the top of the tram car. Once they flew out over the boards, they picked up speed, zooming past the Convention Center and first pier until they reached the second ride pier.

Vassago and the demons were so close now, the wicked cold pricked like pins at his feet.

We're running out of options.

Making a snap decision, Michael sharply turned the corner onto Mariner's Pier, zipping straight through Jumbo's Grille.

Flying right over the heads of the patrons seated at the tables, they headed out the back of the restaurant. Worse came to worst he might be able to safely deposit Sarah in one of the many towers of the Raging Waters Waterpark at the far end of the ride pier. Hopefully, the demons wouldn't be able to pass over the water to get to her. Then, he could turn and defend their position until he came up with a better plan.

There was only one problem.

In his panic and haste, he had forgotten just how packed the boardwalk would be on Memorial Day weekend. The gorgeous weather earlier in the day had brought tons of tourists out for the official start of summer at the Jersey Shore.

Mariner's Pier now teemed with people.

Sarah held onto his hand tightly, as the two of them wove around and through the kiddie rides, heading toward the high extended incline of the Sea Serpent rollercoaster which stood in the middle of the pier. In the back of his mind, he hoped maybe all the electricity from the lights and equipment might help to somehow confuse the demons, and make it harder for them to track their prey.

A moment later he paused at the funnel cake stand, as his suspicion seemed to be confirmed. Vassago and the swirl of demons flew past them and further out onto the pier. *"Look, they're leaving!"* he exclaimed to her with his mind.

When Sarah didn't say anything, he turned around to see what was wrong.

Instead of being relieved, she nearly doubled-over alongside him. With a glazed-over look in her eyes, she gripped her stomach. "No, Michael...they're not." Absolute terror blanketed her face, as her body began to shake. "They're going to topple the Ferris wheel!"

The demons hovered near the middle of the pier next to the incline of the Sea Serpent Coaster, still at least forty yards away from the Giant Wheel.

How can she know what they'll do next?

He clutched her hand and wrapped an arm around her waist to support her. "Sarah...what makes you say that?"

Her next words came out in strained gasps. "I...I don't know...I can see blurry images...of the aftermath."

She turned her face up to his and the pain reflected in her eyes told him all he needed to know.

You're seeing what will happen.

A whimper of agony escaped her lips, as she gave a somber nod. *I think so.*

At the same moment, they both looked up towards the Ferris wheel which sat at the end of the pier in front of the Raging Waters Waterpark. The vampires and demons were converging on the center joint of the wheel, many of them taking turns passing right through the axle as if threading a needle. It didn't take a mechanical engineer to figure out what they were doing, *they're somehow weakening the metal which is holding the wheel together.*

Only a short distance away, Vassago glanced back at him to acknowledge and answer his thought. *That's right. If you don't surrender, I'll keep killing until you do.*

Michael's gaze strafed over the hanging cars. Each one filled with the souls of the innocent. Aunts and uncles, mothers and fathers, *children*. Dozens and dozens of children. All laughing, smiling, even a few couples kissing. Completely oblivious to the mortal peril they were now in at the hands of the devil's disciples.

Sarah squeezed his arm. Her eyes held an intensity he'd never seen before. "Michael...all those people are going to die. But they're not meant to," she said, shaking her head slowly back and forth. "Not today. Not like this..."

His breath came out in a rush, "How do you know?"

Her expression fogged over as if she were trying to recall a long lost memory. "I can see glimpses of...the lives they're supposed to lead...the things they're supposed to accomplish..." She glanced up at the couple kissing in one of the cars. "The love they're supposed to experience." Her voice shook. "Michael...we *have* to do something." Her tear-filled eyes told him it was both a hopeful statement and a desperate question. "They're telling me this is not the appointed day, not the appointed hour for all these souls to die."

So, she's definitely a Seer...

But there was no time to think about that now.

They had to take action.

He let go of her hand and flew a few feet away. As he headed into the fray, he called over his shoulder, "I'll try to distract the demons. You get the attention of the man

259

operating the Giant Wheel and somehow make him stop the ride!"

"How?" she shouted in exasperation.

That's an excellent question.

"I don't know," he yelled back at her. "Just do it!"

Now hovering near the center hub of the Ferris wheel, he sent blast after blast rocketing into the circle of vampires and demons, all having little affect. Each time one got hit, more slithered forward to take their place. And as he flew this way and that to dodge their shots, he came to one hard and fast conclusion, *this is much more than I can handle on my own.*

Telepathically he called out to his Protector, pleading for his help. "Tom! Tom, we're in big trouble. We need you!" he implored from within his mind, all the while directing blasts of energy at the hideous creatures tangled around the hub of the Ferris wheel.

A fraction of a second later, Tom materialized in mid-air next to him. "I was already on my way," he said quickly, as he fired off a fresh round of shots. In retaliation, one of the crazed vampires flew straight at him.

In a blur, Tom transformed from earthbound spirit to heavenly angel, the white light flowing all around him as he wielded his sword, striking the vampire down with one powerful stroke. The angelic white-fire of the blade sunk into the rabid creature, exploding his ghastly soul from the inside out.

Michael couldn't help but be impressed with the weapon. *I have got to get me one of those.*

Dodging blows and flying left and right, the two of them

fired and slashed at every evil entity in their path, but the onslaught continued.

No matter how many they hit, more demons joined the battle, slithering out from every dark corner of the boardwalk.

Michael took one look at what they were facing, and it was obvious what he had to do. Whether he trusted him or not, it was time to call in that favor. *Matt! Matt!* He cried out with his mind. *We could use some help over here!*

Within minutes, his friend appeared at their side. At the sight of the battle, his eyes went wide. "You rang?" he said with a touch of sarcasm, as he sent a burst of energy soaring towards a nearby demon.

Now that help was here they spread out with a three pronged attack. Tom took on most of the vampires, while Matt took the back of the Ferris wheel near the hub.

Michael elected to take the front so he could keep an eye on Sarah, who was weaving in and out of the crowd below. In his mind he wondered why no one down below could see the vampires? Then it him. The uber-demons obviously had the ability to be ethereal or corporeal at will. *No wonder they're so damned dangerous.*

After a few minutes of the most harrowing fighting he'd ever done in his life, he looked around at the ever-increasing number of demons.

We're getting our asses handed to us, he thought out loud.

From a short distance away, Tom must've heard him. "I think we're going to need even more reinforcements," his mentor shouted. For a moment, Tom closed his eyes, opened his arms and fell backwards, his whole body going limp.

"This is no time for a nap!" Michael cried out in panic.

When Tom opened his eyes again, pinpoints of light surged forth from every sign, every fixture, every light bulb, indeed every energy source around them.

His mouth hung open in shock. The tiny glowing orbs reminded him of a field of summer fireflies coming alive in the darkness.

The streaks of bright light surged into the battle, now fully manifesting as angels. With beams of energy, some of them bombarded the demons, splitting their ranks and pushing them back. Others swung blades of pure white light, directly hitting every demon within their reach.

The sight was so awe-inspiring, he almost couldn't believe his eyes.

As impressive as the heavenly show of force was though, each time they managed to make a dent against the enemy, others only crept out from the darkness to take their place.

Worse yet, their assault on the Ferris wheel's axle had already done its damage.

A distinct whine and groan of bending metal echoed across the ride pier, so loud the sound momentarily drowned out the other music and noise on the boardwalk.

Michael paused in mid-shot.

People on the pier turned their stunned faces toward the ride, wondering what was happening. Suddenly, the Ferris wheel could be heard grinding, the engines straining to move the axle, which was pinned and locked against the vertical support beams.

Upon hearing the sound, the ride operator hit the red

emergency button. With a frightening shudder, the Giant Wheel ground to a halt, jerking the cars in place, the brakes shrieking under the tremendous strain.

With growing dread he realized, *the axle holding the hub has slipped off its anchors.*

He looked over at Sarah, who was standing next to the ride operator. *That shouldn't be enough to topple the wheel though, right?*

In answer to his question, she frantically pointed at the front left side of the ride. "Stop them!" she screamed. "They're going to set it afire!"

As if things couldn't get any worse, Vassago and two other vampires hovered near one of the triangular support beams that held up the Ferris wheel, flames dancing on the ends of their fingertips.

Michael flew straight at them as fast as he could, but Vassago intercepted him with a bolt of evil energy that came hurtling at his feet.

The shot hit its mark, grazing his toes.

For a moment he couldn't move, as a stabbing pain traveled up his legs and into his torso.

Now, with devilish glee etched on their hideous faces, the vampires sent a burst of flame into the boardwalk below the base of the upright, setting the wooden pier ablaze.

"Surrender!" Vassago screamed in a seething voice.

Gritting his teeth against the ice-cold pain in his paralyzed toes, he yelled back, "Never going to happen, you ugly SOB!" Despite his outward defiance, his heart sank. Sarah's second sight had been just a few seconds too late to stop the vampires.

Now, as if there wasn't enough to contend with, engorged blue flames leaping up from the boards told him the fire was already burning with unnatural intensity.

Oh great, just what we don't *need...a funeral pyre.*

Out of complete frustration he sent a blast shooting towards the trio of vampires.

They dispersed, but not before firing off a few bolts of energy that nearly took his head off.

Luckily, the feeling came back in his legs at the same moment, and he ducked and spun away.

Once he recovered his bearings, he flew back into the fray near the hub. Matt was fighting off to his left, while Tom and a few more angels were to his right wildly slashing away at a half dozen vampires.

In between delivering his own bursts of energy, he chanced a glance down below.

At the sight of the fire, all manner of chaos had broken out. People on the left side of the boardwalk now ran from the ungodly heat, screaming for help.

One by one, each of the ride operators closest to the Ferris wheel began an emergency shutdown of their own rides and a wild evacuation of the riders, but it was going to take a few minutes. Complicated mechanical rides like the Spinning Seashells, Riptide Rocking Ship, and Maelstrom couldn't just stop with the flip of a single switch. They took time to slow down, release hydraulic pressure, cycle through the gears, and descend.

But time was ticking against them.

The tremendous heat of the fire was taking its toll. The diagonal front leg of the Ferris wheel frame had already begun to buckle, the boards underneath burning through, ready to give way at any moment.

Which meant one thing.

The entire metal structure was now in danger of imminent, catastrophic failure.

His mind grappled with the awful possibilities.

If the Giant Wheel fell forward, not only would many of its riders die, but the one hundred and fifty foot tall structure would also crush all the other rides and unsuspecting people in its path.

And if that happened, he would forever blame himself for inadvertently leading the demons here.

As the riders on the Ferris wheel now spotted the flames and realized the ride was beginning to tilt, several screams and shouts went up.

"What the hell?"

"What's going on?"

Terrified men, women and children grabbed the sides of the cars, holding on for dear life.

"Help us!" Many of them screamed, now fully in panic.

Some of the people who were able to, started climbing out of the cars closest to the ground, while others higher up and at the top of the wheel urged them to stay put.

"Don't move!" A few of them shouted. "You're shaking the wheel!"

"Stop! You'll make it worse!"

As Michael traded rapid bursts of energy with one of the demons, he couldn't help but think, *I'm not really sure how things could get too much worse.*

Everywhere he looked angels and demons exchanged

blows with swords of fire and ice, the clash of good and evil energies reverberating through the air.

In the sky above, their fighting seemed to be whipping up a thunderstorm from out of nowhere. Thunder rumbled in the distance and a bolt of lightning flashed, spidering its way across the night sky.

Here and there, some of the colored lights on the spokes of the Giant Wheel flickered ominously from the intermittent surges of energy.

After firing off several more shots, he looked down again at the boardwalk below, hoping and praying the people were getting out of the way, but to his dismay the natural inertia of the crowd had caused a bottleneck on the pier.

Now fully grasping the danger many of the people further out on the pier who had merely been curious at the Giant Wheel's sudden stop started to yell for help, gesturing frantically toward the ride. Others close by who had loved ones on the Ferris wheel, stood paralyzed in fear.

All of them had only a handful of seconds, maybe minutes, to run.

To make matters worse, the people near the kiddie rides at the front of the pier weren't moving fast enough. But it wasn't their fault—it took time to stop dozens of rides and get hundreds of little ones safely off and loaded into strollers. They also couldn't see the fire at the back of the pier, so they had no idea what was going on.

Meanwhile, the crowd coming from the Ferris wheel area urgently pushed forward to evacuate, but the people with small children and strollers had blocked their escape like a human logjam.

Amid the chaos, the police, fire, and emergency personnel were desperately fighting to go in the opposite direction and get onto the pier, but the crowd wouldn't budge.

In sheer panic, he shouted to Sarah down below and pointed toward the kiddie rides. "Talk to the people at the front! Get them to move faster!"

Immediately, she darted off to the entrance of the pier, weaving her way through the crowd, whispering into the minds of the men and women to instill some urgency.

After a few moments, it appeared to be helping, but only a little.

Everyone on the Ferris wheel and down below was watching as the catastrophe unfolded, but they were blind to the true drama taking place directly over their heads—the forces of heaven and hell locked in an aerial battle for the fate of so many souls.

All of a sudden, Sarah flew back towards him with a wide-eyed look of pure terror.

But she was a split second too late to warn him of the next vision she must have seen.

With an enormous cracking sound, the front left brace holding the Ferris wheel collapsed into the burning boardwalk.

For one gut-wrenching moment, the Giant Wheel swayed precariously in the air, its metal frame groaning and bending ominously.

Then it started to fall.

Blood-curdling screams filled the air as the Ferris wheel swung forward. Riders grabbed onto anything they could so they wouldn't be catapulted from their cars.

Lights bursting, metal crunching, rivets popping, the wheel plummeted towards the first ride in its path, a thin elevated track for an aerial ride called the Flying Galleons, a set of hanging cars that resembled pirate ships.

He froze, praying the track might be enough to stop the wheel's descent.

But the weight of the Giant Wheel proved to be too much for the thin track, snapping the metal like a toothpick. The track crashed down, crushing the pirate ships which thankfully were now empty.

As the wheel continued its fall towards the Sea Serpent ride, the vampires sent up a blast that acted something like an EMP burst, tossing angels aside as if they were nothing more than common house flies. The sinister beings obviously wanted nothing to get in the way of the death and destruction that was to come.

The heavenly forces came back stronger than ever though, linking their arms together and pushing upward beneath the Ferris wheel with an enormous parabola of pure white light.

It was the most wondrous sight he'd ever witnessed.

Good is winning.

The angels were managing to slow the Ferris wheel's fall for a few extra seconds, buying the riders on board precious time, ensuring there would be as few victims as possible.

With a deafening roar of metal hitting metal, the top rim of the Ferris wheel slammed into the top of the Sea Serpent's incline track, the wheel crashing with such force that the boardwalk shuddered as if from an earthquake.

A few poor souls fell from their cars.

For one brief second, the forces of heaven and hell seemed to hold their collective breath.

When they realized the Ferris wheel had come to a final rest on top of the Sea Serpent's incline and wasn't going to fall any further, a collective cheer rose up from among the angels fighting.

Now defeated, the legion of vampires and demons began to shrink back away from the battle.

Cars still hung precariously threatening to break free, but at least the worst of the fall was now over.

Yes! Yes! Michael punched at the air over and over. *Damn, it feels good to be on a winning team again.*

His jubilation was short-lived though, as his eyes struck upon a horrifying sight.

A young girl about eight or nine years old dangled from one of the top cars on the right side of the wheel. Clinging to the swung open door, legs kicking, face contorted in abject terror.

He only had maybe three or four seconds tops to save the little girl.

As he launched himself toward her, he realized he would have to will himself to be as solid as possible, otherwise she was going to slip right through his grasp.

"Michael, don't!" Tom screamed from below. "You must leave her alone! You're not supposed to interfere!"

He ignored him completely, speeding ever faster toward the top of the Ferris wheel, concentrating instead on willing himself to be solid enough to catch her.

Before he could reach her, the girl lost her grip.

Horrorstruck as she plummeted thirteen stories towards

the boardwalk, he dove back around in a hairpin arc.

Praying for all he was worth, he swooped beneath her not a second too soon.

She fell with a solid thud into his outstretched arms, right before his feet touched down on the boards.

Heaving a sigh of relief, he set the stunned girl down on a red bench behind a refreshment stand. "You're going to be okay now," he said to her.

With her mouth still hanging open, the girl merely nodded.

He smiled. The crowd had already moved away, but just in case anyone had seen what happened, he decided he better disappear again, so he allowed himself to fade from sight.

The fire department and other first responders had finally made it to the back of the pier and were now further evacuating the crowd, rescuing passengers and putting out the fire.

So that's what it feels like to be Superman. He couldn't help but be fairly proud of himself for making such a spectacular catch. Part of him wondered if Sarah had seen it.

He looked around, but she was nowhere in sight. Now that all of the demons and most of the angels had retreated, he easily found Tom near the bottom of the Sea Serpent.

"Where's Sarah?" he asked.

Tom pointed across the beach toward the middle of the Surfside Pier to a shrinking black mass. "I'm so sorry, Michael. They took her while you were saving the girl."

CHAPTER TWENTY-THREE

GATEWAY

PANIC-STRICKEN, MICHAEL launched himself into the air again.

Sword still drawn, Tom flew upwards getting directly in his path. "No, Michael! Don't!" he implored, thrusting his blade in front of him. "They want you to follow! It's a trap!"

He now lunged straight at him, raising his hands as if to strike. "I know! And I also don't care!" He screamed ferociously. "Make one more move to stop me and I swear to God, I'll blow a hole right through you!"

This was no idle threat either. He meant every word.

"Fine," Tom said in stern, yet sympathetic voice, "but remember…we *can't* help you once you willingly cross over to the other side. You'll be on your own."

Of course he fully realized, *this is probably what they want*.

Still, he had no choice. Even if it meant battling the devil himself, he had to save Sarah.

Matt now joined them, hovering above the boardwalk with a look of concern. "Be careful," he said. "I've been in that place, and it's no picnic. It's a dark mirror of this world, reflecting all your pain and all your fears. And the demons are everywhere. They'll try to mess with your head."

"I'll take it under advisement," he answered him with annoyance. *The thought of her in that awful place is only making me feel ten times worse.*

Not wanting to waste another second of precious time, he left them behind, propelling himself over the beach and toward the next pier, the last one on Wildwood Boardwalk.

With a few minutes head start, the swirling vortex of demons had already reached the Surfside Pier.

He was just in time to see them descend and disappear into the gaping mouth of one of the amusement rides—the winged devil of Dante's Dungeon.

You've got to be kidding me. How freakin' perfect. No wonder Sarah got a sickening feeling when she walked by the outside of the ride the last time. She had probably sensed something like this might happen, or seen flashes of what lie ahead.

But no matter what that was...all he could think about was rescuing her. What would he have to do to get her back? Make a deal with the devil?

Well, if it came to that...he wasn't going to rule it out.

Gathering every last scrap of his courage, he followed the demons through the swirling black portal.

Before him, an endless tunnel of primeval darkness stretched all around him. The unfathomable despair and torment of the place palpable, overwhelming.

Nightmare sounds in the distance left little doubt.

Every fiber of his being told him he was standing at some threshold of hell.

If he hadn't already been dead, he would've been scared to death.

With the darkness so vast, so complete, he was totally blind. He stepped forward but had the feeling he had gone no further. He ran forward but felt no satisfaction that he had made any headway. He flew forward this time, but with the same effect. He tried the same thing, this time in what he thought were different directions, only to realize he had lost any sense of direction.

Now, he stood stock still, reaching out with the fabric of his soul and all his senses, but the only feeling that returned to him was a deep, mind-numbing void. An oppressive loneliness hung all about him.

A sickness began to permeate every inch of his skin.

Cold, he was so cold.

He shivered as much from the frigid temperature as he did from the fear, but one unwavering thought propelled him forward, deeper and deeper into the darkness, *I have to get Sarah back.*

Suddenly, a distorted inhuman scream emanated from the never-ending blackness, like the shrill feedback from a microphone. He covered his ears against the piercing sound though he somehow knew it wouldn't do any good. The scream reverberated straight through the consciousness of his soul.

They knew he was here.

And they were coming for him.

He remembered that night he had been crossing through the Pine Barrens and had grown afraid of the malevolent murmuring in the dark. Now he knew why.

Demons didn't just dwell in the darkness. They *were* the darkness.

And they were all around him now in this black landscape, closing in. He could sense them, hear them, almost feel them, they were so close. An ever-tightening thread of tension wound its way up his spine.

The next minute, dozens, no…hundreds of fingers and hands were touching him, clawing at his very soul…the icy pain crippling.

His fear mounted, until he was sure he was going to scream, until he was sure his mind was teetering on the brink of insanity, but then he remembered something Tom had said to him, *you are a light in the darkness, that is why you are more well-defined there.*

He only prayed it was true.

There was no outward source of energy to draw from, so he closed his eyes and drew from deep within. When he opened his eyes again, shaking with relief he saw it had worked. The demons had slithered back to whatever corner of hell they had come from. He had banished the worst of the darkness…for the moment.

And though it was still quite dark, he could at least see *something.*

As he ghosted through a metal entrance gate, he was surprised to find he was right back where he had started—in front of Dante's Dungeon on the Surfside Pier, except everything was cast in shadow. All of the restaurants, shops and stands were open, but abandoned. None of the rides were running. Nothing was lit up. The place was deserted. As if someone had simply whisked away the crowds and turned off all the electricity. It reminded him of what the boardwalk must look like after hours.

Only worse.

Glancing over the side of the pier at what should be the ocean, even that didn't look right. The water was as murky as an obsidian slab and frightfully stagnant. No motion or waves at all.

He couldn't help but notice something else, too. Normally, there was always at least a slight breeze coming off the ocean. Here, not a single flag or fake palm tree moved. The air was dead. No wind, no breath, no life.

Instead, the atmosphere was thick with a wickedness, so foul, so vile, he feared it might infect his soul at any moment.

Matt was right. *I must be on some different plane of existence.*

It was as if he were looking into a mirror at a dark reflection of the real world. As if he had walked into some hellish nightmare version of the boardwalk he knew and loved.

But the creepiest part?

It was quiet.

Deathly quiet.

Except for the murmuring. Or was it moaning? He couldn't be sure.

A short distance away, he saw the first one. A small, young woman. Shuffling haphazardly in his general direction.

Behind him, he saw another. An older, bald man.

A tremor of fear moved through him again, as more and more of them now came into view, shuffling and moaning, shuffling and moaning.

They didn't speak, but they also didn't have to. He could sense their pain, anguish, and loneliness from halfway across the boardwalk.

As they got closer, he understood why they couldn't speak.

Their mouths were completely missing.

Even more disturbing, jagged scars covered their eyes, as if they'd been gouged out and then left to heal over.

Whatever atrocities these souls had committed to bring them to this God-forsaken place, he could hardly imagine. The regret spilled and flowed out of them, a spigot that would never shut off.

He moved to avoid them and stay at a safe distance, but a few strayed too close and somehow he now sensed their crimes and evil deeds. These sightless creatures with no eyes and no mouths, moaning and shuffling aimlessly in the darkness were among the worst of the worst—murderers, rapists, child-killers, drug pushers.

The Damned.

So deep was their despair, it started to seep into his soul.

He fought to keep it at bay.

Was this purgatory for all these souls while they awaited judgment? Would they be forgiven, or condemned to some final version of hell?

As he walked further toward the front of the pier in an effort to evade the mutilated creatures, a flicker of movement caught his eye. One of the rides was in motion…but only one.

And he found this to be the creepiest, most unnerving of all, though he didn't quite know why.

Eliciting no sound, the double-tiered carousel was slowly rotating backward…inch…by inch…by inch…

Mesmerized watching the painted horses, Vassago's sudden appearance in front of the ride caught him completely off guard.

Immediately he thrust up his hands, preparing for a fight.

"Tsk, tsk, tsk," the vampire mocked. "Such violence from a child of God." The uber-demon choked on that last word as if it felt vile on his tongue. "All I want to do is talk. Matt said you would come to me and he was right."

A phantom breath hitched in his throat. *Matt?*

His eyes went wide as fog lamps, as Matt slowly stepped out of a darkened corner near the ticket booth with a shameless smirk plastered on his ugly face. Yellow and sickly, his skin had already begun to pull tight over his skull and pucker with sores.

"*You?*" he said, incredulous. "After everything you've seen? Even after Emily went into the light? You chose to go back to this side?"

A slimy grin crept across Matt's face. "What makes you think I ever left?"

The revelation rocked him. He shook his head back and forth, refusing to believe it. Could he and Tom have been so easily fooled?

Matt chuckled at his reaction. "I have to admit, you almost had me convinced I might be forgiven," he said, taking a few steps closer to him. "But once I saw Emily go into the light without me, I knew I'd never be invited."

"That's ridiculous," he shot back. "You've had every

chance to make amends. You're not evil! You were helping us fight!"

"Oh, but I am," Matt replied, shaking his head up and down. "The rest was only a show for your Protector until we could lure you here." His eyes danced with excitement. "The truth is, when you read my mind, you didn't see everything about me. There was a side of me even my dear sister, Emily, never knew." He smiled a sick, twisted smile that made Michael's skin crawl. "Let's just say when I got drunk I liked to have my fun."

The next moment, the demon's memories invaded his head. Against his will, horrifying emotions and scenes assaulted his consciousness.

Matt luring young girls back to his apartment.

Girls he raped.

Girls he tortured.

Girls he buried.

With a painful and monumental effort, Michael finally expelled Matt from his mind. He shook his head, trying to dispel the gruesome images that had flashed before his eyes, but there was no way to un-see them.

Matt seemed to be enjoying his revulsion, as he sauntered over to stand beside Vassago. "Finally convinced I might be evil?" he said, laughing.

Vassago joined in with his own sickening chorus of shrill laughter.

"You unimaginable bastards!" Blind with rage, Michael sent powerful bursts of energy rocketing towards the two of them.

With one flick of his hand, Matt knocked both blasts

away and continued talking as if nothing had happened. "Yeah, so that's why I figured I better stop fighting the inevitable, and make the most of out of a bad situation." An even nastier grin snaked its way across his face. "Declare my allegiance, and help them capture you. Besides, the afterlife won't be so bad," he said, turning to look toward the carousel, "I've been promised a few *perks*."

As the ride slowly spun backwards a few more inches, Michael's ghostly heart seized in his chest.

Sarah writhed on the floor of the carousel, tied with thick coils of energy to one of the horses on the top tier.

The excruciating pain in her face nearly shredded his soul to pieces.

"You see, I told them you would be a tough nut to crack." Matt cocked his head to the side and shrugged. "Without the proper leverage, there was just no way you'd willingly give yourself to Lucifer."

Maddened fury took over. One after another, after another, he shot blast after blast, first at Matt, then at Vassago.

Unfortunately, they deflected each of the blows as fast as he fired them off.

"Such confidence!" the vampire hissed with sickening admiration. "So, you finally know what you are."

Out of energy for a moment, pure rage pulsed through him. "Yeah, a Warrior angel," he shot back proudly, though his soul was filled with such vehemence right now he doubted there was any room left for any sort of angelic goodness.

"Not exactly," Vassago corrected. "You haven't been fully claimed by either side yet. So this could go either way," he said with a shit-eating grin on his disgusting face. "Join us and we can put all that magnificent power to good use."

A split-second later the vampire disappeared, only to reappear on the top tier of the carousel next to Sarah, a ball of green light spinning on the ends of his clawed fingertips.

Game over.

Throwing his hands up in the air in a gesture of surrender, he shouted, "Take me! Let her go and take me!"

Vassago flew down from the carousel to stand in front of him, ready to fulfill his wish and complete the bargain. "That's more like it," he said, triumphant. "Now, *kneel.*"

Biting the side of his cheek, he reluctantly started to take a knee…

"No, Michael! Don't!" Sarah screamed through the pain. "That's what they want! Don't think of me! Think of what you *are*. Think of how *important* you are! Believe in yourself." Her eyes wild with panic, she yelled, "Believe in *us!*"

Believe in us. Her words hit him with all the force of a meteor from the heavens—why hadn't he seen it before?

Plain and simple, if he submitted and pledged his allegiance to Lucifer, he would never see his beloved Sarah again.

When he thought of it that way, his choice became as obvious as the morning sunrise.

I shouldn't give in. I should fight with every last fiber of my soul.

Besides, he knew this woman better than he knew his own basketball shoe size. *She's telegraphing me the outcome.*

The only thing he had to do was believe her.

Tom's words now echoed in his head, *you have the power to create light in the darkest of places.*

All of a sudden a deep, yet indistinct voice cried out to him from beyond the darkness, "Draw your sword!"

Michael had no idea what he was doing. He didn't know if it would work or not, but some primal instinct took over, rising up within him.

Using all of his strength, he jumped to his feet and slammed his arms together.

With a thunderous crack that reverberated through the air, a long sword of light appeared in his right hand. The enormous, broad blade was more than half the size of his body, glowing and flowing like a giant tesla coil.

He held the sword aloft and pure energy unlike anything he had ever felt surged through him, making him feel stronger, more powerful than anything he could have ever imagined. He shook under the force of it, but held steady.

For a split second he stared at what he held and then realized…Vassago had drawn a similar weapon.

With a mighty reckless hand, he swung.

Not at the vampire, but at Matt, slicing him in two from shoulder to torso with one bold stroke. A last look of shock blanketed the demon's face, as his evil soul disintegrated into tiny flecks of ash before vanishing into the air.

Swift and final.

Vassago now let out an unholy scream, lunging for him.

As Michael spun around their two blades met, clashing with a shower of sparks and flicks of flame. He had no idea where the ability to wield a sword had come from since he'd never even seen a fencing match, but he sure as hell wasn't going to question it now.

With all the strength he could muster, he aggressively thrust at the vampire, only to be blocked with a vicious blow that nearly knocked his sword from his hand. He counter-hit with a brutal attack of his own, forcing Vassago to take several steps backward toward the carousel.

Back and forth they violently parried, neither one gaining the upper hand.

Until his weapon struck Vassago on the forearm, slicing into his thick and hairy skin, but only deep enough to leave a scorched scratch and really piss him off.

"You're going to have to do better than that," the hideous uber-demon hissed, raising his hand in a circular motion as if manipulating the wind.

Suddenly rising from out of the darkness, dozens of demons formed a circle around them, closing in on all sides.

Michael's gaze darted from left to right, assessing the growing threat.

Only one plan came to mind. Trash talking on the basketball court had always thrown his opponents off their game. Maybe it would work here. Anything was worth a try. He didn't have too many other ideas. "What's the matter? Can't fight me by yourself, you weak piece of shit?"

Enraged and eyes bulging, Vassago lost control, wildly flying at him with his teeth bared.

Their blades now locked against one another, as they grappled to throw each other off balance.

Careful to avert his eyes, Michael suddenly thrust his sword up toward the vampire's face.

The blade connected, tearing through his demon flesh. Vassago let out a blood-curdling scream, clutching his face as he spun away.

But it didn't take long for the rest of his minions to pounce.

Michael now took the advantage, swinging his sword in front of him like a mad man. Connecting with any demon in his path, a renewed strength surged within him.

Yes, he was the one battling the demons. But a powerful force was battling right alongside him. He could feel his power increasing exponentially with each successive strike.

He still held control of the sword but someone or something was helping guide the blade and every one of his blows. The unseen force coursed through his body—a strength, a potency, a fierceness such as he had never known.

He gave in to it, not wanting to get in its way.

He was going to have to trust it if he wanted to save Sarah.

As he doled out some much-deserved payback to the demonic creatures, a momentary flash of light in his periphery caught his attention. The soft glow of the Ferris wheel shining off in the distance on Mariner's Pier. On this side of the veil, the ride was still upright.

His phantom pulse kicked into overdrive, *it's a sign.*

Like a beacon beckoning them toward a safe harbor, someone was showing them the way out.

He knew it with every thread of his blessed soul.

If they could get to the light, they could cross back over to the other side.

Again some heavenly instinct took over, and he raised his

sword in front of him, directing the energy outward to all four corners of the boardwalk.

The writhing tangle of demons viciously wavered and twisted like a bucking bronco against the energy he poured into it. They shrank back far enough to give him some room to maneuver.

With not a second to spare, he took flight to the top tier of the carousel, slashing through Sarah's bonds with one swift but precise motion. He grabbed her around her waist, weak as she was, and zoomed for all he was worth toward the distant light on Mariner's Pier.

"I knew you could do it," she gasped in a strained voice.

"Hang on," he said, pulling her tighter. As good as it felt to have her back in his arms, they weren't quite out of this yet.

He shot a quick glance behind them.

With a murderous look on his disfigured face, Vassago led a swarm of demons in a tight formation.

As Michael turned back around, he realized they had reached the edge of the pier.

His phantom pulse raced. Sure enough, up ahead a swirling fissure had opened at the base of the Ferris wheel.

The way out.

But the demons were so close now.

Raw terror fractured through him, as an ice-cold pain spiked up his legs. *We're not going to make it!* He cried out to Sarah with his mind.

"Yes we are!" she screamed back.

Clutching her with a vice-like grip and praying as if their souls depended on it, he dove for the exit to the gateway.

Once again, the darkness swallowed them.

The last sounds he heard were the angry shrieks and screams of the demons, as one side of the gateway suddenly closed in upon itself, sealing shut.

As he and Sarah emerged from the blackness of the tunnel and back onto Mariner's Pier, they both collapsed onto a nearby bench. Numb and drained of energy, he wrapped her in his arms and cradled her as she softly wept.

Mysteriously, his sword had disappeared.

With every fiber of his soul he now thanked the heavens for letting him have the weapon while he needed it, and for having led them both out of that place of never-ending darkness and despair.

Only a few feet away, a news crew, one of several, was beginning an early morning broadcast near the remains of the Giant Wheel.

"Good morning," the young female reporter said in a serious tone. "Some are saying that a miracle occurred on Mariner's Pier in Wildwood last night as hundreds of people were saved when the Ferris wheel toppled, but seemed to have almost been caught and held upright by the highest track of the Sea Serpent ride which stands several hundred feet in front of the Giant Wheel. Many riders clung to their cars in terror for hours until first responders could safely reach them." As the cameraman panned over, the reporter gestured to the Giant Wheel teetering on the edge of the track behind her. "Surprisingly, only three people were injured as a result of the Giant Wheel falling and I'm told one of them remains hospitalized this morning. Authorities are just beginning their investigation into the cause of the ride's fire and collapse."

Again, the cameraman swiveled around to show the investigators photographing and surveying the damage.

"Eyewitness accounts differ greatly as to what happened here last night," the reporter continued, "with many saying the trouble began when they saw flames at the base of the Giant Wheel, while others remain adamant that the ride suffered some type of equipment malfunction before the fire even broke out. Investigators are pointing to a possible lightning strike as a cause of the malfunction and fire, and they're not ruling out the possibility that a direct strike to the Ferris wheel may have occurred. Lightning can strike so quickly and from such a great distance that it can often go unseen by the naked eye."

"Authorities from both the NOAA and the National Weather Service reported unusual electrical surges in the area last night and speculate that a fast moving lightning strike may have directly hit the center axle of the Ferris wheel. Instead of going to ground as it's supposed to do, the lightning may have caused the fire near the bottom of the ride's uprights, causing the support to fail," she said, gesturing to the still smoldering boardwalk.

"The only thing we know for certain is that we're hearing many tales of heroism by fire fighters and other first responders who helped rescue the stranded ride passengers. We'll be bringing you some of their stories during our noon broadcast. Eyewitnesses are telling us all kinds of incredible tales of bravery. One man even claims to have seen a child fall from the Ferris wheel only to be caught by a stranger on the boardwalk. That man, Anthony Sardoni of Hoboken joins me now."

The eager reporter stuck the microphone in front of the young man's face. "Anthony, tell our viewers what you saw."

"All I know is I saw this girl, about nine or ten years old," he said in a thick North Jersey accent, "fall from the car that was hanging way high up near the top of the Ferris wheel," he said wide-eyed and pointing, "and a young guy standing on the boardwalk jumped up and caught her in his arms. Never saw anything like that in my life."

The TV journalist turned back to speak directly to the camera. "And that little girl's name is Mia Rodriguez. Authorities are having trouble finding the girl's rescuer though. Mia was so shaken up she apparently can't remember very many details about the man who caught her." The young reporter placed the microphone under her witness' chin again. "Mr. Sardoni, can you describe him to us?"

"Nah, you know...I can't," Sardoni said, slightly shaking his head as if trying to jar a memory. "The police asked me the same question, but I guess it all happened so fast...I never really got a good look at the guy or somethin'," he mumbled, as if struggling to make sense of his own thoughts. "And that's the weirdest thing of all. Next thing I know, I blinked and there's the girl standing there all by herself. The guy who caught her was nowhere around. I know it sounds crazy, but I swear to God...it was as if he just up and disappeared."

The young reporter addressed the camera and her audience once more. "Well, there you have it folks, guardian angels intervening to avert disaster on Wildwood

Boardwalk," she said with a light touch of sarcasm. "More on this story after the break."

Even though they didn't have an ounce of energy left, he and Sarah took one look at each other, and smiled with pride.

CHAPTER TWENTY-FOUR

JOINING

WHEN THEY GOT back to the Angel, Sarah was still shaken up from their ordeal. Drained of energy, they spent the better part of the day, resting side by side on the bed up in Room 27.

Little by little, they shared with each other all that had happened and all they had seen while they were in that terrible place of darkness.

As she lay in his arms, she buried her face in his chest and wept. "How much worse is it going to get?" she said through tiny sobs. "What else are we going to have to go through?"

"Shhh, shhh, it's okay," he said, stroking her hair. With one finger he lifted her face to his.

Much to his delight, her eyes were large green emeralds, speaking directly to his soul in a secret language only understood by lovers.

Brushing away her spectral tears, he slowly traced his thumb over her lips. When they both couldn't stand being apart another second, he kissed her, his lips moving hungrily over hers.

She sighed into his mouth, as he felt the tension ease out of her. In between kisses, his hands roamed over her body, touching, teasing, loving her.

Now, his body found hers as quickly and perfectly as steel would find a magnet.

He pulled away for only a second to gaze into her eyes. "I want you, Sarah," he whispered, savoring the heat of her aura. "I'm tired of playing by the rules." He kissed her again, this time skimming her neck and the top of her breast.

Her body arched toward him, as she let out a small moan in answer.

"Hang the rules. I'm not going to wait another minute," he said giving an involuntary moan of his own as he brought his mouth down upon hers once more.

As he cupped her breast she cried out, "Michael... please...don't stop."

Easing on top of her, the magnetic pull of their energies was stronger than ever. Stronger than he could have imagined. Stronger than he could control. It was like trying to keep two powerful electromagnets apart.

With a twinge of fear and a flood of exhilaration he realized he was slipping...

Slipping...

Slipping...

Rings of brilliant light and extraordinary energy swirled around them.

He was totally unprepared for the intensity, for the heat. Now, he was practically burning up in passion's flame. Nothing had ever felt quite like this.

This was much more than a flesh-filled fantasy. This was pleasure, this was abundance, this was everlasting love. Meta-physical and mind-blowing, as goodness and love enveloped them both.

The friction, heat and bliss built to a crescendo.

All at once, their souls became one. He slid into her and she melted into him.

As their souls blissfully intertwined, she screamed out his name.

He thought of the lyrics of an age old song, *you take me straight to heaven*. Those words hadn't been so far off from the truth.

If this is the closest to heaven that I'll ever be, then I'm fine with that.

He'd been with a woman while he was alive, but that was nothing compared to this. This went far beyond anything he'd ever experienced.

Sex sure as hell never felt this *good.*

Just when he thought he couldn't take the climax a minute longer, he sensed the magnetic flux releasing them.

Holy crap, he thought, as they both flopped back down on the bed.

It took them both several minutes to recover.

Breathless, Sarah reached out to entangle her fingers with his. *I love you*, she said with her mind and her soul.

I love you more.

Now, he finally understood why the joining was forbidden.

Because once it was over, the relentless craving began.

CHAPTER TWENTY-FIVE

CATALYST

MICHAEL SAT ON the porch at the Angel of the Sea, gazing out at the ocean as the sun set and reflecting on all that had happened over the last few months. To say it had been an emotional whirlwind would've been the understatement of the millennia.

His brother had been discharged from the hospital some time ago, but it took him a while to gather the courage to see how his family was doing. Finally, Sarah convinced him not to wait any longer.

"Are you ready?" she said, extending her hand.

He nodded. "Yeah, let's go."

Holding onto her tightly, he drafted to his house on Fieldpoint Drive, touching down on the driveway.

He took a deep breath, preparing himself for what he might see, and trying to keep his expectations in check.

Then, a flare of hope lit within him. He pointed to the front porch. "That banister was broken last time I was here...and it looks like someone fixed it."

Sarah turned her sympathetic eyes to him. "Maybe that's a good sign."

As they drifted through the front door, his gaze swept

around the living room. He almost couldn't believe how much the house had changed.

He squeezed Sarah's hand, as his ghostly heart threatened to explode with joy.

It was as if a miracle had occurred and restored his house back to the way it had always been. His mother had cleaned up everything, nothing was lying around, everything was in its place, exactly as it had always been.

With a few remarkable additions.

On the mantle, sat a bunch of new family pictures in wooden frames. One of his dad, smiling behind the barbecue grill on Fourth of July a few years ago. One of him, holding his championship trophy. And one of the four of them on a family vacation at the Jersey Shore.

As he reached out to touch one of the pictures, he became aware of a familiar sound. He glided out into the hallway near the stairs. Sure enough, the grandfather clock was actually ticking, the pendulum beneath swinging back and forth in a comforting rhythm.

They're moving forward, minute by minute, one step at a time.

The rhythmic pulse of his family had started again. They were on the road to recovery. He could tangibly feel it in his bones. The dark energy that had fallen over the house had lifted, replaced by the warmth, comfort, and happiness he'd known and cherished as a child.

He almost cried.

Then, he heard the best sound of all. His mother's and brother's voices coming from the other room. *They're speaking to one another again.*

As they floated into the kitchen, he heard his mother say, "I talked to the lawyer on my lunch hour again today. He told me as long as you finish the community service and the court appointed out-patient rehab on time, and have no other trouble in the next year, he should definitely be able to get the charges expunged since this was your first offense."

"That's awesome," Chris responded. "Thanks for talking to him, Mom."

His mother stirred a pot on the stove. "I also called Principal McClure."

"And what did he say?" his brother asked, looking anxious.

"He said you would need to complete APEX over the summer and finish up the classes that are incomplete right now, but then after that you should be on track to graduate on time next year," she said with a broad smile.

Chris breathed a huge sigh of relief. "Thanks for all your help, Mom."

"You're welcome," she said sweetly. "But that means now we have to get caught up with your college search. Junior year's almost over." She paused for a long moment. Michael could sense she was struggling with the best way to breach the subject, since focusing on baseball was no longer an option for him. "Have you given any thought about what you might want to major in?"

He held his breath waiting for his brother's answer.

"I've been thinking a lot about going into physical therapy or maybe sports management," Chris replied in a hopeful tone, which made Michael's heart soar with pride.

So instead of being bitter, he's going to make lemonade

out of lemons. He couldn't have been more pleased or more proud.

Now, he took a good long look at his mother. She looked so much healthier, he guessed she must be going to AA to help with the drinking.

Sarah squeezed his hand, saying to him in her mind, *maybe the spirits at the Cocoanut Grove were right after all. It may be difficult to see at the time, but eventually good truly does come out of bad.*

She was right. He saw it plainly now. His brother getting shot had been the catalyst for his mother and brother's reconciliation and recovery.

It's possible it wouldn't have happened any other way.

. . .

Later that evening, he and Tom meandered along the beach in the Outerbanks. He still preferred meeting his mentor here, for reasons he couldn't quite understand. Maybe it was because it was the first place they'd met. Maybe it was because the Outerbanks had meant so much to him when he was alive. Or, maybe he just liked sticking with a tradition. Whatever it was, he certainly didn't mind the breath-taking coastline, especially right before sunrise.

He hadn't seen his mentor since the night the demon's attacked the Ferris wheel in Wildwood and he had to rescue Sarah from that terrifying portal of hell. Now, they strolled over the sand, discussing all that had happened.

Michael shook his head. "I still can't believe Matt managed to fool us both like that."

Tom turned to stare at him with wide eyes, as if insinuating he was too naive. "That's what demons do, Michael. And they're good at it," he said, sounding remorseful. "But I have to take part of the blame. I had a hunch there was something off about him, but I never acted upon it."

Something else now struck him that he hadn't given much thought to before. "So, it must've been Matt who hit Sarah that night on Diamond Beach."

"I guess so," Tom mumbled under his breath.

They both fell silent for a moment, lost in the sound of the ocean waves and their own thoughts.

Finally, Michael said, "My ability to wield a sword sure came in handy in the nick of time."

"You've always had the power my dear," Tom said in a high falsetto voice, "you just had to learn it for yourself."

"Really? Is that who you think you are now?" he said jokingly. "Glinda, the good witch of the North?"

Tom laughed, but then his expression turned much more serious. "You know...we have to talk about something. You didn't obey me when I told you not to move at the casino, or when I tried to stop you from intervening in your brother's shooting, or about not saving that little girl who fell from the Ferris wheel," he said sternly, counting each incident off on his fingers for emphasis.

Michael sighed. "I don't mean to be difficult. But I don't understand why I can't make my own decisions. It's just so frustrating. *I* used to be in control of my life. Now all these things are happening to me that are beyond my control," he replied with an angry edge to his voice.

Tom stopped and faced him. "Were you in complete control of your life? Or did you only think you were?" He folded his arms, giving him that all-too-familiar knowing look. "Have you learned nothing from the ghosts at the Cocoanut Grove, or from your mother and brother's situation?"

In equal parts, he had come to both respect and loathe his mentor's preaching. "Okay, okay...I get it," he conceded. "Good can come out of bad. My brother getting shot was a catalyst for change."

"Well, that's a start," Tom said, unfolding his arms. "Listen, I want you to do something for me, Michael. I want you to take a look at the living people around you. If they had a crystal ball and could see even just five years ahead into the future, they wouldn't recognize their life or anyone else's. There would be acquaintances made, marriages bound, births announced, deaths grieved, divorces finalized, fortunes won and lost."

"So what are you trying to say?"

"Life is a complicated business," Tom said in a meaningful way. "I want you to think about that."

"I know," he said with a tang of bitterness on his tongue, "but I still feel bad that my brother will never play baseball again. He'll never be the pitcher he was meant to be."

Tom leveled his gaze on him once more. "Have you considered the possibility that maybe it *wasn't* meant to be?"

He fell silent again, as he let the implications of Tom's question sink in.

After a few minutes, his mentor finally said, "Look, the past is the past. What's happened to Chris can't be undone.

Your brother will have to learn to let it go." He pointed a stiff and purposeful finger at him. "And so will you."

Tom's words struck him like a sucker punch to the bread box. "That's not going to be so easy," he admitted.

"I'm sure," Tom said with a slight nod. "But remember what I told you about regret, Michael. The past is like a broken mirror. You can only see fragments. Fragments that will never be whole again. The only way to truly move forward is by looking to the future where the reflection is not yet broken."

The future.

His future certainly had changed.

He thought his death had destroyed his life, yet here he was reborn as an angel with a new direction, and a new profound purpose.

Still, he couldn't help but wonder what the future held for him and Sarah.

Tom must've overheard his thought because he now said in a slightly annoyed way, "Like I've told you before, Michael. Have patience."

"Patience isn't easy for me," he shot back.

Tom heaved a sigh, showing his own impatience. "Remember," he said, looking down his nose at him, "no one is begrudging you a little impatience. Just be careful that you do the right things and make the right choices while you're waiting."

CHAPTER TWENTY-SIX

REPRIMANDED

THE LAST FEW days had been quiet and peaceful. It was a welcome change from everything they had been through the past few weeks. As he sat on one side of the porch at the Angel of the Sea watching the sky turn a perfect shade of sapphire, he couldn't help but feel incredibly grateful.

From across the way, he lounged with his gaze fixed on Sarah.

He loved her so deeply, he now knew what it meant to truly cherish someone.

She had no idea his eyes were on her, because she was busy reading over the shoulder of a guest who had her nose in a romance novel.

After a few minutes, she came back and sat down next to him on the wicker sofa. "I really do miss being able to curl up with a good book," she said with a heavy sigh.

He took her hands in his while he thought for a moment. "Well...now that we've learned how to lift things, why can't you?"

Her face lit up. "You know what? You're right!" she squealed. "There's this book I've been dying to finish ever since I read part of it one day over a guest's shoulder a few years ago."

As usual, her enthusiasm was so infectious, he couldn't help but smile. "Do you know the title?"

"No, I never saw the cover and I was so absorbed with the story I never thought to look at the top of the pages," she said, somewhat dismayed. "But what little I read of the first few chapters was amazing. The book was about a young boy named Harry who finds out he's a wizard and attends a school of magic. Do you know it?"

He grinned broadly from ear to ear. "Oh, I think I might." It was all he could do to stifle a chuckle. "Come on, I know this cute little book store in town."

Pulling her into his arms, they flew off toward the Washington Mall. Within seconds, they had touched down on the sidewalk. At this hour of night, all the stores were closed and the Mall was deserted. Not even any spirits around.

"Cape Atlantic Books is right inside here," he said, gesturing toward the indoor shops of the City Centre Mall, a brick building that was part of the larger pedestrian Mall. "My family and I visited the bookstore every time we came to Cape May on vacation. Each of us would pick out a brand new book to read at the beach. My mom always got a romance novel, my dad usually got something by Tom Clancy or Dean Koontz, my brother would pick the latest Captain Underpants, and I would of course choose a book by Neil Gaiman or Terry Pratchett."

Floating up and down the aisles, it didn't take him long to find what he was looking for. Concentrating intently, he slowly plucked the book off the shelf for her. "Is this the one you read part of?"

Carefully, she levitated the book from his fingers to her own, flipped forward a few pages, and began reading. "Oh yes, this is the one," she said excitedly. Settling down on the floor between the bookshelves, she looked up at him to ask, "Do you mind?"

"Not at all," he replied. "You've waited a long time to finish it and there are six more books in the series," he added with a smile.

"Really? Seven all together?" She craned her head at him again. "However did you know which book I wanted anyway? Was it a bestseller or something?"

"Um…yeah," he said with a cheeky grin. "I guess you could say the series was a bit popular."

"Huh," she said lightly then burrowed her nose back in the book. As she turned each new page her emerald eyes danced with excitement.

He smiled and shook his head. *Only those books could bring joy to anyone, living or dead.*

Moving further down the aisle, he plucked a book by Neil Gaiman off the shelf and began to read. As he was finishing the first chapter, Sarah called out, "Oh, there are *ghosts* in the castle. How cool is that? This book is *brilliant*."

He laughed inwardly. She never ceased to amaze and delight him. "If you like that, just wait until you get to the second book. There's a chapter in there about the ghosts throwing a death day party for one of their own."

Several hours later with dawn approaching, Sarah had finished the first book in the Harry Potter series. "That was amazing!" she exclaimed. "I can't wait to read the rest."

Grinning, he said, "Okay, but not tonight." He was trying

to find a nice way to tell her he was getting a bit bored. "There are only seven, so the books need to be savored."

"Oh, all right," she begrudgingly agreed, "but promise me we can come back tomorrow so I can read another?" She said it in a babyish voice, sticking out her bottom lip in a pout and giving him these lost-puppy-dog eyes.

And it slayed him.

What would I ever do without this woman?

Day after day, her unbridled enthusiasm, infectious laughter, honesty, curiosity, empathy, and passion gave him a reason to keep going.

Reaching out his hand, he helped her up from the book stack she had been leaning against. Slowly, he took the book out of her hands and placed it back on the shelf. As he turned back around, he wound his arms about her waist and pulled her close.

Instantly, his lips found hers, his tongue playing gently in her mouth, as her heat wove its way straight to his core. With the memory of their joining still fresh in his mind, it took nearly all of his restraint to stop before he could get carried away again.

By the time he did pull away, he could've sworn he was breathless.

"Come on," he said, "let's go home before I get myself into trouble."

She gave him a wicked little grin, but shook her head in agreement.

As they walked arm in arm back toward the Angel of the Sea, he said to her, "You know, I never had a chance to ask you what it felt like to be a Seer."

Sarah's expression turned serious, as she took a moment to think. "To tell you the truth, it's a lot like when you're having a bad dream you want to wake up from, but can't," she said, shuddering at the memory. "But when you and the other angels started to win the battle, and the picture changed for the better, it flooded me with such tremendous relief and peace. Somehow I just knew things had gotten back on track as they were supposed to be. Of course, it went downhill after that because the demons snatched me, but—"

As they rounded the corner of Trenton Avenue, they both stopped short.

Tom stood on the front porch of the Angel, looking for all the world as if he had bad news to deliver.

"What are you doing here?" Michael asked, leery. At the same time he was wondering what was up, he noticed something else odd.

For once, Tom wasn't blocking him from reading his thoughts. The only problem was his thoughts were completely unsettling. *I'm here to take Sarah to the Elders. I have no choice.*

Over my dead body. He joked.

His Protector glared at him. "This is no joke, Michael. Don't make this any harder than it needs to be," he said in a stern, yet pleading voice. "You've already read my thoughts. You both have." He now turned to Sarah with a gentle, fatherly expression. "And you both know exactly why I'm here. I'm sorry for this, but she has to go to the Elders...*now.*"

Michael heard the apology in his words, but also the resolve. "Fine, but whatever happens don't get in my way," he said threateningly. "You can't expect me to stand by and let them hurt her or reprimand her in any way."

Tom sighed heavily, drawing in a deep, ragged breath. "Michael...you can't come with us."

"Wait...what?" he shouted in disbelief. "Why not?"

"Because they want to speak to Sarah...alone." Tom set his jaw and advanced across the street towards them.

Instantly, Michael's whole body tensed as he stepped in front of Sarah, shielding her. A well of guilt overflowed inside of him for having gotten her in some kind of trouble with the Elders. "Why only her? Why not both of us? It takes two to tango." He squeezed her hand. "We both should be in trouble."

Tom's eyes filled with sorrow. "I honestly don't know. I only know I'm supposed to bring her there now...without you."

"That's bullshit!" he shouted, balling his hands into fists. "There's no way I'm letting you take her!"

Sarah moved to step around him. "Michael, it's okay—"

"No, it's not!" He pushed her back behind him again as gently yet forcefully as he could, and took several steps closer to Tom. His father's warning was still in the back of his mind, echoing in his head. "I said you're *not* going to take her," he growled, raising his arms to strike him down if it came right down to it.

"Stand down, Son," Tom responded through gritted teeth, "...and consider very carefully what you're doing. I'm not going to fight you again."

Sarah put her hands on his chest. "Michael, calm down. I'll go with him. It's okay."

"No, it's not!" he shouted, shaking from head to toe. "Why are you punishing her? Punish me!"

Tom put his arm out in front of him as if to say stop. "No one's punishing anybody," he said in an unconvincing tone, "the Elders simply want to talk to her. You're overreacting."

"No, I'm not!" He shook with rage and fear for Sarah. "You have no idea what they want with her and if you say you do, you're lying!"

"Fine, you're right," Tom conceded, his words grave, almost mournful. "But that doesn't change the fact that I have to take her to them and if you try to stand in my way there will be *consequences*."

He wasn't just going to take that veiled threat lying down. Not when Sarah's fate was at stake. Raising his hands, he sent a bolt of energy shooting at Tom.

Unfortunately, his mentor must've anticipated he might not easily comply, for a blast of pain suddenly radiated through his legs before he even knew what hit him.

Tom had stunned him with a glancing blow.

Luckily, his energy only wavered, but didn't dissipate.

But that slowed him down enough to give Tom the time he needed to grab Sarah and take flight with her in tow. "Do yourself a favor, Michael and for once, please *listen*," he called over his shoulder. "And do *not* follow us!"

Momentarily immobilized, all he could do was silently fume while he waited until he could move again.

Luckily, it didn't take that long.

I certainly don't need his permission, he thought sourly, as he reduced himself to an orb. *I already know exactly where he's going.*

Half out of his mind with worry, he sped faster than lightning toward the observation deck of the Chrysler building.

By the time he got there, Tom and Sarah were nowhere in sight. He hadn't expected them to be. Tom's little stunt had probably put them at least a few minutes ahead of him.

No matter, he would easily catch up. He just needed to be on the side which faced the Atlantic Ocean. Rounding the corner, he paused mid-step.

Tom and Sarah were preparing to jump from the precipice over-looking the city. Except, they weren't alone. Two of the same type of muscle bound guards he'd seen with Catherine the Elder stood nearby, one on each side of the entrance to the ley line. Both of them at least seven feet tall.

"No, wait!" Michael shouted.

Tom rounded on him. "Don't take another step."

"Just let me say goodbye," he lied, taking a step closer.

One after another lightning bolts struck the deck in front of him.

Damn.

They weren't even going to let him near the ley line.

Fine. Then I guess I'll have to make my point from over here.

All at once, he threw several bolts of energy at the guards.

With one sweep of their arms, they cast the blows aside. In return, they sent several powerful blasts straight at his head.

He barely managed to duck in time, as the energy ricocheted off the deck, scorching a nearby wall.

"Michael, stop fighting them!" Sarah screamed. "You don't need to fight them! I'll be back. You don't have to worry. I *know* I will be back."

Immediately, he understood what she was saying, she had seen a vision and knew she would return. The only question was when.

He stared at Tom with a dagger-like gaze, but reluctantly put his hands down and surrendered.

As Tom and Sarah jumped from the observation deck, she turned around to mouth, *I love you.*

With his heart nearly ripping in two, he said, *I love you too.*

A second later, the two guards took up positions in front of the eagle on the corner of the ledge.

Now, the only thing he could do was wait.

And pace.

And pace.

And pace.

All the while, a singular thought looped through his mind, keeping him sane, *I'm going to love Sarah for all eternity and no force in heaven or hell is going to stop me.*

• • •

To be continued...

AUTHOR'S NOTES

The Angel of the Sea is an award-winning bed and breakfast in Cape May, NJ. This spectacular inn has been featured on several television programs and in magazines throughout the world. Most notably, it was chosen by Oprah Winfrey as one of the "Best Vacations in the World" and included in her television talk show. The Angel of the Sea is one of the most recognized Victorian structures in the United States. Legend has it that in the late 1960's, a girl did fall to her death at the Angel of the Sea and did at one time, haunt the inn. The story of the girl has been included in several non-fiction books about ghosts in Cape May. Sarah's character in THE GHOST CHRONICLES series was inspired by this legend. You can learn more about the Angel of the Sea by visiting: http://www.angelofthesea.com/

THE COCOANUT GROVE FIRE

On the night of November 28, 1942 nearly one thousand patrons packed the famous Cocoanut Grove supper club in Boston. Around 10:15, a fast-spreading fire of unknown origin broke out in the Melody Lounge.

In less than fifteen minutes, the second worst single-building fire in American history claimed the lives of 492 people and injured hundreds of others. Famed Hollywood actor, Buck Jones, the star of many popular cowboy films of the day, was among those who perished as a result of the fire. Many of the people died from inhaling toxic smoke and fumes caused by the highly flammable wall coverings and decorations. The club's signature feature, a revolving glass door at the front entrance became a deathtrap. In addition, the fact that many other exits were blocked, obscured, or bolted shut undoubtedly contributed to the tremendous loss of life.

A Grand Jury would later indict ten people, but only one was ever convicted of a crime—owner, Barney Welansky, on one count of manslaughter. Sentenced to 12-15 years in Charlestown State Prison, he would only serve three and half, having been pardoned by Governor Maurice Tobin for medical reasons. In 1947 he died of cancer at the age of 50, shortly after his release from prison.

The exact cause of the fire has been investigated for decades, but no final or definitive conclusions have ever been reached. Though a busboy admitted to having lit a match, other theories abound as to the how the fire truly started. Some witnesses (who left the club before the fire even began) testified that shortly before the visible fire broke out, one of the walls was intensely hot to the touch, which may indicate that an electrical fire had already been brewing behind the wall where the air conditioner was located. Another theory suggests that the refrigeration systems may have been leaking a highly flammable gas—methyl chloride—which may have caused the fire's inevitable ignition and intense flashover. After nearly seventy-five years, the case still remains open.

Both Massachusetts General Hospital and Boston City Hospital were flooded with hundreds of burn and smoke inhalation victims that night. The over-whelmed staff at Boston City Hospital experienced one of the highest admittance rates ever recorded at a hospital. Some sources say higher than the treatment rates after the attack on Pearl Harbor, or in London during the Blitz.

However, it is said that necessity is the mother of invention. In a desperate attempt to save lives that night, hospital staff and doctors, using their courage and ingenuity came up with several medical breakthroughs and innovations that would have lasting effects on medicine to this day.

Two surgeons at Massachusetts General Hospital, Oliver Cope and Francis Daniels Moore, pioneered the use of a relatively new 'soft' technique for treating burn victims, by wrapping the skin in cotton cloths treated with boric petroleum jelly. To aid the healing process, skin grafts were also utilized. All in all, ground-breaking advances in burn treatment were made at both hospitals in four areas: fluid retention, infection prevention, treatment of respiratory trauma, as well as, skin surface and surgical management. The tragic event also saw the first major use of the hospital's new blood bank, one of the first of its kind in the nation.

In 1942, penicillin was new, expensive and had yet to be used on the general population. The patients from the fire were among the first people to ever be treated with this new antibiotic. Shortly after the fire, Merck and Company rushed a large supply of the drug from New Jersey to the hospitals in Boston. The drug proved helpful in combating staphylococcus bacteria, which can cause serious and potentially fatal infections in skin grafts and other wounds. As a direct result of the use of this new antibiotic in Boston, the United States government decided to support the production and distribution of penicillin to our armed forces. This move would have a tremendous positive affect for our soldiers in World War II, and eventually lead to penicillin's widespread use throughout the nation and the world.

Another consequence of the fire was the work done by Erich Lindemann, a Boston psychiatrist. His work with the families of those that lost their lives in the fire would become a classic study on the symptoms and management of severe grief. Another scientist, Alexandra Adler, also conducted some of the earliest research on what would become known as post-traumatic stress disorder (PTSD).

The fire was one of the worst in our nation's history, yet it also laid the groundwork for sweeping reforms in public fire safety, not only in the city of Boston, but eventually nationwide and even worldwide. The most notable advances were made in the areas of exits, combustible materials, emergency lighting, and automatic sprinklers. The definition of places of public assembly was also expanded. In addition, fire laws now specifically require all revolving doors to be break away (meaning, if you push hard enough, the center axis is designed to collapse), and to have at least one adjacent standard easement, such as a door.

Though largely forgotten today, the tragic fire at the Cocoanut Grove had a lasting impact on lives nationwide, and indeed, throughout the world.

The truth is there are some events in human history so tragic, their echoes are endless throughout eternity. Perhaps that is how they must be, so we may hear them and never forget the lessons learned.

Source:
Grant CC. "Last dance at the Cocoanut Grove." NFPA Journal 85 no.3 (May/June 1991): 74-86

ACKNOWLEDGMENTS

As always, much love and thanks go to my family: my husband, Chris, my sons, Michael and Andrew, and to my Mom, Dad, sister and brother for their unwavering support and faith in me.

When I wrote the acknowledgments for the first book in THE GHOST CHRONICLES series, I was terrified I was going to forget someone. And unfortunately, I did—author Amy Patrick. When I was facing rejection after rejection with my first book, Amy didn't even know me, but she sent me a very encouraging email after reading some of my writing. Her kind words came at the exact moment I needed them most, and gave me the nudge I needed to persevere and not give up. For that, I will always be grateful.

To all my writing friends everywhere, there are simply too many of you to mention by name, but know that I am always grateful for your tremendous knowledge and never-ending support.

To all my wonderful fans and readers, especially those who reached out to let me know that you loved Book One and couldn't wait for Book Two, I am forever grateful. Your enthusiasm for this series helped me to keep going and write this next installment, despite life throwing all sorts of obstacles in my way.

Special thanks to Casey C. Grant P.E., Executive Director of the Fire Protection Research Foundation, and Nicole Dutton MLIS, of the National Fire Protection Agency for helping me with information about the Cocoanut Grove Fire. Thanks also to John Corbo retired captain of the Branchburg Fire Department, Kristen Christiansen EMT-B of Branchburg Rescue Squad, and Sharon Huff RN, for your expertise in your various fields. Also, many thanks to Scott D. Banks, James Martin, and Anthony Scott, for giving me my own private tour of Boardwalk Hall in Atlantic City, and my own private concert on the grand organ. I will cherish the memory of that haunting place forever.

To my fabulous cover designer, S. P. McConnell, for his incredible talent and extraordinary patience.

To all the fantastic writing organizations and groups that have brought me so much knowledge and camaraderie over the years, New Jersey Romance Writers, Romance Writers of America, YA-RWA, NJ-Society of Children's Book Writers and Illustrators, TeenLitAuthors, and WritingGIAM.

And last but certainly not least, to Ronald and Theresa Stanton, owners of The Angel of the Sea, for their continued friendship and hospitality, and for allowing me to use the name and image of their 'beautiful angel' once again.

ABOUT THE AUTHOR

Marlo Berliner is the award-winning author of THE GHOST CHRONICLES, her debut book which was released in November 2015 to critical acclaim. The book won the 2016 NJRW Golden Leaf Award for Best First Book, was named FINALIST in the National Indie Excellence Awards for Young Adult Fiction, received the Literary Classics Seal of Approval, was awarded a B.R.A.G. Medallion, and was named one of the "best indie YA books we have seen in the past year, from both self-publishers and small presses" by IPPY Magazine. Marlo is represented by Eric Ruben of the Ruben Agency and she writes young adult, women's fiction, and short stories.

When she's not writing or editing, Marlo loves reading, relaxing at the beach, watching movies, and rooting for the Penn State Nittany Lions. After having spent some wonderful time in Pittsburgh and Houston, she's now back in her home state of New Jersey where she resides with her husband, two sons, and a rambunctious puppy named Max.

You can connect with her online at www.marloberliner.com or on Twitter @MarloBerliner or Instagram @marloberliner.

You've finished! Before you go…

- Please visit my website http://marloberliner.com and be sure to sign up for my newsletter so you can receive advance notice of the next installment of THE GHOST CHRONICLES and other upcoming releases.
- Rate/Review this book on your favorite retailer's site and Goodreads. Reviews are like candy for authors.
- Tweet, or share on Facebook, that you finished this book.

MORE BY THIS AUTHOR:

THE GHOST CHRONICLES, Book 3
coming soon!

LESSONS OF HOPE AND LIGHT
A COLLECTION OF INSPIRATIONAL SHORT STORIES
available now!